Cover and Chapter Art by S. Kersey
Derived from photos "our road" and "toward Lovejoy"
by normanack licensed under CCBY 2.0

ISBN: 0615718809

ISBN-13: 978-0615718804

This is a work of fiction. Names, characters, places, businesses and incidents are either the
product of the author's imagination or are used fictitiously. Any resemblance to actual
persons, living or dead, businesses, events or locales is purely coincidental.

.

"I am alone and miserable; man will not associate with me; but one as deformed and horrible as myself would not deny herself to me. My companion must be of the same species and have the same defects."

—Mary Shelley, *Frankenstein*

STRANGE FALL

1

"I know," Faeriwyn McKeller said softly as she placed a basket down on her picnic blanket. "Fried chicken. It's always fried chicken. And you're right, it will be the death of me. I'll probably have a heart attack by the time I'm twenty-five."

She sat on the blanket next to the basket and held her head back to allow the cool autumn breeze to blow over her.

Though her name was Faeriwyn, she hadn't gone by that name for as long as she'd had a say in the matter. To everyone outside of her family and close friends, she was known only as Winnie. It was a somewhat more common name, though it often led to rather obvious jokes about bears and excrement in school.

She hated school—especially now.

"I brought coleslaw," she went on, "The kind with extra...

coleslaw juice. Whatever it is. I know you like that kind."

She was sixteen years old, with black, shoulder-length hair. Even if the color hadn't been natural, she would have chosen it. It suited her, inside and out. She felt dark; like a shadow which constantly moved about, without true form or definition. It had been that way ever since...

She continued, "But there's fruit. That's healthy, right? It's in the pie."

She waited patiently for the response that she knew was coming from her sister, but she was met only with silence. Another cool breeze blew past her, sending a strand of hair over her eyes. As she brushed it away, she nodded and smiled, just slightly.

"I know," she sighed. "Once again, you're right and I'm fat."

That was a lie. She hadn't ever been fat. Up until a year before, she might have been called *curvy* perhaps, but never fat. Since then, she'd thinned considerably as her appetite faded.

Her sister, Cindy, had been blessed with good looks and a normal name. She was the popular girl in school, which seemed to happen effortlessly. Cindy glowed, and everyone who had been fortunate enough to know her marveled at that light.

Faery was another name that Winnie had been called, but only when she was younger. It was the name that Cindy had given her and nobody in the world had referred to Winnie by that name but Cindy and her best friend, Tami. On most days, Winnie would love to hear herself referred to by that name.

In her sleep, Winnie often dreamt that she was lost in the woods. In the dark and cold, as search lights moved across distant trees, *Faery* was the name that she heard called to her.

She could never find the voice to respond.

"Mom and Dad were out all night again," Winnie told her sister, opening the container of coleslaw. "I guess that's nothing new. I just wish..."

She didn't know how she wanted to finish that sentence. There were so many things that Winnie wished for these days, and none of them seemed to be the normal priorities of a sixteen year old girl. She didn't care about prom dresses and homecoming. She didn't care about dating boys and gossiping with her girlfriends.

Looking up at the sky, Winnie found herself staring at the clouds overhead. They were various shades of gray and white, with not a spot of blue to be seen. They looked as though snow could fall from them at any moment, but it was too early for snow.

Pre-winter, she liked to call it; that short span of time when the leaves had changed and fallen and autumn's peak had come and gone, but before that first freeze or snowfall. In this time between seasons, Winnie seemed the most at home. There was a sense of calm that filled the air during the pre-winter. A quiet remembrance of what had been and the anticipation of what was yet to come. It seemed like a proper match for Winnie, who had felt as though she had been stuck between seasons for just over a year—ever since Cindy had died.

School was no refuge for Winnie. There, she felt the constant comparisons to her sister, whom everybody had loved. Cindy's friends had once been Winnie's friends, but that link was gone. Those who hadn't graduated quickly found new friends and new joys, while Winnie seemed frozen at a crossroads with no idea which direction to go. Part of her didn't want to move at all. To put distance between this place and wherever those roads led would mean putting distance between herself and Cindy. It would be a betrayal, to turn her back on her sister.

Winnie didn't bring two servings of fried chicken, coleslaw, or pie to the graveyard. She hadn't convinced herself that Cindy was capable of sitting there with her, or of eating food. She only wished to feel as close to Cindy as possible, without the prying eyes of her parents or the school kids who had begun to talk about her when they thought she couldn't hear.

She didn't talk to Cindy because she believed that her sister was with her, or could hear her from wherever it was that Cindy had gone. The talking was for herself, because there didn't seem to be anyone else who would listen without judgment or analysis. She didn't need therapy. She didn't want someone turning her own words against her. All she wanted was for someone to listen, because she had grown tired of eating alone.

As she finished eating her chicken and coleslaw and was just about to move on to the pie, Winnie heard a slight *beep*. At first, she assumed that this was the sound of branches knocking together on a nearby tree, or perhaps a container shifting in her basket. It took her mind a few moments to process this sound and properly identify its source.

Mechanical. Technology. Not her phone, or her iPod, yet it was familiar. She'd heard this sound before, many times, but it made no sense here. It was outside of its proper context, since she was alone.

The urge to confirm her mind's conclusion was too strong for Winnie to ignore. She put away her pie and stood. She looked around the cemetery to make sure that she was alone. Nobody was around.

The sound was not intended for anyone else who had been buried in the cemetery. It was a sound meant for Cindy. Winnie didn't need to worry herself with a large-scale search of the area. The source of this sound was close, and there weren't many hiding places around her sister's headstone.

As Winnie looked toward the headstone, a surge of adrenaline ran through her—not because she was frightened or nervous, but because she was fuming with anger.

Her suspicions were proven correct as she looked behind her sister's grave. On a slight ledge around the headstone, just off of the ground, Winnie found a digital audio recorder.

2

She drove her car down the twisted, leaf-covered streets which led the way from the morgue to her small, stone home in the middle of the woods. Few people traveled those roads, because few people needed to.

Obell had made her home from the stone remains of a house which was rumored to have belonged to a woman in the 18th century, murdered by locals on suspicion of being a witch. The woman hadn't been a witch, of course. Few of those cases involved real witches. Still, the house was charged with the energy of that history; the lies, the suffering and the death. All of the wrong that had befallen that poor woman now served as the welcome mat at Obell's door.

Real witches did exist. There were those who worshiped the

earth and were one with the moon, who were peaceful and took offense at the fairy tales which painted them as trolls who lived in the woods and preyed on the innocent.

These witches were oblivious to the other kind—The kind who *did* live in the woods and *did* prey on the innocent. This was the type of witch that Obell had become over the course of many, many years. This metamorphosis took time. It required the soul to rot inside of its human shell, until there was nothing left but the darkness, the ugliness and contempt.

A *true witch*, as Obell referred to herself, would not have been tried for being a witch in those days of paranoia. One of her kind would go unseen by anyone that they wished to remain hidden from. A true witch would blur a stranger's vision and erase any memory of their visit, should she choose to remain unknown. More than that, a true witch would not be drowned, or burned at the stake. Death is the process by which a soul leaves its human body. A true witch's soul has already rotted away, and the human shell is nothing more than the vessel for the creature that has replaced it. Death would kiss Obell on the cheek like a nervous prom date, and run away screaming when she proved more than it could handle.

It amused her to think of all of those lowly, common people walking around, oblivious to the power she held. They would never know, unless she chose for them to know. They would never see her unless she wished to be seen. She was a figment, and that meant that she was free to do whatever she pleased.

In her forty-five years on Earth, Obell had never met another of her kind, but she knew that they were out there. They could not die, and that meant that someday she would meet her brothers and sisters, and their reunion would begin a new chapter in the history books: *The Age of the True Witch*.

She wondered how many of them had grown up as she had. She wondered if they'd all been found as babies on the doorstep of an unsuspecting stranger and raised without a family until they were old enough to be on their own.

She wondered how many of them had watched, time and time again as other children were chosen for adoption, while they were overlooked. A witch is invisible at times, and Obell hadn't yet known what she was. She couldn't control her power as a child. Surely, she would have been adopted if they had seen her. But could they *love* her?

One needed a soul to be loved, she theorized. She didn't have a soul. It had rotted out from under her when she was still a young child. The exact moment, she didn't know. She went back and forth with herself over that small detail, but she knew that it had to have been a while.

It was in high school that Obell realized her true nature. She read the history books and the tales of the falsely accused, and she laughed. If only those poor people had known that there were true witches in their midst, watching them and giggling at their lunacy.

The years passed, and she could feel herself becoming

something new. Her soul was gone, and in its place there was now something which even she could not define. An *abyss*. A portal into something darker and more powerful than anyone around her could ever imagine. She was no longer one of the lowly. She no longer dreamed of being adopted or loved. She was complete on her own.

Thirteen years after her realization, Obell had been fooled by an agent of her enemy. He made her believe that she was human and could be loved. He gave her the illusion of a family, with a son of her own. She lived in this illusion for years, until her enemy, whoever or whatever it was, decided to reveal the truth of its spell to her. In one swift move, her family had been taken from her and her weakness had been revealed. She'd fallen for the lie, but that would be the last time.

If any hint or fragment of her mortal soul had remained from childhood, it was now surely destroyed and in its place there was nothing more than a thirst for vengeance. She would find her enemy and she would make him pay.

She poured herself into her work, and for the next several years she continued to surprise herself with all that came from the abyss inside of her. The pit was the source of great power, and she used that power to plan her revenge.

The house she lived in, with its history of persecution, served as a focal point for that power. The wood that she'd used to rebuild the home around the stone structure had been painted white, to mock the world which surrounded her. Weeds were growing all around her home, and vines had begun to overtake her porch.

Crows and snakes enjoyed her garden, where she grew the herbs needed to perform her spells and create her potions. Sometimes, those same crows and snakes managed to find their way into the pot, along with the deadened basil.

The driveway that led from the main road and down to her home was made of dirt and stone, as she imagined it had been when the original house stood, centuries before. To come home was to leave the world of the modern day, where the only curses consisted of text messages and spam e-mails. To enter that house was to return to the proper order of things. It was the place where curses consisted of blood rituals and animal sacrifices, just as nature had intended.

Home, sweet home.

She stopped her car walked around to the trunk, still swimming in the glory of the spell she'd placed on the morgue technician. It was the first time she had ever attempted something on that level before. It had confirmed to her that her power was without limit. It proved to her that she was capable of completing the task at hand.

As she opened the trunk of her car, Obell found the body of the young man staring back at her with glazed-over eyes. Its mouth was just slightly open, as though it continued to breathe. His skin was the color of death, and cold to the touch.

The smell was something that only a mother could love, and as she looked down at the boy she did feel as though she were a mother-to-be, just waiting for labor to begin.

She ran a hand over his face and brushed his hair away from his eyes. He was beautiful, her boy, and would only become more beautiful once he was back on his feet.

3

Marion McKeller enjoyed the quiet. She enjoyed the moments
in between the chaos, when none of life's many troubles could
grip her around the neck and squeeze. She'd been through a lot in
the past year, and each minute of each day seemed like a struggle
of its own.

She'd had two daughters; each different and special in their
own way. Each could bring a smile to her face with the simplest of
expressions. She had *made* them, and watching them grow was
perhaps the most amazing thing she would ever witness.

One of those girls was now dead. The very notion of that
sentence seemed absurd to Marion. It was not the natural order of
things. It was wrong. It had to have been some sort of mistake, but
there was no way to make that case. There was no manager that

she could speak to. There was no going back.

After spending ten years specializing in family counseling, Marion knew all of the stages of grief. She knew how many families in this situation fell apart, and how many mothers or fathers could find themselves in a never-ending free fall into a dark and cold pit. She refused to become one of those families. She refused to put that burden on Cindy's memory. To do so would be unfair to that beautiful girl.

In those quiet moments, Marion never felt alone. She was a firm believer in a life beyond what can be seen with the eyes. She believed with every fiber of her being that when the human body is shed, the soul emerges like a butterfly from its chrysalis. Because she believed this so firmly, she would not allow the loss of her daughter to destroy the soul of anyone else in her family. When they were reunited with Cindy, she did not want to have to explain such a downfall. She wanted a joyous reunion.

For the most part, things seemed to be working out as well as could be hoped for. The after-hours business that Marion ran with her husband, Mark, kept them from ripping each other apart. At first, it was difficult. The process of mourning was one that each member of the family had to go through on their own, and at times their methods conflicted, but the business served as a constant reminder of what they believed.

For nearly seven years, long before Cindy's death, Marion and Mark had been investigating claims of the supernatural. Usually, this meant investigating reports of ghostly activity in a person's home. On a few occasions, they'd explored the woods or an abandoned carnival, following urban legends about unusual creatures or cursed objects. More times than not, these claims were easily debunked. However, on that rare occasion when something truly unexplainable took place, the couple felt closer to understanding the universe around them.

They were not the type of people who would abandon science in favor of imaginary creatures. They were also not the types of people who believed that everything that exists in the world was known, or that we could measure everything in the universe with our current perspective and our limited technology. They believed that the best, most logical path toward truth could be found somewhere in the middle. Science, with the understanding that we have only just begun to scratch the surface of reality.

There were times when their hunt for the paranormal would lean toward Cindy. There was an urge to search for her. There was a desire to catch her voice on tape, or find some evidence that she was still around. These urges were powerful, and if not kept in check, they could become all-consuming.

Not every person remained on Earth after they had died. If the souls of every person who ever died were roaming the planet, there would be no need for investigation. The world would be a year-round Woodstock of souls. Most moved on to wherever they were meant to be. Nobody knew why some chose to stay behind. There were many theories regarding unfinished business, or penance, but since nobody had ever sat a ghost down for an in-depth interview, nobody could know for sure. Still, Marion didn't want Cindy to linger. As much as she wanted her daughter to be with them, the idea of her daughter being unable to move on scared Marion more than soothed her.

And yet...

"How could you?" came the angry voice of Marion's second daughter, Winnie, as the front door slammed shut behind her.

The sudden break in the silence caused Marion to jump in her seat at the dining room table, where she was reviewing video tapes from the previous night's investigation.

Since her mind had been wandering toward Cindy, she would have to go back and start over.

"How could you do this? To her!" Winnie continued, waving an audio recorder in front of her.

The recorder was one of Marion's. That much was obvious. Yet, Marion didn't know why Winnie was holding it, or why she was so upset.

"Honey, calm down. We can talk about this," Marion said, standing up and trying to cool her daughter's ever-growing temper.

"Don't do that. Don't pull your psych-101 crap on me. I'm not a patient," Winnie fumed as tears fell and she her free hand twisted into a fist. "How could you treat her like one of your stupid little role playing games, Mom? My sister is not a game."

Marion put the pieces of this puzzle together in her head. She hadn't set up the recorder. She was not the person that Winnie wanted to yell at.

The previous night, Marion and Mark had taken separate cars to an investigation, both having gone straight from their day jobs. Afterward, Mark told Marion that he needed to stop for gas on the way home and they parted ways. Obviously, he had placed the recorder.

Winnie was angry, and that was understandable. It was a normal response. It was healthy for her to vent that anger, rather than keep it bottled up. At least she was sharing her feelings, and that was essential for keeping the family together. Communication. Honesty.

Of course, Marion would not tell Winnie that her father had been the one to set up the recorder. Turning daughter against father would only drive a wedge between Marion and her husband. She would discuss this with him later, but for now she would allow Winnie to take her anger out on her.

"Say something," Winnie demanded. "Explain to me why you would do something like this. She's your own daughter, not some campfire story."

Marion wasn't sure what to say. She never would have put the recorder by Cindy's grave, but this was a situation that she had to resolve as smoothly as possible.

She took the recorder in her hand and looked down at it. In a soft tone, which sounded surprisingly unconvincing, even to Marion herself, she said, "We all have different ways of dealing with our grief."

Winnie said nothing. She looked Marion in the eyes, seeming to get more upset by the second. When she couldn't stand the sight of her mother any longer, she turned and stormed upstairs, leaving Marion alone with the recorder.

Seconds passed, and Marion knew what was coming next. She waited for it. Waited. Waited...

SLAM!

Nobody could ever claim that Marion did not know her daughter well. Even after Cindy's death caused Winnie to pull away and retreat into her own world, some things could always be relied upon. This was comforting to Marion. She could have faith in Winnie.

Mark, on the other hand, had proven to be a mystery that Marion had not expected. She had believed that they were communicating and including each other in their mourning process. She believed that this was essential to the survival of their relationship.

She held the audio recorder in her hand, running her thumb over the buttons and trying to decide what she should do with this evidence. It was Mark's attempt at closure. It was something that he felt the need to do for himself, and that was understandable.

Marion scrolled her way through the menu on the audio recorder's display screen until she came to the final option: *DELETE*.

There, she hesitated.

4

She hated them. She hated every single person who had ever claimed to love her or her sister. Her so-called *friends.* Her parents. Her neighbors. They could all rot, as far as she was concerned.

Nobody cared. Nobody felt the loss of Cindy. Winnie was alone in her mourning. She was the one who had truly loved Cindy. She was the one who would feel the pain of her sister's death in her heart forever. Everyone else was a liar.

After slamming the door to her bedroom, Winnie couldn't sit down. She couldn't calm herself. She paced across her floor, jaw clenched, trying to think of some way to make everyone suffer the way she was suffering. They deserved to know this pain after their constant lies.

At Cindy's funeral, half of the student body from their school had shown up, wearing their stylish black clothes and pretending to care. Speech after speech was given by supposed friends, talking about how beloved Cindy had been and how their loss would be felt forever.

Apparently *forever* really meant *a couple of weeks*. Before the last of the lilies could dry up at Cindy's grave, those friends could be seen smiling and having fun at their parties and football games.

Liars. None of them cared. If they had truly loved Cindy, their worlds would be as dark as Winnie's was. Or perhaps Winnie's world would be less so. Maybe if those friends had shown signs of feeling that loss, Winnie would not feel so alone in her pain. Maybe she wouldn't feel as though she were drowning in death.

Maybe she wouldn't feel drawn to it.

If Winnie had ever spoken that truth out loud, her mother would have had her popping ten kinds of pills, three times per day. She would be evaluated, probed and placed on a strict treatment plan for whatever serious disorder she was diagnosed with. She knew better than to reveal all to her parents.

The world is a hard place, and Winnie hadn't felt the slightest relief from the pressures of her life since her sister's death. Every day seemed like a constant reminder of what was stolen from her. Students at school, laughing at jokes which had nothing to do with Winnie, were mocking her without realizing it. Her parents always felt a need to comfort her and give her a shoulder to cry on, never realizing how each of those gestures seemed so fake and heartless to her.

The fact that the sun continued to rise each day, and the skies weren't constantly filled with thick clouds and bolts of lightning annoyed Winnie. She knew that these were her own issues, but nothing that anyone could do would ease those feelings. She needed to figure them out on her own. She needed to make sense of how someone she'd expected to have around for her entire life could suddenly be gone. She needed to know that her relationship with Cindy wasn't a huge waste of time; that it meant something.

Cindy's death was filled with questions that would never be answered. She was found at the base of a steep hill, next to one of the roads between the high school and her home. Cause of death: Head trauma.

No witnesses. Nobody to tell Winnie why her sister was dead. Though it was believed that Cindy's death was a random accident, nobody would ever know with complete certainty. Winnie didn't need to know. Those mysteries were for someone else to worry about. Winnie's concerns were far more personal—far more selfish. Cindy was dead, and that was Winnie's reality now. It was her entire world. Understanding why things were the way they were would be as useful to her as knowing why Earth revolves around the sun. It might be interesting, but knowing wouldn't change anything. It happened because it happened. It was because it was. Winnie was more concerned with what happens next than figuring out what happened before.

She'd done more than a little bit of research on the topic of death. The internet was a wondrous thing for the modern teenager, seeking comfort in knowledge, even if that comfort would not be found.

She had read theories on the afterlife, from fluffy white clouds, to the river of blood that all noble Klingons crossed upon their noble death. None of it made her feel any better, because what all of this research boiled down to was the simple fact that nobody knew a damn thing about what came after. Nobody was an authority on the subject. There were no focus groups or surveys taken of residents from the great beyond, with charts and graphs depicting overall satisfaction of their post-life experience.

Perhaps this was why she felt such contempt for her parents and their foolish attempt at solving this great puzzle. For thousands of years, people have asked the question of what happens next, and her parents—a family counselor and a videographer—assume that they will find that answer? They might as well make a career out of playing the lottery, because they had just as much chance of figuring out the winning numbers.

There were no answers. There was no way of making this feeling go away. The closest anyone had come was the atheist theory which says that when we die, we're gone. Blackness. Nothing. Only, Winnie thought this theory had it backwards. Instead, she figured that when Cindy died, those who remained were the ones who ceased to exist. This was Cindy's world, and without her, all that remained was limbo.

She continued to pace back and forth, turning thoughts and ideas around her head. Trying to figure out why everyone around her insisted on making her mad; trying to understand why these things made her so mad in the first place.

She just wanted it to stop. She wanted the thoughts in her head to go away, even if only for a little while. She wanted to have quiet inside of her own mind. Maybe then she could see things more clearly.

One thing was certain: The noise inside of her head would not be going away as long as she was surrounded by constant reminders of her former life. The pink paint on her walls had become like nails on a chalkboard. The princess wand that she'd played with as a small child now mocked her from the bookcase where it had been placed for the sake of nostalgia. The girl who had grown up in that room felt as dead as Cindy; replaced by something else entirely. She didn't know who or what she was anymore, and it was becoming more and more difficult to pretend for the sake of her parents.

At long last, a plan came into Winnie's mind. She knew what she wanted to do. She wanted to run. She wanted to be free from the constant reminders that her sister was dead and that the lesser sister had lived, but she also just wanted to feel as though she were moving in any direction at all. She wanted to feel her legs ache, and her lungs screaming for breath. She needed to escape.

In the back of her mind, Winnie had always wanted to try

sneaking out of her bedroom window. Ever since she was a little girl, she would look down and wonder if it were possible to slip out of the house without anyone noticing—and without breaking her neck.

Just below her bedroom window there was a bay window, which created a shingled ledge that angled downward. In her mind, she had always seen herself slipping out onto this ledge and jumping down to the ground like a super-powered action star. She had always wanted to try it for real, but had always been too scared.

Fear meant nothing to her in that particular moment. If she died, she died. At least she would finally have the answers to all those questions. And as for her parents... Well, she could always talk into one of their stupid audio recorders and answer their questions too.

She opened her window and a rush of that cool pre-winter air washed over her. It energized her and gave her confidence in her ability to safely make it down to the ground below. In that moment, Winnie had faith. Faith in herself, and faith in something greater.

She sat in the open window, letting her legs dangle over the ledge below, and slowly lowered herself toward it. As she grew closer, inch by inch, she couldn't believe that she had been scared of trying this for so many years. It was actually very simple.

Her right foot touched the ledge first, followed quickly by the left foot. Winnie had made it to the ledge without killing herself.

She smiled at her own success. She was strong. She was liberated.

She let go of her open window, and allowed the full weight of her body to rest on the ledge, and time seemed to slow to a turtle's pace.

Her right foot slipped, throwing her off balance. Her left ankle twisted, and she felt herself bending backwards. Her hands reached out, trying to grab onto the side of the house, but there was nothing for them to hold onto.

She was falling. The air was blowing her hair into her face and everything inside of her seemed to shift upward, away from the ground, as she fell. It took her breath away, and tingled just a little bit.

As she fell, she thought a dozen different thoughts. She cursed and screamed at herself for being so stupid, though she remained outwardly silent. She tried to think of ways out of this fall which wouldn't result in any pain. There were none. She anticipated the pain. She feared its inevitability. It took less than a few seconds for her to slip and fall to the ground, but those few seconds seemed to last for hours.

Her right shoulder hit the damp ground first, and time resumed its normal pace. Her right arm was crushed behind her back as she hit. It didn't hurt right away, but she knew the pain was making its way through her system and up to her brain.

She waited for it. Waited for it.

Ankle throbbed. Shoulder throbbed. Her butt felt like she'd been spanked by a sledgehammer. Her head was spinning. Her lip was bleeding where she's apparently bitten it. It hurt. It did.

And still somehow, she didn't feel a thing.

5

Obell grabbed the corpse under its arms and pulled as hard as she could, but it appeared to be stuck. Something about the way its legs were bent, or the angle at which it had been placed inside the trunk was making it incredibly difficult for her to pull it free.

I should have put it in the back seat, she thought to herself, though she knew that it would raise an eyebrow or two if anyone happened to catch a glimpse of a dead, naked young man, spread across the back seat of her car—and that didn't even take the autopsy wounds into consideration.

For the first time in the three years since buying the car, Obell wished that she'd sprung for the tinted windows.

She stepped away from the car and looked down at the body, rebuilding her strength and planning her course of action for the next attempt. Of course, there wasn't much to plan. What could she do, except grab the body and pull?

Walking back to the trunk of her car, Obell was beginning to get annoyed. The feelings of a loving mother-to-be were replaced by the frustrated feelings of the pissed off mother of a teenager.

"Get out of the car," she murmured through her gritted teeth as she once again pulled without success. "Get out of the car!"

Finally, the corpse shifted and seemed to pull loose from whatever had been keeping it in the trunk. This freedom came with a very distinct *crunch,* which she knew could not be good.

Considering the size of the body, Obell was surprised at how light it was, once she'd pulled it from the trunk of the car and dropped it onto the muddy ground. Of course, she knew that an autopsy had been performed and that meant that all that had once been inside of the boy was not necessarily still inside of the boy. Blood and fluids had been drained. Organs had been removed.

It made her job a little bit easier. After all, she wasn't looking to *resurrect* the dead. That was an absurd notion. No, she only meant to reanimate the corpse. He wouldn't need organs and blood. All he would need was magic.

She grabbed the corpse's arms and dragged it through the mud, to the front door of her house. It was not a very neat process, but Obell was never one to care about muddied floors. Dirt was primal and savage. It connected her with the core of her nature.

As the body rested by her feet, Obell struggled with her keys, fumbling through a collection which all looked the same to her. The products of a cookie-cutter world.

When she finally opened the front door, she stepped over the threshold and looked down at the body. She did not look forward to hauling that thing through the house. Though lighter than she'd anticipated, the body was awkward to maneuver and dragging it around was beginning to make her back ache. She could not wait until the corpse could get up and move on its own.

Her house was not as large as some in town. It was a single-story home, with a kitchen to the back and living area to the right. To the left was a spare bedroom, where she kept her many volumes of long forgotten lore, old potions, and the stamp collection she'd started in college. To the rear of the house, an extension had been added for a master bedroom and bath. It had been built in the style of the original house, mimicking the stone remains that she had built upon. It blended in well enough, but Obell loathed it for its lack of history. She spent no more time in that room than was necessary.

The walls of the house were plastered and painted in a drab gray. Their wooden supports maintained a natural look, as did the worn, wooden floors.

There was electricity in the house, but she preferred to use fire and candlelight. Electric light was cold and impersonal. The flicker of flame was warm and nurturing, yet threatening at the same time.

Only the smallest amount of daylight sneaked its way through the closed shutters that covered the windows. Sunlight purified, and made clean what had been soiled in the night. Obell savored the night. She believed that the darkness of night revealed the truths of the world. All that was hidden in the shadow of daylight was set free at night, when the world was convinced that nobody was watching.

There was one mirror in the house, located in the master bathroom. This mirror was usually covered with a black cloth, as Obell hated to look at her own reflection. She despised her own appearance. The eyebrows which arched too high, giving her look of a cartoon villain. One eye which opened slightly wider than the other. A smile that not even the Grinch himself could love. She hated her hair because it was too frizzy. She hated her skin because its color threatened to reveal the heritage of the people that had abandoned her as an infant—if they were people at all.

Her clothes were like potato sacks, hanging loosely from her body and made of materials that were more suited for curtain making than fashion.

She did not need to look at herself to know that she was not beautiful. It was the price she had paid for allowing her soul to rot within her. However, with that rotting of the soul came power. Just as she had controlled the mind of the morgue technician, she could make most of the world see her as she wished to be seen. Only a select few could see through her guise, and they were easily dismissed by everyone else.

Once she had dragged the corpse far enough into the house to allow the door to close, Obell decided to take a rest and consider her plans for the night. There were a lot of variables to consider when it came to reanimation. Anything that touched the body during the process could alter the outcome. Any scent in the air, or miscalculation of ingredients.

Pulling up a wooden chair and taking a seat, Obell gazed upon the body on the floor and allowed her mind to slip away. In her head, she combined each ingredient and applied each element, trying to account for the results as best she could without having actually performed this ritual before.

She could almost see the lifeless eyes blinking as the corpse awoke and stood before her. After that, she could do whatever she pleased. She could use it as a slave, or keep it as a pet. It didn't matter. All that mattered was that she could harness this power unlike anyone who had come before her. She would become the master of Death. She would be the strongest person to walk the earth.

As she considered the glory that awaited, a small mouse crawled across her feet. At the sound of the mouse's slight squeak, Obell was startled from her daydream and let out a scream that could wake the dead... So to speak.

Out of reflex, she kicked her foot outward, sending the mouse through the air and onto the corpse where it regained its composure and began to sniff around.

She knew that she had to get the mouse away from the corpse

before it began to nibble, but the thought disgusted her. She hated rodents.

6

Mark McKeller sat in his small office with all of the lights turned off and the window blinds shut. He preferred the dark when editing video, so the details on screen would stand out. But he was finished editing now and the darkness was for his own comfort.

On the twenty-four inch wide-screen computer monitor in front of him, Mark's most recent project was playing. It was the sweet sixteen party of a young girl named Tabitha Howser. He didn't know the family very well. He didn't know the guests very well. He had simply shown up at the party with his camera, done his job and left. Now, he couldn't take his eyes off of the screen.

The party could have been for any girl—*his* girl. The smile on Tabitha's face could have been Cindy's. The dance music could have been of her choosing. He didn't focus on the faces. If Mark allowed his vision to blur just a little bit, the details would be washed away and his mind could replace strangers with family members.

In the year since Cindy's death, Mark had tried to pick up the pieces of his life and move on. He tried his best to resume normalcy for the sake of his wife and his second daughter, Winnie. He had no choice but to be strong for them. They needed to mourn in their own ways, and his falling apart would only hurt them more.

His time alone was different. In the darkness of his office or car, he could stop smiling. For a year, he had felt as though he was walking around in a daze. His senses were dulled. Food had lost its taste, and the colors of the world weren't as vibrant as they had once been; everything seemed darker. The most troubling change to Mark was his sense of touch. At times, he could not feel a thing. He could punch a wall and it wouldn't faze him. He could jam a key into his leg, and while he knew that the pain logically had to be there, he couldn't care enough to feel it.

He stopped the video and ejected the disc from his computer. Keeping the lights off, Mark placed the disc in its case and turned off the monitor. The darkness was now complete.

He believed in a great many things. He believed in God, and in Heaven. He believed that those deserving of Hell were sent there to burn, and prayed that he would not be one of those people. He believed in demons. He believed in undiscovered creatures, which some might call monsters. He believed that there was a chance of life on other planets, but if truth be told, he didn't really care if they existed or not, since there was not much for him to do with that information either way.

Mark also believed in ghosts. There were several types of hauntings, based on all of the information gathered over the centuries. *Residual hauntings*, were images of the past repeated over and over again, like videos without a camera. There were *intelligent hauntings*, which were believed to be the actual spirits of the dead, capable of interaction with the present. The list could go on, depending on the country you happened to be in, or the people telling the story. Mark wasn't sure where the truth was, but he believed that there was something to be discovered. It was only a matter of time.

Having lived in a haunted house as a child, with a ghost who he had seen in vivid detail, Mark had always wanted answers. He had always wanted to know how the universe worked and how many levels of reality there were, which current technology could not measure. He had opened his eyes to the possibility of the supernatural, while remaining objective and discriminating in which stories he would believe and which he would shrug off.

And then Cindy died. His beliefs were tested on that day, and for a long time he couldn't bring himself to think about ghosts or monsters. It all seemed so childish and stupid. More than that, it seemed to dishonor her memory by mocking the true nature of death.

Death meant forever. If someone could stay with their families after death, *everyone* would stay with their families after death. Cindy wouldn't choose to abandon those she loved. She would have to be ripped away, kicking and screaming.

The thought hurt Mark. He didn't want to think of his daughter kicking and screaming, calling for her father's help. He couldn't think of it that way.

Time went on and those thoughts continued to spin around his mind. Maybe it hadn't been a struggle. Perhaps there was something powerful, drawing her away. Certainly, Heaven would have a lot to offer.

Then again, maybe there had been a struggle, and maybe Cindy had won. Perhaps there was a chance that his daughter hadn't moved on, but was still around them. She could have been too inexperienced as a ghost to manifest as a full-figured apparition, or to move objects. She could have been in their house, waiting for one of them to use their gadgets and listen for her.

Marion would see an investigation into their own daughter as an insult. She needed to process Cindy's death in her own way, and Mark understood that. Certainly, Winnie would not support such actions. She barely believed in any of those stories of the supernatural, as far as Mark could tell. He couldn't drag them into this process. If he tried, he could hurt them even more.

At the same time, he couldn't rid his mind of these thoughts. His dreams were plagued by images of Cindy, begging him to listen to her. He didn't know if these dreams were truly visions of his daughter, or products of his own imagination, but he couldn't write them off. If he truly believed in the existence of ghosts, how could he take the risk of not looking?

Every now and then, Mark attempted to investigate this possibility in his normal ways. Audio recorders placed in Cindy's room, or someplace where she might visit. Usually, these recordings were filled with nothing but the occasional audio glitch, which was common in Mark's line of work.

If he chose to, he could listen to a digital artifact and convince himself that it was a voice, but this was akin to looking up at a cloud and seeing a bunny rabbit. To date, he hadn't picked up a true and distinctive voice on any of those recordings.

In the pocket of Mark's jacket, he could feel the weight of a business card pulling at him. The card was given to him by another member of the paranormal investigation community. It was the card of a dentist, which was of no use to Mark. However, on the back of this card was a name and a location.

Warren Oster, was the name that Mark's friend had scribbled with rather poor penmanship, and the *Angel of Mercy Nursing Home* was the location.

Warren Oster was—supposedly—a psychic. If Mark's friend was to be believed, Warren could not only see the future, but gaze into the great hereafter and receive messages from the dead. Mark wasn't sold on the idea.

Psychics, in Mark's experience, were usually little more than illusionists. Tricksters, who enjoyed targeting emotionally needy clients, and manipulating them into believing that they were talking to the dead. They sometimes convinced themselves that they were doing a good deed by easing the minds of these clients, but in Mark's eyes they were con artists. The talented ones could pick up on small details and read people like a criminal profiler might, and the less talented would use partners to gather information and feed it back to them through various methods.

In Mark's opinion, if someone went public with their psychic talents and used them to sell books or charge for readings, they were probably fakes. That said, Mark had met one person in his years of investigation who stood a chance of being a legitimate psychic.

Martin Blue was a man in his early thirties when Mark met him. Together, they worked on a couple of cases, investigating paranormal events. Martin made no profit from his gift, and kept it a secret from people, including Mark. While he sometimes joked about knowing the date of his own death, three weeks after his thirty-third birthday, Mark thought those comments were simple, dark humor.

After Martin's death from a brain aneurysm—three weeks after his thirty-third birthday—Mark received a six page letter in the mail, detailing Martin's abilities and several predictions for the future. The dates for most of these predictions were still too far in the future for Mark to confirm or deny, but one sentence from this letter now stood out for Mark.

Ten-ten... God, I'm sorry.

For years, this sentence was a mystery to Mark, but when Cindy died on October 10th, it became clear. Martin Blue had predicted the death of Mark's daughter. He knew what was coming, and he said nothing.

The one true psychic he had ever known, and Mark would hate Martin forever.

Warren Oster fit the bill as a potentially legitimate psychic, as far as Mark could tell. Never went public with his abilities. Never made a profit from them. He had been a police officer for four decades before retiring, and now lived a quiet life in a nursing home. He would have died undiscovered if Mark's friend hadn't had a great-uncle in the same home. This lack of attention-seeking made Mark wonder if Warren might just be the answer to all of his questions.

There was an urge to see Warren, and to discover whether or not he could be believed. If Mark did trust the man, he could find out whether or not Cindy's spirit lingered, trying to communicate with her family. There was really no reason not to investigate the supposed psychic. It was Mark's job to look into these matters. Yet, despite his constant push for answers, there was some part of Mark that wondered if he really wanted to know the truth. Perhaps the lie would be easier. Maybe the con would be more comforting.

7

Each step was painful, but Winnie kept walking. She had no destination in mind, she simply needed to move. She needed to put distance between herself and her home, her family, and if possible, the rest of the world. She would just have to move more slowly than she would have liked.

Whatever lapse in judgment had convinced Winnie that it was a good idea to jump out of her window had obviously been a mistake. Her ankle was hurt, but as far as she could tell, it wasn't broken. Her shoulder was undoubtedly going to have the mother of all bruises on it, but the injury did not feel life threatening.

The pain in her ankle was a sharp, stabbing pain. Each time she put her weight on that side of her body, the pain shot through her entire leg. It was very unpleasant, and yet somehow reassuring.

The capacity for pain was there. The urgency of that pain was present. The desire for it to go away was overwhelming. If Winnie didn't know better, she'd have thought that she was a normal person, living a normal life.

If only she could feel joy as sharply.

It was only a year ago that Winnie and Cindy had crept their way out of the house together, trying not to make a sound as they went to the annual Blackout Ball. Sure, their parents weren't home at the time, and they probably would have allowed the girls to go to the party even if they did know about it, but the secret was half of the fun.

The Blackout Ball was not related to a power outage of any kind. It was named for its communications blackout. Every aspect of the party was meant to remain secret, from parents, police, and most of all, from any classmate not deemed cool enough to be invited. Each year, the location of the party would change. In the case of the previous year's party, the location was a clearing in the woods, where teens could get away with doing all of the things that would probably get them in trouble if they were ever caught.

Winnie knew that the Blackout Ball was being held that night, as she hobbled her way down the street. She didn't know *where* it was being held, but the fact that she had been left off of the guest list didn't surprise her in the least. Cindy had always been her gateway to all the best parties.

She could remember the previous year's Blackout Ball as clearly as if it had happened the night before. She and Cindy tiptoed through the dark house, tripping over objects in their path and trying to remain quiet, though bursting into a fit of laughter that would have gotten them caught if their parents had been home.

They ran across the lawn and down the street like fugitives being chased by blood hounds.

Winnie nearly smiled as she remembered that night. Yet, before her lips could turn upward, everything that happened shortly after that night flashed into her mind. Those memories were even more vivid. The aftermath of Cindy's death played out in front of her like a movie, yet the memory of their laughter as they crept through their dark house overlapped those horrible images.

The pain was like a knife stabbing into her heart. In that moment, the throbbing of her ankle faded. There was only so much hurt to go around.

In the distance, she heard a loud engine roaring down a road. The horn honked and the cheerful howls of teenage boys could be heard. Somewhere out there, life went on.

Winnie once again found herself growing angry at that thought.

8

The corpse was wet. This was the cause of great perplexity in Obell. Initially, she thought the corpse had been too dirty to be reanimated. Any hint of an uncalculated ingredient could throw her entire spell off. A spot of dried mud from just outside her own door could have any number of unexpected results.

Part of her was curious to see how the mud would affect the zombie once it had been reanimated. Perhaps the mud of her doorstep would bind the creature to Obell's home, or to Obell herself. If this were the case, it might be a convenient addition to the potion. She would hate to have her zombie wandering the streets, eating the brains of anyone it encountered. Then again, a servant is far more useful when it can run errands.

At the end of her internal debate, she decided that while the experiment might have been a worthy one, it would need to wait for another day. This corpse was meant to test her potion, and she could not risk throwing off the balance that had taken her years to perfect.

After casting off the horrible rodent from the corpse and out of her home, Obell felt a need to shower. It was as this thought occurred to her that she first noticed the mud that had gathered on the corpse as she dragged it into her home.

She hauled the body through her house, into her bathroom and spread it out on the floor of her shower. For the next half hour, she scrubbed that corpse until she was sure that every particle of mud was gone. Once it was cleaned, she dragged the corpse back to her kitchen and hefted it onto the table.

As she turned to consider her next move, she noticed the trail of water across the floor. The corpse was wet. Water was a foreign ingredient. Just as the mud might bind the zombie to her home, water could do any number of things. Water was used to baptize, and the last thing Obell wanted was a God-fearing zombie, evangelizing her ear off at the dinner table. The horror of that thought sent a chill up her spine.

Water was a powerful symbol, which could not be ignored, so she would have to wait for the corpse to dry before she attempted to perform her wicked deeds.

As she returned her gaze to the corpse on the table, studying each of its youthful features and imagining all of the evil—yet entirely tasteful—uses that she might have for such a creature, there were several more factors which danced through her head.

The soap from its shower. Obell didn't know what went into making commercially available bath soap, with a hint of floral scent. She could not begin to imagine what impact it might have on the corpse, but hoped that it had been rinsed thoroughly enough so that it wouldn't matter.

The dust on the floor of her house, through which she'd dragged the corpse on its way back to the kitchen. The air which surrounded the corpse. The fibers of the towel that she used to dry it. The oils from her own skin. The stitches that were holding its chest closed.

It was a shopping list of possible failures which would have driven Obell insane if she allowed them to. She stopped those thoughts dead in their tracks. Surely, her spell would account for the normal pollutants of the world. The body was not covered in dust, as it had been with mud, and whatever small amount of soap remained on the thing was surely not enough to turn her zombie into a day-spa employee.

Her mind began to settle. She had spent years working on the formula for her zombie, and she had taken many factors into account. She was prepared to perform her spell. There was no place in her brain for stage fright; only sweet success.

Placing her hand on the cold, lifeless flesh of the corpse's head, Obell closed her eyes, savoring the moment.

"Soon, my son of darkness, you will take your place by my side" she whispered.

She opened her eyes and hesitated for a moment, saying to

herself, "Son of darkness? Or... Son of twilight?"

Obell walked toward the kitchen, dragging her hand along the corpse as she made her way past it, "Child of destiny?"

9

In his mind, Mark had imagined the home as a large, Gothic building. He expected gargoyles to watch him as he approached the building, and intricately carved dark wood to surround him as he walked inside.

Instead, the home looked like a wing in a hospital. Though dated, the interior of the home reminded Mark less of Dracula's castle, and more of the all-girls school featured on *The Facts of Life*. While the 1970's decor was certainly scary, it was not creepy in the least.

The lobby was empty, for the most part. Next to the entrance sat an old woman, sleeping in a wheelchair. Though the doors squeaked loudly as they opened and closed, the old woman remained asleep.

After pressing the button for the elevator, Mark spent several minutes waiting for it to arrive. Behind the closed doors, he could hear the workings of the elevator humming and churning, bringing the car closer and closer, but taking far too long in doing so. Just as he began to wonder if it might be faster for him to take the stairs, the elevator doors slid open and a gust of air blew over him, carrying with it the scent of mothballs and bleach.

Before stepping into the elevator, Mark glanced toward the stairs which led upward, once again considering the option, but deciding against it. When he did finally step inside, the elevator car shook just enough to make Mark uneasy. The doors slid shut behind him.

The ride from the lobby to the third floor of the home was slow, and the mechanical sounds that Mark had heard the elevator making from the lobby were much louder inside. He stared at a piece of paper that had been placed behind the glass of the emergency call box, assuring passengers that the elevator had been inspected only three months earlier. Rather than resting at ease as he stared at this paper, Mark began to question the validity of any and all inspectors from the state.

Once he arrived on the third floor of the building, Mark wasted no time in hopping out of the elevator. He could hear the car shake once again as his weight was removed from the smelly box and he decided right then that he would be taking the stairs on his way out.

The elevator was the only unnerving aspect of the home. On

the third floor, residents slowly roamed the halls, and sat in the dining room playing board games while nurses and other employees went about their business. There was a definite smell to the third floor, which was neither mothballs nor bleach. It smelled organic, yet not at all like food.

Right outside of the elevator, there was a nurse's station, which was empty at the moment. There were three hallways which branched off in different directions from that spot. One to the left, one to the right, and one which led straight ahead. Each of these hallways had signs which indicated which room numbers could be found down each hall.

Mark followed the sign which pointed the way to room 342, where Warren Oster lived. He walked slowly and quietly, as he had walked through his grandmother's home as a child. Somehow, being around the elderly always had Mark on his best behavior, even as the gap between their ages and his own grew smaller. Though in his forties, Mark felt as though he would be scolded for rushing through the halls, or making too much noise.

The door to room 342 was closed, but not entirely. It hung open, telling passersby that Warren was inside, but did not require total privacy. Mark knocked anyway, and waited for an answer. When none came, he knocked again. This time, he opened the door just enough to glance inside.

As Mark's eyes swept across the room, Warren Oster looked up from his chair and said, "Who are you?"

Mark smiled politely and walked into the room, but making

sure to leave the door open just a little bit, as he had found it.

"My name is Mark McKeller. I was told that I could find you here."

Warren was a fragile looking man. He was not the type of elderly person that one would find on television, running in parks and leading an active lifestyle. He was the traditional old man, sitting in a recliner and watching *Matlock* reruns on TV, with the volume turned down. He wore a pair of gray pants and a belt, though neither seemed to fit him properly. His red and black flannel shirt was tucked into his pants, and also seemed baggy. If Mark were to guess, he would say that Warren was losing weight quickly. It was not a good sign.

"What?" Warren asked, squinting in an attempt to see Mark's face more clearly, "Who are you?"

A little more loudly than before, Mark replied, "My name is Mark. I was told that I could find you here."

"Right. By who?" Warren asked in a tone which reminded Mark of Jimmy Stewart in some undefinable way.

"Evan Flannery. He's a friend of mine."

When Warren heard the name, he sat back in his chair and rolled his eyes. He looked to the television for a moment, leaving Mark to guess what he was thinking. After some time, he turned back to Mark.

"I told that son of a bitch that I never wanted to hear from him again," Warren told him, "That went for his little spooky friends too."

Mark wasn't sure how to respond to this. Evan hadn't mentioned any sort of feud between Warren and himself. It was a detail that Mark would have preferred to have known.

After a moment of consideration, Mark nodded to Warren and said, "I understand, sir. I'm sorry to have bothered you."

Mark turned and walked toward the door. He planned on making a phone call to Evan Flannery on the way to his car, thanking him for the time wasted. As he reached for the doorknob, he heard Warren behind him.

"They call this place the *Angel of Mercy* nursing home," Warren said.

Mark turned around, finding Warren staring at the television once again. For the longest time, the old man said nothing, leaving Mark to wonder if he was still supposed to leave, or if Warren had meant to engage him in some sort of conversation.

After a moment of consideration, Mark took a step toward Warren and said, "No offense to those in charge, but it smells more like the angel of death."

Warren smiled. Apparently Mark had replied in the proper fashion. He took another step toward Warren.

"I really didn't mean to bother you, sir."

"Tell that to the old woman with the bonnet."

Mark tried to think of a response that would fit Warren's comment, but nothing came to mind.

Warren shook his head, "Walk right through and don't tip your hat or say please. It's just rude. Ruder than the shadows, and they're a bunch of squatters."

For several seconds, Mark tried to run Warren's comments through his mind, hoping that they would eventually make sense after being processed and filtered like one of his investigation recordings in a computer. When that didn't happen, he pressed his lips together and forced an awkward smile.

Warren nodded slightly and reached for the remote control to his TV. Turning it off, he said, "So, you were told that you could find me here?"

"That's right, sir."

"Why is that?"

Mark shifted his weight, suddenly feeling uncomfortable in Warren's room, with the door slightly open behind him. He felt as though he was being watched by someone just outside the room.

He walked to the door and shut it, though he saw nobody on the other side.

"We need privacy?" asked Warren.

"I thought you might prefer to keep this conversation to ourselves."

Warren chuckled and said, "Boy, there's no such thing as privacy in a place like this. If a good ear ain't listening, a dead one is."

Mark scanned the room, wondering if he and Warren were truly alone. The investigator in him wanted to pull out his audio recorder and electro-magnetic field detector, but this was not the time to investigate. He was there for a reason.

"You see dead people," Mark blurted. "Ghosts, I mean."

"Sometimes. I'm not like that gal on the TV, but I've had an uncomfortable conversation or two in my day. They very rarely know they're dead."

"Right. That would be... uncomfortable."

"I see things that other people don't. Sometimes, that's a lost soul. Other times, it's a different angle on the big picture."

Mark was once again unsure how to respond. He was not entirely clear on what Warren meant with that last comment.

Rolling his eyes at Mark's obvious puzzlement, Warren said, "People like to call themselves psychic. They like to think they see the future and know what's going to happen. That's bull; all those crystals and card games. It's crap, just like fairies and witches with potions. There is no future to see. It hasn't happened yet. And if anyone ever did see it, there'd be no way for that future to remain the same. I don't claim to see the future. I see the world around me. Sometimes close to home, and sometimes not so close. If it seems like I'm claiming to know what's going to happen, it's because I see all the pieces on the board."

"Remote viewing," Mark commented, "The government experimented with the idea during the second World War and up until the 1970's. The idea was that these people—the remote viewers—could see our enemies and gain intelligence from thousands of miles away."

With a slight smirk, Warren said, "You don't say."

"I read a book on the subject," Mark replied, sitting on the corner of Warren's bed.

"I had a dream a few weeks back. I saw this girl. This lost little thing, trying to find her way..." Warren trailed off, and his eyes wandered toward the window.

Mark waited for Warren to continue his thought for what seemed like minutes. He said nothing, because it didn't seem as though Warren had forgotten to finish what he was saying. It seemed as though Warren was trying to remember exactly what he had seen, and to figure out how to properly convey those images.

"You need to find your daughter," Warren said at long last. "That's why you came to me."

Mark nodded, and looked at the ground. He said nothing.

"I saw that girl. She was searching too. Lost. Scared."

Mark's eyes went back to Warren, now filled with concern for Cindy. His fears of her becoming one of those lost souls that he had spent so much time researching were becoming a reality.

"Can you help me find her? Talk to her?" Mark asked. His voice was weak and shaky. His palms were beginning to sweat, though he felt cold.

Warren hesitated for a moment, studying Mark's eyes. He was reading something inside of Mark, but Mark didn't care what the old man saw. He only cared for his daughter. After Warren was finished studying Mark, he pointed to a sketchbook on his nightstand.

"Hand that to me, and the pen next to it," he told Mark.

10

Marion paced back and forth in the kitchen. All things considered, it was a calm pacing; very slow and graceful, showing none of the many emotions that were swirling through her gut.

The audio recorder was on the counter nearby and her eyes went to it each time she passed. It was not only the representation of so many issues within her family, but also the possibility for change. She was at a crossroads, and her decision could have determined the path that she and her family would go down.

To delete the recording would deny Mark the chance to work through his feelings and bring him to his natural resolution. It could drive a wedge between the couple and push them apart forever.

Statistics showed that losing a child often led to divorce.

Marion didn't want to lose Mark. She didn't want to lose the family that they had created or the life that they had built together. They were two halves of one whole.

On the other side of her internal struggle was her relationship with her only remaining daughter. If she could show Winnie that she was on her side, it could bring her daughter to the realization that she was not alone in this world. Winnie had been so isolated since Cindy's death, and perhaps some show of solidarity would begin the healing process.

There was no simple answer. No matter how many times she ran through the potential outcomes in her mind, she could not convince herself that this issue would be resolved without further conflict. There did not seem to be a way of containing or controlling the situation, which annoyed Marion. It made her angry. It made her want to scream.

But screaming would resolve nothing, she told herself. *Losing control of myself will only make matters worse.*

It had been her motto all along. She needed to remain in control of herself, for the sake of everyone around her. She could allow her family to cry, but she needed to remain detached for their sake. She needed to look at each situation from an outside perspective, as she would with any other patients.

She took a deep breath and calmed herself. It would be too simple for her to base her actions on emotional response—To scream at Mark for planting a bug at their daughter's grave, without even telling Marion; to scream at Winnie for taking it so personally. To scream, just for the sake of screaming.

There were moments when—just before falling asleep at night —Marion found herself angry at Cindy. For leaving the family. For never fulfilling her potential. For entire seconds, the anger directed toward Cindy brought Marion's daughter out of the abstract and back into the present. In anger, Marion felt almost as though Cindy were still present. Entire seconds, before the inevitable rush of remorse, followed by a renewed sense of loss.

On those nights, she sometimes found herself crying. It was the only time that she allowed herself to lose control, even if only for a minute or two and even if she managed to keep her weeping silent so that Mark would not hear. By the time she fell asleep, she was in control once again. By morning, the tears on her pillow would dry and the puffiness of her eyes would fade. Nobody would ever know. Their perfectly calm, rational shelter from the storm would remain intact.

The audio recorder was a line in the sand. On one side of that line stood her husband, and on the other side, her daughter. The choice was impossible.

She stopped pacing and sat on a stool next to the island in the center of the kitchen. She closed her eyes and covered them with her hands, shutting out the world.

"Okay," she said to herself, "I am a professional. I do this all the time. So, how would I handle any other family?"

After considering this question for a few moments, Marion decided that her best course of action would be to defuse the situation before it became more volatile than it already was. Perhaps if she could talk to Winnie, she could spin the situation in a new direction.

Manipulation was not something that she regularly suggested to her patients in a situation such as this, but it seemed to be the best option in that particular moment, so Marion stood from her stool and walked toward the stairs.

As she walked, she tried to plan her words carefully. She wanted to make sure that she sounded caring and concerned for Winnie, so that she didn't further alienate her daughter. At the same time, she wanted to direct her daughter toward a cooler, calmer reaction to the recorder so that there would be no anger toward Mark.

The best thing for everyone in the family was to know that their emotions were valid and that there was a safe environment for them to explore those emotions. That had to include Mark as well as Winnie.

As she ran through the speeches that she might give to Winnie, she found each of them leading toward conflict rather than rational conversation. It seemed impossible to plan for such a conversation, since her daughter had become so angry that even the simplest *hello* could lead to Winnie screaming. There was no understanding Winnie's logic, because her response came from a place of emotion, not reason. So, Marion decided to wing it. She could more easily navigate the situation if she had no firm plan.

Once she reached Winnie's bedroom door, she stood in the

hallway and gathered her thoughts. She took deep breaths and straightened her clothes, preparing herself for deep and meaningful conversation. She then knocked on the door.

There was no answer.

11

Winnie limped down the street, trying to put as much distance between herself and her home as possible, but any attempt to hurry along would have been futile. With each step, there was pain and a wince, and the sucking of air through her teeth. The pattern was almost rhythmical. If she were in a better mood, she may have started singing Sam Cook's *Chain Gang*, but since there was no song in her heart, it remained in her head, where it played on a constant loop.

The pain was no longer as sharp as it had been at first. It was getting better, but even if it wasn't, she would have felt no need to rush to the hospital for help. Hospitals had never been of any use to her anyway. She hated them.

The chill that she had felt during the day had grown sharper as darkness fell. Though the clouds had thinned enough to let the light of the full moon shine down like a spotlight across an otherwise dark area of town, the feel of night hadn't been lost.

Night had a way of settling Winnie's mind in a way that daytime never could. There was a stillness to night that could not be matched, even on the calmest and most quiet of days. Sounds seemed to carry differently at night. The air seemed somehow cleaner. There was also a mystery to the nighttime—a danger that might have been too scary for some, but which thrilled Winnie.

From the darkness of night, anything could jump out at her. A bear could attack, or a mugger could charge. She had seen enough movies to convince herself, on some deep and hidden level, that a vampire might swoop down from the night sky and take her in his arms. From there, the direction of her fantasy would depend on which movie she'd seen most recently. On that particular night, her mind wandered down a path of romance and danger, rather than bloody horrible death.

As a gentle breeze passed, a strand of hair blew across Winnie's face, and the leaves of a nearby tree shook. Despite her limping, she allowed her imagination to cast her as the heroine from one of her supernatural romance novels. The hair across her face was like the image from a steamy book cover. The rustling leaves were where her vampiric lover awaited.

She wasn't delusional enough to believe that an actual vampire was watching her. She hadn't lost touch with reality, no matter how desperately she may have wanted to. She wanted nothing more than to imagine herself in a fantasy life, with no memory of anything that had come before.

From behind her a car's horn honked. The unexpected noise pulled Winnie from her daydream so suddenly that she couldn't help but jump. Placing a hand over her chest and feeling the pounding of her own heart, she turned to face the car.

"Jerk!" she called, before completing the turn or seeing who was behind the wheel.

When she did see the driver of the car, she recognized the face of Tami Hurd. Tami was a young woman of mixed decent, and with features which seemed to capture all of the best elements of her different ethnicities; dark skin, light eyes, full lips, and brains which matched her beauty. She was a cheerleader, student body president, and a friend to almost everyone.

Tami had been Cindy's best friend for as long as anyone could remember, and had been like another big sister to Winnie for most of her life. The three girls played together, laughed together and swooned together over whichever movie star they happened to have a crush on at any given moment. After Cindy's death, all of that ended. Winnie lost both of her sisters.

"Winnie!" Tami called from her car, "Get in! Blackout tonight!"

Winnie wasn't sure how to respond to Tami at first. It was as though Tami had forgotten everything that had happened. As though Cindy had never existed.

Winnie wanted to look Tami in the eyes and ask her how she

could even consider going to a party. How could she move on, as though everything was perfectly normal?

Three weeks after Cindy died, Winnie saw Tami out on a date with some guy from the football team. *Three weeks* and Tami was back to eating pizza and hanging out. Winnie could have punched Tami in the face, but she chose to be the better person. If Tami didn't care to mourn for Cindy, Winnie would do it alone. If Tami wanted to abandon Winnie when she needed her the most, that was fine too. So, Winnie moved on from Tami as quickly as Tami had moved on from Cindy.

Now, Tami wanted to take Winnie to a party. It seemed almost funny. It was moments such as these that brought Winnie to the realization that she was truly alone. Nobody else in the world felt the way that she felt. Nobody cared. Cindy was dead, and as far as the rest of the world was concerned, it was *good riddance*. It made Winnie sick to her stomach.

"Get in!" Tami called again.

Winnie wanted to spit in her face. She wanted to drag that perky cheerleader through her open window and rip the hair out of her head. She wanted Tami to—for once—feel a fraction of the pain that Winnie felt every day of her life since Cindy's death.

But Winnie was a better person than that. She was better than all of the friends who had simply moved on since Cindy died. She would not lower herself to their level of inhumanity. So instead, she turned and began to walk away.

Tami put her car into *park* and hurried to catch up to Winnie on foot. When she was close enough to put a hand on Winnie's shoulder, she stopped Winnie and stepped in front of her.

"What's happened to you?" Tami asked. The look in her eye feigning concern and making Winnie feel even sicker than before. "Why won't you talk to me anymore, Winnie?"

Again, Winnie wanted to spit in Tami's face. She wanted to rip the girl apart for abandoning not only Cindy, but for abandoning Winnie in her time of grief. Of all of the people in the world, Tami should have felt the pain of loss as much as Winnie did, and yet she was living life as though everything was normal.

Winnie shook her head and grinned in disbelief. She said, "What's happened to me? Let me think about that for a minute. What could have possibly happened to me?"

She took a moment to pretend that she was deep in thought. It was an act that was carried on for just a few moments longer than absolutely necessary. She then looked Tami in her perfect little eyes and said, "My sister died. Your best friend died, and you want to party like it's friggin' Mardi Gras."

"What do you want me to do, Winn? Do you want me to die too?"

"I want you to feel something! I want you to at least pretend that you care."

Tami said nothing for a few seconds. What was there for her to say? Winnie knew that there was no good response for Tami to fire back with. There was no good excuse. Instead, Tami pushed out some obviously fake tears.

"Do you know how often I reach for the phone to call Cindy and tell her about my day?" Tami asked, "How often I wake up from a dream where I see her, and for a few seconds, I forget she's not here anymore?"

Winnie couldn't help but roll her eyes. Cindy was dead, and Tami wanted to make it all about herself. It was the shining image of selfishness.

"I miss her, Winn. Every day," Tami said, wiping a fake tear from her cheek, "But I didn't die. I'm *here*. I have to live every day for the rest of my life, and I can't do that if I pretend that I died with her."

"Well, aren't you heroic? You're living for today, because life is beautiful and important. How convenient for you. You get to be a skank for the greater good of humanity."

Tami smiled. She actually smiled, and then tried to play it off as though she were the one being insulted. Once again, it was all about her.

Then, Tami said, "So your big plan for life is to walk around like a zombie? Do you really think that's how Cindy would want you to mourn for her?"

"Don't say her name. You don't get to do that anymore. You want to dance on her grave, that's fine. But you don't get to pretend that you care."

"I care!" Tami yelled, and seemed to grow better at her crying act as she pretended to hold back sobs. She turned and began to walk toward her car, but stopped herself. She then walked back to

Winnie and said, "Don't do this. Please, Winnie, I am begging you not to let this destroy you. Please. Don't go down like this."

Winnie pretended to consider Tami's words. She acted as though she cared what that backstabbing prom queen had to say. She then looked Tami in the eyes and told her, "I don't have a choice. See, I actually give a damn about someone who isn't me."

With that, Winnie turned and walked away. After a year, she had finally told Tami what she thought of her and it felt great.

She could feel Tami watching her. She knew that Tami was trying to think of the perfect comeback, and the silence proved that she could not think of one. This made Winnie smile.

"Cindy is dead, Winnie!" Tami finally yelled, stating the obvious, "You're not!"

If that was supposed to hurt Winnie in some way, Tami had failed. Winnie wasn't even sure what the insult was meant to be. All that she knew was that she had put Tami in her place. She had defended her sister's memory. Once again, Winnie had proven that she didn't need anyone else. If she was meant to be alone in this world, that was fine by her.

12

Creating the potion to reanimate the dead was like creating the perfect recipe for chicken soup, as far as Obell was concerned. It required not only an understanding of each individual flavor that went into the mix, but also a talent for understanding how those flavors would interact with each other.

Shakespeare would have been proud of Obell. Her plan was grand and dramatic. Her spell was nothing short of poetic. As she watched the giant pot of water boil on the stove, she could not help but grin and repeat to herself that classic line, *Double, double toil and trouble; Fire burn and cauldron bubble.*

Boiling water was not merely for the dramatic impact of standing over a boiling cauldron. Though the classic witches of *Macbeth* were always strong inspirations to Obell, the work that she was performing on that night was far more important than the smoke and mirrors used by stage actors in some play.

Water was a form of purification. When used in the potion— and not merely on the body itself—it cleansed the body of its previous life, and prevented John Doe from running home to Mommy as soon as he awoke. Boiling the water also allowed the rest of Obell's brew to blend and stew as needed.

Into the pot of boiling water, she added three quarters of a cup of graveyard soil. She'd collected dirt from a nearby cemetery just that morning, making sure that it was as fresh as possible.

The purpose of the graveyard soil was to tie her spell to the dead. She imagined that this was something like dialing an area code before a phone number. After all, an improperly directed spell could result in *resurrection* rather than *reanimation*, and she did not want a teenage boy running around her house, nagging her to let him borrow her car.

Double, double toil and trouble; Fire burn and cauldron bubble.

Next came the dirt from a hospital's lawn. This was an ingredient that Obell had debated with herself for a very long time. It seemed like a bad idea to her at first, incorporating a link to the living and a potential sign of healing. Hospitals were hardly the symbol of wicked deeds and magic. Yet, she could not shake the feeling that she needed the soil to complete the symbolic circle in her spell. Tying death to life seemed like the thing to do, in some strange way. She was trying to get a damaged corpse to stand up and walk, after all. That would require some amount of healing energy. However, she wanted to make it very clear that death would outweigh life in this equation, so she only added one quarter of a cup of the hospital dirt.

Double, double toil and trouble; Fire burn and cauldron bubble.

The line from *Macbeth* that echoed through her thoughts with each addition to the pot was really beginning to annoy her, like a pop song that was stuck in her head. Though she tried to bring in images of other witches from different films and books and recall their more memorable quotes, nothing seemed to knock that line from *Macbeth* out of her head.

She was beginning to hate Shakespeare.

Deadened basil from her own garden provided a nice, fresh scent to the brew. It was the first of several herbs, chosen for their medicinal properties. Many ancient cultures had depended on herbs for thousands of years before the advent of Tylenol. The herbs would help her corpse to move around, preventing tightening of the muscles, easing the circulation of her potion through its body, and taking the edge off of its awakening, so that it would not panic and cause harm to itself or—more importantly —to Obell.

Even more herbs would be placed in the mouth of the corpse before the injection of the potion, further aiding the process.

Next into the pot, she tossed the petals from three roses of different colors. Red rose petals were, in Obell's mind, a symbol of beauty and perfection. They represented her wish to have a zombie whose flesh was not rotting and who could refrain from drooling all over the floor.

Pink rose petals symbolized the grace and elegance that she wished her new pet to possess. She did not want a zombie who stumbled around at a snail's pace, taking an hour to make its way across the room. She had seen enough movies in her day to know the pitfalls of zombification.

The lavender rose petals that she added next were a token of whimsy. In every spell, there should be an element of the fantastic, and this was her way of supplying that element.

She stirred the pot, and the line from *Macbeth* played once more in her mind.

After allowing the rose petals to steep, Obell added moss from a nearby tree. Years earlier, she had read that moss was a symbol of motherhood. If successful on that night, motherhood is what she hoped to achieve. For so long, she had imagined herself as pregnant, with the idea for this spell growing inside of her and maturing like a baby. Now, she was ready to bring that spell into the world and the thought of that final moment sent a chill up her spine each time she pictured it. She couldn't help but smile as she added the moss.

She added juniper next, as a symbol of protection. After everything that had happened in her life, it seemed as though an element of protection would be useful to any of her creations.

Three drops of her own blood. No more. No less. This was a

vital aspect of the spell. It was a piece of her own life force. It was a means of giving herself as a blood sacrifice, without the need to go overboard. She did want to live to see her creation, after all.

After her blood was dropped into the pot, Obell watched the liquid bubble and churn. It was almost ready. She could feel the power within that liquid. If she listened closely enough, she could almost hear the voice of the grim reaper who was sitting at the barrier between life and death, waiting to deliver her prize. It was beautiful, but it was not yet ready.

She walked to a nearby cabinet and pulled open its squeaky door. Inside the cabinet, there was a small metal box which was tightly secured by chains and locked with a heavy-duty padlock. Inside of that box was the most vital of all ingredients that Obell would need to make the dead rise. It was something so simple, and yet nobody would think twice about the power it possessed. It radiated life. It contained hopes and dreams. It was the symbol of what could be, and what could be lost forever.

She had locked this ingredient away so long ago that she could barely remember what it looked like, or how it felt to hold it in her hands. The very thought of seeing this piece of the puzzle once again brought a lump to her throat, because even she could not ignore the complete corruption of something that had always been so innocent.

She barely looked at the thing as she removed it from the box and dropped it into the pot. She did not stop to examine it or appreciate its beauty. She held her breath, so that she could not smell the sweetness of this thing, which threatened to burn through her very core with a mere whiff.

Somehow, of all that she had done in her life, and all that she was about to do still, nothing had ever made her stop and second guess her actions quite like that one deed—That one ingredient and what it meant.

For minutes afterward, Obell felt the evil that she had inside of her, and for that brief time, she did not delight in its flavor.

The moment passed, however. In a remarkably short amount of time, she pushed those thoughts and feelings aside and she once again marveled at the power of her own creation. Soon, the dead would walk the earth.

She turned to face the body that would soon rise. As it rested on the table, there was nothing for her to connect with. She did not view the lifeless thing as a boy whose life had been cut short. It was merely an empty vessel. She viewed it the same way that she would view an empty Honda, parked outside of a used car lot.

It was not in pristine condition. There was damage to the body, both from the actions which claimed the life of its former occupant and from the autopsy that was performed afterward. Beyond that damage, however, she saw potential. It had sleek lines, and curves. There was little excess fat to weigh it down once it was on its feet. All that she needed to do was rebuild the engine, and maybe buff out some of the dings, and her project would be completed.

Her brew had a very distinctive smell to it. The herbs and

flowers were not entirely unpleasant when each flavor was singled out on their own, but when taken as a whole, the potion would hardly sell at any of the finer perfume counters. It was earthy and bitter. The steam that rose around her brought tears to her eyes.

It was through these tears that Obell first noticed an odd occurrence on the body which she had been studying. She wasn't sure at first whether she had really seen what she thought she saw, or if her eyes had been playing tricks on her. As she stepped closer to the body, she confirmed that it was very real.

Placing a hand on the corpse's chest, she leaned closer to its face and looked at its lifeless eyes. A haze had formed over the dried out eyeballs, giving them an almost porcelain appearance.

There was a thick black liquid dripping from the corners of each eye. She was not a medical examiner and had very little familiarity with corpses or the various liquids and gasses that they might secrete. To her, this black liquid seemed out of place. It seemed... wrong.

Black liquid or not, her plan was in motion. She would not allow any strange goo to interfere with the project that had been so long in the making.

Hurrying into the kitchen, she snatched a paper towel from its roll and returned to the body. She wiped the eyes clear of as much of the black goo as she could remove, and tossed the towel into the garbage can as she walked back to the stove to check on her potion.

Giving the pot a good stir, Obell could not help but recite that annoying Shakespearean line, "Double double, toil and trouble; Fire burn and cauldron bubble."

If her plans worked, she decided that her next project would involve reanimating the body of William Shakespeare and using it for target practice. Obviously, his religious bigotry had seeped so far into human culture that even legitimate witches could not perform their most sacred rituals without hearing that parody echo through their minds.

Her recipe called for the evil to stew for an hour before being used, but Obell was growing impatient. She glanced at her watch, seeing that only minutes had passed since she had mixed her potion.

Letting out a sigh, she was just about to return to the body and make sure that everything was in place for her ritual, but as she turned away from the stove, her attention was drawn elsewhere.

Out of the corner of her eye, Obell saw a dark figure dart across the room. Startled, she turned to get a better look at the intruder, but saw nothing. Aside from herself and her would-be zombie, the house appeared empty.

13

Winnie was content to be alone. She didn't need friends or boyfriends. If she'd learned one thing in life, it was that people were unreliable. If their own egos didn't cause them to disappoint, their mortality would. Having people in her life would be a weakness. It would set her up for inevitable suffering.

When she was alone, she was free to be herself. Winnie could think whatever she wanted without worrying about hurting someone's feelings. She could wear whatever she wanted without caring whether or not the color of her top would jive with whatever season it was.

In addition to the freedom that came with being alone, there was also a realization: Winnie hated people, generally speaking. Sure, she might like the rare being who happened to not suck as much as everyone else, but for the most part, people were annoying, selfish and stupid. She was better off without them.

She sat on a park bench as she pondered these thoughts for what must have been the millionth time. It was dark out, and the shadows of the trees hid her bench from the moonlight. This gave Winnie the opportunity to see without being seen as she rested her ankle.

Years earlier, Winnie had enjoyed the park during the daylight hours. She loved to run through the open areas with her friends, watching other people go about their lives, and imagining what those lives could have been like. Somehow, in her imagination, nobody's life ever seemed horrible when they were wandering through a sunny park.

Now, she preferred the park at night, in the dark. She preferred the playground to be free of screaming children and mothers who had nothing better to do with their time than gossip. She preferred the shadows to the light. She enjoyed the mystery of not knowing what was hiding around the next corner. It was honest. Daylight provided a false sense of security, making you believe that what you see is what you get, but nothing is as it seems. At least nighttime was man enough to admit it.

If she could have her way, the park would always be empty at night. She could sit in silence in a place where nobody would think to look for her. She could listen to the silence. She could wonder if some hidden danger was coming for her and for some reason, that threat would thrill her.

Unfortunately, Winnie was not alone on that night. Sitting on the swings was a young couple, apparently in love. They were a bright and happy couple. Both blond and dressed in light colors; both disgustingly attractive. They made pouty faces at each other as they whispered sweet nothings and rubbed noses.

Winnie wanted to gag. She wanted to throw something at the couple and scream at them to wake up and realize that the world was not a place for Eskimo kisses and sappy love letters. In the real world, people cheat on each other. They spread pictures, taken in private, all over the internet. They hurt each other.

She watched that couple, smiling and happy. She wondered what it must be like to be them. She would hate to be so ignorant. She would hate looking herself in the mirror if she were so content with the nature of the world. She looked at them and wondered if they had made a conscious decision to ignore all of that, or if they truly were as stupid as they seemed.

As that couple on the swing set kissed, Winnie cringed with disgust, and yet she wondered how it would feel to... feel.

14

Mark sat for what seemed like hours, waiting for Warren to complete his work. The old man had fallen silent. His eyes had closed, but he was not asleep.

Warren was breathing deeply. His eyes moved back and forth behind his eyelids. The pen in his right hand danced across the paper so quickly and chaotically that Mark was certain that nothing productive was being accomplished. Still, he said nothing.

Instead, Mark's mind drifted. He thought about the daughter that he had lost, yet feared for on a daily basis. Of all things, the tone of her voice when she was annoyed with him was what stuck out the most on that night. He could almost hear Cindy's high-pitched screaming, and though he never would have expected it when she was alive, the memory brought the slightest of smiles to his lips.

He wondered what he would tell Marion when he finally arrived home that night. Of course, he had never told her that he was going to visit Warren, in the hopes of contacting Cindy. She wouldn't be happy about that at all. Still, he did not wish to lie to her. He couldn't look her in the eye and tell her that he'd been working late, editing videos.

It would have been so much easier for Mark if he thought that Marion would support his mission. Throughout their relationship, they had been partners in most things. They investigated together. They raised children together. They'd gone through phases of *Lord of the Rings* and *Star Wars* fandom, all together. They had kept no secrets until recently. It went against his nature to keep those secrets, but opening the most painful wound possible for Marion would also go against his nature.

Warren ripped a sheet of paper out of the sketchbook and allowed it to fall to the floor, next to several others that he had dropped since his work began.

Mark looked at the floor, hoping to catch a glimpse of what Warren was scribbling, but each sheet of paper fell face down, as though Warren had spent years practicing the art of drawing out the mystery. Except, Warren did not seem to be one for shows. Unlike most supposed psychics or mediums that Mark had encountered over the years, Warren was not trying to sell himself. In fact, Mark got the distinct impression that Warren wished to be left alone. Yet, the pen danced. Warren was helping Mark for reasons that were not entirely clear.

Staring down at the pen in Warren's hand, Mark tried to imagine what all of this could be leading to.

In some practices, mediums would scribble freely as they channeled the dead. Eventually, as the spirits began to communicate, those scribbles would become words. Many sheets of paper had been wasted in Mark's presence over the years, all for the sake of what would usually be single-word messages, too vague to be of any use.

If, after all of the waiting that Mark had done that night, Warren had only managed to produce the word *help* or *love*, Mark would call the man a liar and walk out. It would not be the first time. His patience for such acts had been lost many years earlier, along with his patience for supposed paranormal investigators faking their evidence on reality TV shows. He had a respect for the field, and a passion for answering questions that he had been asking for as long as he could remember. Anything that mocked that passion angered him.

Warren's expression turned more intense. Though his eyes remained closed, it was as though he had looked into a bright light and he needed to look away. Yet, he didn't. With his pen still hard at work, Warren fought the urge to stop. His grip on the pad in his left hand grew so tight that Mark thought it must have hurt the old man.

In his right hand, Warren was still holding the pen, but his fingers had slipped at some point, and were now dragging across the paper, making a horrible scratching sound with each movement. At any moment, Mark expected to see blood drip from Warren's fingernails and swirl across the paper, but that did not happen.

Warren leaned his head back, breathing even more heavily than before. Mark's worry was increasing. He began to wonder if he should call a nurse for assistance, but something kept him seated. It was more powerful than curiosity; more powerful than fear. It was selfish desire. He would get help for Warren, but he needed for the old man to finish his work before a nurse came in and ripped away the only hope that Mark had.

Even sitting there, having made the decision to wait, Mark knew that he was wrong. His soul could not be undamaged by such a choice. He hated the feeling of that darkness, crawling inside of him like a worm. It brought tears to his eyes, but still he remained seated. Cindy was his little girl. For her, he was capable of a great many things that he never could have imagined.

Warren ripped one last sheet of paper from his pad and dropped it to the floor before his frantic scribbling came to an end and the old man's head fell to his chest. He was still breathing. He was alive, but Warren was not at all well.

"Are you okay?" Mark asked, as his eyes drifted toward the mess of papers on the floor.

Warren tried to speak, but could not form words. His tongue searched for moisture in his mouth, but found none. Instead, he dropped the pen from his hand and gestured toward a glass of water sitting on a nearby table.

Mark, still not a complete monster, brought Warren the glass of water and allowed the man to drink before pushing for answers.

"You can look at the papers," Warren finally managed to say, "But I'm not sure you're going to like where they lead you."

Mark was confused. "Lead me?"

He grabbed the stack of papers off of the floor, keeping them in the same order in which they had fallen as he straightened them out. When he looked at the first sheet, Mark didn't know how to react. Certainly, it was more than a single word, and yet he didn't quite know what to make of it.

15

When Obell was a teenager in high school, she was forced to endure a home economics class which she found both disgusting and tedious. She rolled her eyes and insisted that she would never need to know such dreck in her real life.

Oh, how things had changed.

In one of those classes which fell near the Thanksgiving holiday, Obell's teacher taught the class how to prepare a turkey. She taught them how to make the stuffing and to cover the wings with aluminum foil to prevent burning. She also taught them how to inject seasoning under the skin with what she'd called a *flavor injector*, but which was really just a large, somewhat menacing syringe.

Many of the kids had laughed at the flavor injector. They began waving them in the air and pretending to be doctors or addicts as the teacher screamed at them to behave and calm down.

That teacher may have been a little bit too gourmet for high school Home Ec., but that lesson was now proving useful as Obell prepared the corpse for reanimation.

There were several points across the body which would need to be injected with her brew if it were to walk again. She began with the left foot, which she held in her left hand as she prepared to inject with the right.

As she pushed the syringe, which could no longer be referred to as a flavor injector, through the corpse flesh, she found that it required less strength than she'd anticipated. Something about puncturing a human body seemed like it should be difficult, but it was surprisingly simple.

She pressed down on the injector's plunger and could have sworn that she felt the foot twitch ever so slightly as the potion was released into it.

There was no blood when she pulled the syringe out of the foot. There was only a slight dripping of excess potion, which fell onto the table.

Obell stood back for just a moment, observing the work that she had just done. She didn't know how long it would take for the potion to work. It might have been hours before the body began to come to life, or it could have been seconds. She found herself holding her breath as she waited.

Nothing happened.

She refilled her syringe and moved to the right foot. Once again, she found the process remarkably simple, and the mess small enough to leave for later. Once again, there was no response from the body.

She injected each knee, hip and shoulder, and still nothing happened. Before moving on to the elbows, Obell stopped and put down the syringe. She stared at the body on the table, wishing for some sign of success. She would settle for a twitch or a shudder.

She placed her hand on its thigh and closed her eyes, but felt not even the slightest tremor. She moved her hand up the body and rested it on the chest, over its unbeating heart. Again, there was nothing.

Was there even a heart inside of this body? She knew that an autopsy had been performed and the corpse's insides had been removed for examination, but had they been placed back inside of the body once the autopsy was complete? Perhaps the organs were back in the morgue, sitting in a jar.

It didn't matter. She didn't need a heart for her spell to work. It was a spell of reanimation, not resurrection. She reminded herself of this fact several times that night. Heart or no heart, brain or no brain. Either way, there would be no soul.

She grabbed her syringe once again and injected the elbows, wrists and palms without stopping to think. She wanted this task completed. She didn't want to waste any more time wondering whether or not her magic was working before she'd even completed her spell. She needed to focus. She needed to bring this body to life and to know that she could do what so few had managed to accomplish before her. She needed to defeat death. To harness it. To command it.

She opened each glazed-over, empty eye as wide as she could and squirted her potion into them, closing the eyes when she was done. She shot her potion into the ears, and through the back of the corpse's head, into its brain... If it had brain.

Finally, when all of her injections had been completed, she stuck a funnel in the mouth and poured what remained of her brew into the body.

Once she had poured every ounce, she dropped the pot onto the floor and took the body's face in her hands. She allowed her breath to wash over it and kissed its lips. Her potion would be its blood. Her breath would fill its lungs. Her kiss was a random act, born in the moment. It was not a romantic kiss by any means. Instead, it was the sort of peck that one would give a dear friend on a happy occasion.

"Wake up," she told the corpse, as she climbed onto the table and knelt next to it, "Open your eyes and enter this world, my dark creation."

Nothing happened. This annoyed her. She didn't want to wait any longer. She was tired of waiting. She was tired of having no say in when things happened.

She slammed her fist down onto the body's chest and screamed, "Now!"

Still, there was no response. Logic dictated that she would

need to be patient, but she had no patience left. Obell's fury was growing stronger by the moment.

Without looking, she grabbed a handful of dried herbs from a nearby bowl. She stuffed the herbs into the corpse's mouth and held it shut once she was done, as though the body could swallow the herbs if she was insistent enough.

From the corner of her eye, she saw something move. At first, she assumed that the corpse was rising, but as she turned to get a better look, she realized that whatever she had seen could not have been the corpse at all. What she had seen must have been on the other side of the room.

Obell climbed off of the table and scanned the house around her.

"I saw you," she said to nothing at all, "I've seen you twice now. I know you're here. Show yourself."

As seemed to be the theme of the night for her, there was no response, but she could feel something in the house with her. The air seemed different somehow, and there was a pit in her stomach which was threatening to destroy the buzz that she was getting from raising the dead.

Her eyes moved from dark corner to dark corner, waiting for something to move or jump out at her. She was prepared to face down an intruder, should the need arise. She was even ready to spot a mouse scurrying its way across the floor. Anything would be better than knowing that she was not alone and yet finding nothing. After all, only crazy people believed in invisible house guests, and Obell knew that she was not crazy.

She turned around, once again facing the corpse on the table, waiting for it to sit up and greet the world with a smile, but to her dismay, the body remained still.

Obell tickled the left foot. Some distant memory in the back of her mind made this seem like a rational idea. Children could be woken by a tickle to the foot, so perhaps a corpse could too. It made perfect sense.

Still, there was no response.

Double, double toil and trouble...

Obell felt as though her mind was slipping away from her. She was losing control of the strict, rational thought process which had driven her to this point. Balance was key. If she lost her grip on her thoughts and emotions, everything that she had worked for would be lost forever.

She took a deep breath and told herself to remain in control. She took a step back, both literally and figuratively, and closed her eyes.

"I am in control," she reminded herself, "I am the most powerful bein—"

Before she could finish that thought, a chill ran up her spine. She felt as though someone was standing directly behind her, preparing to grab her shoulder and pull her to the ground.

It was a baseless thought. She heard no sound from behind, nor did she smell any person, aside from the corpse. Yet, this feeling was overwhelming and she could not resist the urge to open her eyes and take a look.

Once again, she saw nothing... At least, at first. It was only when she turned her eyes toward the floor in another attempt to pull herself together that she spotted something unusual.

There was a paper towel on the floor, next to the garbage can. It was the same paper towel that she had earlier used to wipe the mysterious black goo from the corpse. It had to have been the same towel, because she hadn't used another all night. Yet, it had somehow found its way to the floor.

She was sure that she had thrown it into the garbage can. She was not the type of person who allowed garbage to fall onto the floor unnoticed. She was meticulous. In her mind, there was only one way that this paper towel could have possibly made its way to the floor—the mysterious intruder. There was no other answer.

Obell walked to the paper towel and knelt down to investigate. If she could find something to prove that she was not alone, she could prove that she hadn't been imagining things. A footprint or a hair of unknown origin could assure her that she was sane.

If and when she proved that she was not alone, there would be no end to the level of Hell that would fall upon her intruder. On a normal night, she would throw a curse their way. If she were in a bad mood, she could imagine boiling their blood and delighting in their agony. After all, the world deserved more pain.

This was not a normal night. This was the night that she had been waiting for her entire life. This was the night when her destiny would be fulfilled and her power would be proven to all.

Any person or thing that threatened to interfere with that would experience a sort of pain that no human being had ever experienced before.

As she picked up the paper towel and took a closer look at it, she discovered that she must have been mistaken. There was no black goo on this towel, so this could not have been the same one from earlier. She must have used another, or perhaps her intruder had, though she could see no reason for her intruder to be using up her paper towels.

She looked inside the garbage can, to find the towel with the black goo on it, just to confirm her findings, but there was no second paper towel inside of the trash can.

Questions rushed into her mind. Was this the towel that had once been used for the goo? Was it a different towel? Where was the goo now? She needed answers. This paper towel was of utmost importance!

As Obell went about her ponderings, she failed to realize that something incredible was happening. On the table behind her, the corpse had opened its eyes.

16

Winnie had spent nearly an hour staring at the stars in the sky that night, which was why she was surprised to hear a roar of thunder.

At first, this roar was a slow rumble, but it soon built to such volume that Winnie could feel a vibration in the ground beneath her feet. Then, just as steadily as it had built, the roar subsided and the night was once again silent.

Winnie waited for another clash, or a bolt of lightning. She held her breath in anticipation, but neither came. The air was calm and cool, filled with the smell of fires burning in nearby houses.

The thunder remained with Winnie, as she sat and resumed her stargazing. It was such an unexpected event. So out of place. Such a *wrong* thing to happen on a night like this.

Somehow, she had grown to feel more comfortable with things out of place than those which were normal. Everything normal felt like a lie to her. Everything mundane had become unsettling.

On the day Cindy died, Winnie had been sitting on the couch in her home, watching a reality show rerun and eating ice cream before dinner. There could have been no day more normal or uneventful. There was no reason for that day to be etched into her memory. There was nothing special about the old, faded jeans that she was wearing, or the pink and black striped long-sleeve tee that she had on, and yet the outfit was what she now wore in every nightmare she had. Even her more pleasant dreams sometimes featured that outfit. It was how she saw herself.

There was no such thing as normal. There was no such thing as love. No such thing as forever. No use in planning for the future, because the future didn't exist. Nothing was real to Winnie anymore, except maybe the thunder.

The roar of that thunder made Winnie uneasy. It tied a knot in her stomach. She knew that if a storm was coming, she should get home, but there was not one part of her that wanted to walk in that direction. She was content to sit on that bench, whether there be rain or not.

In the darkness of night, Winnie could sometimes hear Cindy's voice. Memories of conversations would float to the surface of her mind, and the world around her would melt away. All that she could see or hear were images from the past. She tried to turn these memories into something new. If she could have convinced herself that she could still talk with Cindy, she would have been happy to, but she could never capture Cindy's spirit. It was easy to say *"Cindy would say this"* or *"Cindy would do that"*, but these were only educated guesses based on past experience. Winnie could not even drive herself crazy enough to buy into her own delusions.

She began to wonder if Tami ever thought of Cindy, or tried to hold a conversation with her. Tami had been Cindy's best friend. As far as anyone was concerned, she had been a part of the family. She'd eaten with the family. She'd gone on vacations with them. Surely, Tami would have felt the loss.

It wasn't enough to just feel it though. Winnie's world was changed. Her life would never be what it was meant to be. She couldn't simply cry every few weeks and then go to a party as though nothing had happened, yet Tami did just that. She moved on.

In her quiet moments, Winnie was not usually an angry person. When she sat alone in the dark, she was sad and scared. She wanted so desperately to be held and comforted. She wanted to connect with her family. But the rage washed over her whenever someone came close. It was a blind, irrational rage. It kept her hidden from the world.

Now, the rage was rising within her even when she was alone. Just the thought of Tami was making her mad. The idea of Tami laughing and dancing and having a good time infuriated Winnie. She felt her fists tightening at the thought of Tami. Her jaw was clenched. She was so full of hatred that she wanted to scream.

Hatred felt a lot like envy. This was a realization that came to Winnie as she sat on that bench. She was pissed off at Tami for finding a way through this mess when she herself was still so lost.

Winnie smirked. Her mother was beginning to get to her. She was beginning to look at her world through the coldness of an analytical eye. It seemed like this should be a good thing, but Winnie knew her mother too well to believe that acknowledging a problem was the same as resolving that problem. Standing back and taking a good look at one's self only served to put distance between a person and their problems. This was why Winnie believed that her mother was perhaps the person most damaged by Cindy's death.

Deep thoughts plagued the troubled soul, but rarely served it any good. Winnie seemed to spend most of her time pondering her life, and the lives of those around her. In the morning, when she woke up, she would imagine what her day would be like if only she could shed her knotted soul and resume a normal teenage life. She could picture it so clearly, and yet she always found herself sitting in one class or another, realizing that she'd let yet another opportunity slip between her fingers.

At lunch, she would see Tami sitting at a table, talking with friends and laughing. She knew that if she could simply walk to them and say hello, her life would be on its way to recovery. She wanted to do this so badly. Each day, she told herself that she would make her move, but each day, she would sit in silence as

Tami ate lunch and walked away. Winnie could never seem to bring herself over to that table.

When she did speak, she would hear words coming from her mouth and would have no idea where they had come from. She would hear herself saying hurtful and hateful things to people that she cared about, and she couldn't stop those words from coming out.

She felt those words. She felt the anger inside of her, directed at her family and friends, and it was real. This new Winnie was a true version of her, and yet it was so far from who she had once been. It was so far from who she was when she sat alone. She felt as though her two personalities were fighting for dominance inside of her; the darker of them always seeming to win.

Alone, she could be more at ease. Without anyone to trigger her rage, she could take a step back and see all that she had become. She hated it, and yet she could see no way back.

She wanted to smile, and love, and laugh. She wanted to be happy, but after everything that had happened, she knew that those things would never be. She could look at the world, but she could no longer touch it. The darkness was her life now. It was who she had become. It was how she would forever be.

It was why she waited for death to claim her, as it had her sister.

17

Obell knew that she wasn't alone. She could feel some hidden thing creeping its way through her home. She heard it scurry, but only in her mind. She felt it brush past her leg, but that too seemed to be her imagination playing games with her.

Of all the nights to be paranoid, she was furious at herself for choosing this one. This was a night of creation and magic. It was a night of celebration, should all go well. It was not a night of looking for monsters under her bed—and yet, she could feel someone's eyes on her back.

A noise from behind startled her. She jumped and let out a gasp that, quite frankly, embarrassed her. For someone of her power to behave in such a way was shameful to be sure, but this noise was not her imagination. This was real.

It was a scratching noise. The sound of fingernails on wood, making their way back and forth, back and forth, as though to purposely leave a mark.

As Obell faced the table upon which the corpse was prepared, she held her breath. She took a step closer to her project, looking for some confirmation of not only the scratching sound, but of her own success.

Years of dwelling and plotting had all boiled down to this moment. It was her moment to shine.

Double, double, toil and trouble...

Inside of her mind, she could not help but laugh as that thought replayed once more. Its annoying, endless loop had driven her to the edge of sanity, but now it seemed so amusing to her.

Another step closer, and finally she could see the left hand of the body on the table. She could see the index finger moving, if just barely. It seemed like a twitch at first; like a reflexive muscle contraction rather than a sign of reanimation. But as she moved closer and closer, and as she listened to the sound of the scratching on the table, it became apparent that this was not a reflex. There was some amount of strength behind that scratching. The corpse was digging its fingernail into her wooden table and scratching it, over and over again.

Once again breathing, Obell turned the corners of her mouth into a smile, which was so unnatural to her that the muscles in her face felt strained by the process. Her heart was pounding in her chest. She experienced very few moments of pure, unquestionable joy in her life, but those were nothing to her now. They were fragments of dreams. This was real. This was happening to her right now.

She could not take her eyes off of that finger as they filled with tears of pride.

"You can do it," she muttered under her breath, "You can do it."

The scratching continued, and she waited for movement to increase and for the rest of the body to spring to life. She could not help but think of the Tin Man, muttering the words *oil can* as he stood rusted and unable to move, yet fully alive on the inside.

She waited for what seemed like an eternity, staring at that one finger. The rest of the world had melted away and all that existed in that moment was her own beautiful creation. Her life's work.

At last, she saw movement in another finger. Now, the middle finger on that same hand began to move. Obell squeaked with delight. She wanted to run for her video camera and capture this moment, but she was scared that she would miss the big event. She probably would have too. Soon, a third finger was scratching the table. Then the wrist began to move as well.

Obell could not have been more thrilled with herself as she stood by that table, staring at the barely moving hand. It was such an insignificant movement in the grand scheme of things, but she felt such validation and satisfaction in that moment that the moving hand could have just as easily been an entire continent shifting under her will.

As the movement in the corpse's hand increased, Obell looked toward the face of her creation and for the first time realized that its eyes had opened.

Staring into the abyss of where death should be, but wasn't, Obell found the endless loop of *Macbeth* quotes in her mind come to a sudden and jarring end. In its place was one word which screamed so loudly through her thoughts that she feared the whole town would hear:

ABOMINATION!

Marion felt as though her life had become a waiting game. Whether she was waiting for Mark to open up to her about his investigation, or for Winnie to come out of the daze that she'd been in since her sister's death, Marion always seemed to be on the sidelines. Forgotten. Alone. Waiting.

She sat on Winnie's bed, staring at the open window, through which Winnie had made her escape. In her hand, she held a glass of wine, which she'd felt a strong desire for after finding that Winnie was missing, but which she hadn't even tasted thus far.

It seemed to Marion that she should want to drink, to calm her nerves. She should have a strong desire to round the edges of her stressful life. To dull the pain of her loss. To sleep a restful sleep. But try as she might, she could not seem to take that first step toward that very predictable downward spiral.

She imagined herself taking that first sip, and feeling relief. Taking another and feeling calm. Another, to feel nothing at all. She closed her eyes and pictured what it would be like. It was an ugly picture—one that she did not wish to bring to life. Though, somewhere in the back of her mind, she wondered what would happen if Mark came home and found her passed out. It would be such an obvious cry for help, but she wondered if he would react to it at all, or if he would simply tuck her into bed with a glass of water by her side, to prevent the hangover that would be sure to follow. Would he be concerned at all?

A clash of thunder ripped through the air, causing Marion to jump and nearly spill the wine all over Winnie's bed. No rain had been predicted. No lightning had flashed. The thunder was completely out of place.

The sound of the thunder echoed through Marion's memory, playing over and over again. A cool breeze blew through the window. A chill ran down her spine. She didn't know whether that chill was caused by the breeze or the memory of the thunder, but with each second that passed, Marion grew more uneasy.

Winnie could be caught outside in a storm. She could catch a cold, or worse. Marion didn't want to even think of a phrase like *Winnie could catch her death out there,* because such phrases carried more weight with her than with most mothers.

She pictured her daughter walking down a dark, winding street. Alone. Cold. Dripping wet from the non-existent rain. It was her motherly duty to go and find Winnie and to bring her back. Freedom to grieve be damned, Winnie needed to come home for the sake her own health.

Marion was thrilled to have this excuse, but she did not pretend to believe it for a moment. There would be no rain that night. Winnie was most likely in no mortal danger. The truth was, Marion was tired of sitting around, waiting for her family to come back to her. She was going to go out into the night and bring her family home, even if she had to drag them back kicking and screaming.

19

It was wrong. It was a bastardization of everything that Obell had worked her entire life to achieve. It was ugly and empty. It wasn't hers. It wasn't victory.

It was now sitting up on her table, having slowly gained movement throughout its entire body. What started as a twitching finger became a moving hand, and then an arm. Its awakening spread through its body like a virus, and as each limb began to function, it reached and grabbed and felt the world around it. It studied the table with its hands. It explored its edge with its feet. It felt its own body, attempting to determine which things were a part of itself and which were not.

Obell stood back and watched as all of this happened, locking her arms across her chest and trying to remain guarded, as though this unliving thing could crawl inside of her and take up residence.

More than once, she saw the shadow out of the corner of her eye. It darted across the rooms of her house like a bird, trying to find a window through which it might escape. She was concerned about the nature of that shadow thing, but she did not dare to take her attention off of the reanimated corpse.

For so long, she had planned for this day. She had carefully crafted her spell in order to make the dead walk. To claim power over the forces of life and death had been the dream that she dreamt every night with a metaphorical smile on her face and warmth in her heart. Now that dream was sitting before her, looking her directly in the eyes—and her stomach turned.

"St—" Obell began to mutter, before her voice gave out on her. Trying again, she barely managed to get the words out, "Stand up."

The thing on the table cocked its head slightly, as though considering the meaning of her words and the options that it had when it came to following her command. Free will had not been part of her spell. There should have been no hesitation.

With a blank expression on its face which seemed to mock Obell, the corpse placed its feet on the ground and stood up.

It looked at its feet, seeming puzzled by the fact that it was standing. To Obell, it seemed as though the creature was more concerned with the feel of the floor and the ability to stand rather than the fact that it had followed her command.

She was not comforted by the fact that the thing had done

what she'd ordered. She felt no sense of authority. Instead, she felt as though the thing in front of her was playing along and would turn on her at any moment.

Obell lived for darkness. She allowed hatred and evil to wash over her like a rose scented shower. Ugly and monstrous things had been a part of her master plan from the beginning. This, however, was wrong. Everything on the surface appeared to be what she had been asking for, but her gut was telling her that nothing had gone as planned.

She stared at the pale, damaged body in front of her. It had once been a man, young enough to be her own child, but old enough to ensure that its nudity was not inappropriate. Regardless of age or the fact that it was now dead, the body looked inhuman to her.

Obell took a step back, unsure of what would come next. Even if her plan had been a booming success, she hadn't thought much about what she would do with a corpse that could do her bidding. She supposed that it could mop the floors or run errands or some such nonsense. Now, she didn't know what to do. She had her corpse, and it seemed to be following orders, but she hated it.

"Stay here," she told the thing, in a voice that sounded far less commanding than she would have liked.

She needed to step out of the room and assess the situation. If she could take a deep breath and clear her mind, without looking into the endless abyss that the corpse's eyes held, perhaps she could find the perspective that she required in order to take charge of the situation.

As Obell took a step toward her bedroom, she didn't take her eyes off of the standing body. She couldn't. She was convinced that as soon as she looked away, the corpse would dart across the room at inhuman speed and snap her neck.

Still moving across the room at a snail's pace, trying her best not to spook the thing in front of her, Obell was watched the entire way. Empty eyes should not be capable of curiosity, but its were. That fact alone taunted Obell. Curiosity was a need for knowledge and understanding. It was the function of a human mind, not a corpse. It certainly was not a part of her spell.

Out of nowhere, the corpse puckered its lips. Obell was unsure what to make of the act. It sent a chill up her spine.

Raising a hand to its mouth, the corpse kissed its fingers. A soft, gentle kiss. It was as though it did not know what a kiss was, but was somehow compelled to learn of this function as surely as it had learned to move its arms and legs.

It gave Obell the creeps. Dead things should not kiss.

She picked up her pace and dared to take her eyes off of the corpse as she hurried into her bedroom. Once inside the room, she glanced back and found that the thing was still staring at her. She slammed the door.

Turning her back to the door and leaning against it ensured that nothing would enter her room without her knowing. Nothing could sneak up on her from behind and grab her. It also meant that she had something to hold her up and keep her from collapsing into a puddle on the floor.

For the first time in a long time, Obell felt weak. She felt as though something had come into her home uninvited. She had intended to animate a corpse, of course. She had no problem with the idea of an empty vessel walking around her home, reminding her of her glorious victory every time she saw it. What she minded was the fact that this thing that had come into her home was not right. Even if she couldn't put her finger on exactly what had gone wrong, she knew that something had. Somehow, this was not what she had agreed to.

"Calm down," she whispered to herself, "It's still just a corpse. It's not alive. It's not capable of life. It is what you created, so just snap out of this and get back out there."

She had always been good at pumping herself up. She was her own best friend. She could lie to herself and make herself believe whatever she wanted. All of those therapists on daytime TV would love how skilled she was at self-motivation and building her own self esteem. She was everything they could wish for in a devoted patient, aside from the desire to reanimate the dead, and general thirst for evil.

Very few people would understand her motivation. People would tell her that she was insane, which she thought was somewhat bigoted.

Obell herself understood her need for power and her thirst for evil. Her desire to control the very forces of nature, and to have everyone else cower at her feet. She understood it all because she was inherently better than all of those small-minded commoners who would be satisfied just to make the mortgage payment on time.

She was better. She was smarter. She was more powerful. They needed other people to survive, whereas she needed nobody but herself.

Each of these thoughts came with a deep breath and a renewed sense of control over her situation. Surely, if she were better than all of those normal people, she was better than one of their mindless, empty bodies.

"Stupid corpse," she reassured herself, "I'm better than a stupid corpse."

Nodding to herself and accepting her perfection, Obell grabbed the stack of folded clothes intended for the body and exited her bedroom.

When she looked back to where she'd left the corpse, she expected to find it still staring in her direction, following her orders to stay put. Instead, she found that the corpse was gone.

From the corner of her eye, Obell once again saw the shadow thing dart across the room. As she turned to look in the direction of the shadow, she found herself staring at the front door of her house, which was now wide open.

"Stupid corpse," she muttered under her breath.

20

It had been a long night. Mark's visit with Warren had been interesting to say the least. Whether or not it proved productive remained to be seen.

The old man had given Mark a stack of papers upon which his gift had revealed the path toward Cindy. At least, this was the claim being made. Mark had yet to see any solid proof of Warren's abilities.

He studied those images as he walked back to his car, barely paying attention to where he was going. His mind raced with questions and theories, which he could have spent the entire night grilling Warren on, if only visiting hours hadn't ended.

"Keep them in order," Warren had reminded Mark, "They will guide you to the child you've lost."

The instructions hadn't seemed the least bit funny in the moment, but as Mark walked toward his car and tripped over an oddly placed flower pot, Warren's words became somewhat more amusing. As the papers flew through the air and scattered in the wind, Mark's only two options were to shout enough expletives at the top of his lungs to send a number of the home's elderly residents into cardiac arrest, or to see the humor in the situation.

While he wouldn't have defined the moment as *funny*, he did choose to vent his emotions through laughter. He was mad at himself for tripping. He was mad at the person who had placed the flower pot in his path; mad at Warren for not numbering the pages; mad at the world for sucking so damn hard. Mostly though, he was just tired. He hadn't slept well since Cindy's death and he had gotten even less sleep in recent days due to a heavy workload, on top of his supernatural side projects.

Picking up the papers, he tried to remember which order they had been in. This task was made difficult by the fact that only some of them made sense to him.

Images were the outlet of most remote viewers. Some scribbled notes about what they were seeing, but many stuck to shapes and landmarks. In Mark's studies, he had found most of these sketches to be rough. Some were so nonspecific that they would be completely useless until long after they might have helped. In most cases, Mark imagined that the connection between remote viewer sketches and the scene of whichever top secret Soviet operation the US government was trying to spy on at the time was made after the fact. The product of active imaginations, rather than a true gift. If the line and circle drawn by a remote viewer didn't turn out to be a street and an arena next to the hotel where a secret meeting was being held, it would turn out to be the knife and plate sitting on the table in the room where those meeting ate lunch.

In short, Mark did not have faith in remote viewers any more than he had faith in the idea that clouds in the sky were made to look like bunnies and dragons on purpose, as part of some grand design. People saw what they wanted to see, and marveled at those visions because it made them feel in control of the situation.

The sketches provided by Warren were different than any that Mark had seen before. If he'd worked with the government on any top secret projects, his sketches had not been included in the declassified material that Mark had obtained. The sketches were not simple shapes and vague doodles, and they definitely weren't random words like *love* or *peace*, which mediums often used to con their customers. Warren's sketches were specific. They were the types of sketches that Mark had seen in art class text books. Rough in some ways, but when it came to the important details, Warren left nothing to the imagination.

Two of the images drawn by Warren were familiar to Mark. The most obvious being Mark's own house. It was a remarkable sketch, considering the fact that Warren had never been to Mark's house.

Rationally, Mark told himself that he'd been sent to Warren by a person who could have fed the old man information about Mark. Skeptics would certainly dismiss Warren's work because of this, but Mark couldn't bring himself to believe that Warren had spent the night conning a man who would never pay him a dime and who would not publish any of those sketches.

If it was a hoax, it was a cruel and pointless one.

The second familiar image was of Cindy's grave, with leaves and a plastic cup blowing through the image. Where the plastic cup had come from, Mark wasn't sure, but the grave was exactly as it appeared in reality. Warren had even included the small stone placed on the headstone by a family friend a few days earlier.

Those were the familiar pieces of the puzzle which was meant to bring Mark together with Cindy. He had no idea where they belonged in the stack of pictures, but he at least knew where to find them in the real world.

There were three more images, which made little or no sense to Mark. The first was what appeared to be the entrance to a building. Though there may have been a sign above the door, it was hidden by shadows.

The design reminded him of a professional building. The doors looked to be automatic sliding doors. In front of them, there were support columns which held a roof above the driveway that led to this entrance.

Unfortunately, this was all that Warren had drawn. His vision did not seem to include a street address or GPS coordinates.

Next in the stack of pictures was a lovely scene. It was a view of a cliff, hidden in a wooded area, with a bright full moon in the distance and a town down below. Mark did not recognize this cliff, but thought that it would be far easier to locate than the mysterious building.

Finally, Warren had drawn a small house, nestled in the woods. Perhaps near the cliff, but perhaps not. The house was overrun by vines and seemed to be neglected. Some might have considered it cozy, but Mark thought it was rather small and knew that the cable company would charge an insane amount of money to run cable to a place like that. It was definitely not someplace where he would like to settle down.

He might have assumed that the house was abandoned, except that there was a car parked in the driveway and the front door stood wide open.

How the mysterious building, the cliff or the house in the middle of the woods would relate to Cindy, Mark had no clue. What he did know was that there was a path for him to follow. The specific order of this path was lost on him, but he would try his best to find those places. He would walk to the ends of the earth if it meant finding his daughter and knowing at last that she was at peace.

21

From the park, Winnie walked. Despite the pain in her ankle which caused her to limp as she went, she just picked a direction and started moving. She was in no need to get to any particular place, nor to be there by any particular time. She simply walked because she felt like walking.

It was liberating to know that she was truly alone. There was not a person in the world who knew where she was. For all intents and purposes, she had simply vanished. She was nobody.

She walked tall through the dark streets. Every so often, a car would speed past, sending a gust of dusty, smelly wind across her face. A weaker person would have coughed and gagged, but Winnie remained steady in her pace.

While she marveled in the freedom of loneliness, Winnie

neglected to pay attention to where she was going. After two or three random turns, Winnie lost track of where she was. She was also unable to remember which turns she'd taken and which roads would lead her back toward the park.

It was a curious moment for her when she stopped and realized that she was lost in her own hometown. That freedom of being alone, with nobody in the world knowing where she was, suddenly took on a new meaning.

She continued to walk.

The area of town in which she found herself had no streetlights. There were no houses with porch lights or spotlights in the landscaping. Even the moonlight seemed to struggle as it made its way through the trees. Even if Winnie had been familiar with this part of town during the day, the darkness would have bathed it in mystery. Every sound was a potential threat. Every beat between breaths was spent waiting to hear the exhale of an attacker from behind.

She wasn't sure if she would describe herself as *scared*. That was the most interesting aspect of that walk. Winnie wanted to feel that danger. She enjoyed entertaining the thought of a vampire jumping out of the woods and attacking her, as she'd seen in so many movies. She didn't believe it would happen, of course, but the night gave her a sense of wonder. Anything seemed possible, no matter how far-fetched it actually was.

She felt vulnerable, and she allowed herself to hold onto that feeling. After spending so much of her time on the defensive, always shielding herself, she enjoyed wondering what would happen if she simply vanished from the face of the earth, never to be heard from again. No more fighting.

A rustling of leaves from off to her right stole her attention and before she had even processed the sound, her eyes were scanning the woods for its source.

"A squirrel," she assured herself, "Or maybe a raccoon, if squirrels don't come out at night."

Having grown up in a heavily wooded town, Winnie was familiar with the sound of animals scurrying around nearby. Over the years, she'd adapted to the point where she didn't even notice those sounds anymore. Deer routinely ran through her front lawn. The rabbits that lived under her front porch were so accustomed to humans that they didn't bother to run off unless you walked directly toward them. You could practically build a house around some of the local birds before they even noticed you were invading their space.

She knew nature, and she normally found those sounds comforting and peaceful. Yet for some reason, that particular sound, on that particular night, caused her ears to perk up and her eyes to sweep the area. Perhaps this was because the cover of night had changed her world, but there seemed to be something else to what she was experiencing on that night. Though she didn't know exactly where she was, she felt that she was on a path toward... something.

Another rustling, this time from further ahead. Winnie picked up her pace as she tried her best to discern the shapes of shadowy trees from the shapes of living creatures. More than once, she managed to convince herself that a rock in the woods was a lurking wolf, waiting to pounce, but still she saw no real living thing that might have made those noises.

She stopped walking and continued to watch the woods. Her curiosity began to turn into concern. The night was still and quiet. Too quiet.

It wasn't difficult to think that there might be an area of woods near a road where there would be no animals, especially when a human was walking nearby. Not every creature was as comfortable with people as Winnie's porch rabbits. Yet, the stillness and quiet of the woods seemed wrong to her.

As the wind blew, tree branches high above knocked together and several leaves fell near her. She tried her best to avoid imagining creatures stalking her from above, but those attempts failed.

Another rustling. This time, from deeper in the woods.

She called out, "Hello?"

There was no response. She didn't expect one. Despite what an entire childhood's worth of animated movies might lead a person to believe, forest animals rarely answered when you spoke to them.

More rustling followed. This time, she picked up on a definite rhythm to this rustling. One-two. One-two. One-two. It didn't sound like any deer that she knew. It sounded too heavy for a rodent. Too light for a bear... At least, in theory. She had never actually seen a bear before.

Winnie wondered how many animals in those woods would walk on two legs, because she was certain that it was a one-two pattern, but could not think of many animals that matched this sound. Of all the creatures that sprang to mind, only one could not be dismissed.

"Hello!" she called again, this time expecting to be answered.

The rustling stopped. The woods went silent, save for that knocking of the branches high above.

This silence was heavier than before. This was not a lonely silence, full of possibility and thrilling mystery. This was the silence of something real lurking in the woods.

She could feel eyes on her, studying her every breath. Whether she was being paranoid or not, she didn't know. Regardless, she pulled her cell phone from her pocket. Until now, she'd kept the phone turned off. Without taking her eyes off of the woods, she powered up the phone, just in case.

Adrenaline surged through Winnie for the first time in what seemed like an eternity. Even when she screamed and fought with people, she could not recall feeling such a rush. She'd forgotten the hum of each of her limbs as they hungered for action; the way her heartbeat would be reflected in her vision; how her mind could be both sharp as a knife and cloudy as a stormy day, all at the same time.

She wasn't sure what would come next. Her most basic

instincts were telling her to turn and run, but something stopped her. Something deep inside of her was drawing her toward the unknown thing.

Another rustling from up ahead, and a thousand images from a thousand movies wherein the hero throws their blade into a tree right next to the source of such a noise flashed through Winnie's head. She gripped her cell phone tighter, not trusting herself to keep from throwing it.

From the corner of her eye, Winnie could have sworn that she saw a dark form darting through the woods on the side opposite to where the sounds were coming from. Out of instinct, she turned to get a better look, only to be met by a sea of shadows. To find anything in those dark woods would have been impossible.

She cursed herself for being so easily distracted and began to turn her attention toward the sounds once again. Her eyes didn't even make it all the way across the street before they locked onto a most curious sight.

Standing on the street, maybe thirty feet ahead of her and hidden by shadows—but accented by just enough moonlight to give Winnie the general idea of what she was seeing—there was the figure of a man. Tall. Lean. Also, quite a bit naked.

22

Marion's memory of the day her daughter died was fuzzy. She didn't remember anything that happened before receiving the news, and what she remembered about everything that came after losing Cindy revolved around emotion rather than any specific details.

Her first reaction to the news was a strange one. She didn't fall to the floor and cry. She couldn't absorb the information fast enough for such a proper reaction. Instead, she remembered feeling as though Cindy were being physically pulled away from her. When she dreamed of that moment, what she saw was an image of herself, trying to hold very fine sand in her hands, only to have it slip between her fingers and blow away. Tightening the grip didn't work, nor did holding the sand close to her body. It always blew away.

She remembered feeling as though there should have been someplace for her to go and someone for her to speak with in order to correct the situation. She'd disputed speeding tickets, test grades and late fees charged to her video rental account. Life was all about fighting her hardest to make things right. When presented with a situation where there was nobody to fight and no way to have this death erased from her family's permanent record, she simply could not process the information. It was too unfair. Too wrong. Too final.

When she heard the news of Cindy's death, Marion denied it. She insisted that it was someone else's daughter. She thought it was a waste of time for her and her husband to drive down to the morgue to identify the body. This was her way of fighting fate, but no matter how desperately she tried to hold onto her daughter, all hope eventually slipped between her fingers.

A year later, Marion still could not look at an hourglass with its sand draining away without feeling a tightening in her chest.

Faeriwyn is next. Marion's gut twisted as those words ran through her mind. She could feel Winnie slipping away from her, but she refused to accept this. Unlike what happened with Cindy, Marion had been given a chance to change this outcome. If she had to, she would face down the forces of Hell itself, to get her living daughter back.

It was classic teenage rebellion, exacerbated by severe emotional loss. Winnie was scared and felt alone. She was angry at the world. She was angry at her parents, whom she no longer felt could protect her. Childhood securities were gone. With proper time and care, these issues could be resolved through discussion, and possibly transformed into something more positive.

It all sounded like such a load of crap when Marion was talking about her own daughter. How she had spent so many years placing people into such neat little categories, she did not know. How she could possibly continue to do such things in order to earn a living was a question best saved for later.

Right there, in that moment, Winnie was gone. She was not a case study. She was not a test subject. She was Marion's own child, and no amount of higher education could tell Marion where to find her daughter or how to bring her home safely.

Outwardly, she remained calm. She was always composed; always ready to repress whatever storm might arise in her own mind.

She stood on the front porch of her home, staring into the night, ready to take off in pursuit of Winnie. The only trouble with this plan was that she didn't know which direction to head in. She didn't even know whether to walk or to drive. Marion was lost already, and she hadn't even made it past the front yard.

To activate the GPS in Winnie's cell phone might be seen as a violation of her daughter's privacy and would surely get Marion screamed at once more, but she didn't care. She didn't live in a world where teenagers got to make their own rules. She lived in a world where her daughter had jumped from a second-story window and had wandered off into the night without informing her parents. Freedom was a privilege that Winnie had not earned.

Marion was already planning her defense for when Winnie began to yell. If she'd had a notebook handy, she might have written down some replies in advance, just so she wouldn't forget them. Since she had no paper, she allowed those words to stew inside of her and fuel her anger. Anger was better than fear. Anger caused a person to take action.

Marion stepped off of the porch, pulling her cell phone from her pocket. After she typed a code into her phone, Winnie's location was highlighted on a map. Marion was on her way.

23

She heard the sound of plastic on pavement, but didn't take her eyes off of the figure standing up ahead. It took Winnie several seconds to realize that she had dropped her cell phone. Even after that realization, she couldn't bring herself to lower her eyes.

At least sixty percent of her hesitation was born from distrust, while the remaining forty percent could be chalked up to curiosity. A naked guy, standing in the middle of the road was not the type of thing that she saw on the average day. It was not a particularly warm night, so even the smarter crazy people should be wearing a jacket. If she looked away for even a second, Winnie felt as though she would be opening herself up for attack.

The stranger did not move. His features remained hidden by shadows as he stood, staring back at Winnie. It seemed as though he found her as interesting and unusual as she found him, and this did not bring comfort to her heart. Most people, naked or not, weren't captivated by the sight of a normal, fully clothed girl, walking down the street. Somehow, being the object of interest to a nude man in the middle of a dark night, was nowhere near the thrill that she'd always imagined.

She remembered the party that was taking place somewhere in town. She wasn't sure where this party was being held, but surely this boy must have been drunk. From what she could see, he could have been a high school student. Then again, he could have also been a middle-aged dentist. Her powers of deduction only worked so well without proper light.

After what seemed like an eternity of staring, she decided that something needed to be done in order to move this situation along, one way or another. If she were to be mugged that night, she'd rather get it over with in time to make it home for the late night talk shows.

"Hello?" she called in a curious tone, with just a hint of the attitude that she'd been perfecting of late.

She was proud of herself for managing to not sound like the weak, helpless victim in a slasher movie.

She waited for a response, but the nudist said nothing. He simply continued to stare.

"So," she started, with no idea what to say next, "Come here often?"

That was a stupid question. Instantly, a hundred better lines ran through her head and she wished that she'd chosen one of those instead.

Still, the naked figure did not respond. Apparently he wasn't much of a talker.

Winnie had waited long enough for something to happen. She was beginning to feel less like a potential victim and more like a participant in a staring contest. The man in front of her was clearly not in his right mind, so the best thing for her to do would have been to call the police.

Unfortunately, she remembered that her cell phone was on the ground, next to her feet. She needed to get to it, but hesitated to take her eyes off of the stranger.

Eyes on the man, Winnie bent down, hoping to find her phone quickly and get back to a less vulnerable position before the stranger would have time to make a move. She hadn't anticipated that the shifting of her weight would suddenly and sharply compound the pain in her ankle. She winced at the surge of pain, sucking air through her teeth and pausing for a moment, allowing the pain to recede.

As she did this, the stranger's head cocked ever so slightly. The move reminded Winnie of a curious puppy. She found it unsettling.

He was staring at her, once again motionless. While the lack of heavy breathing that was usually associated with perverts and serial killers in the movies was mildly reassuring, any comfort gained was quickly lost once again due to his perfect stillness. She had never seen a person stand so still, without a shifting of weight or an involuntary twitch.

She found herself sympathizing with all of those doe-eyed animals in *Discovery Channel* documentaries, chewing on grass or sipping water from a pond, right before the jaws of a predator clamp down around their neck and drag them to their bloody death.

In her mind, she was being surrounded by two or three other naked people, ready to pounce. Though she doubted that this was the case, she found herself wishing desperately to be spared such an incredibly lame death. The last thing she needed was to be on the nightly news as the girl who was murdered by a cult of nudists.

She found her phone on the ground and wrapped her hand around it as though it was the rope by which she could pull herself out of this situation. It was salvation.

As she stood straight once again, the naked figure in the shadows finally shifted his weight. For a moment, Winnie thought that he would lunge at her and attempt to drag her back to his cave. Except, he did not run toward her. Instead, he ran away.

The shadows all around her seemed to shift as the stranger ran into the trees and out of Winnie's sight. Once again, the night fell into an eerie calm.

She looked around the dark woods next to the street, wondering if the mysterious stranger would leap out and grab her. She caught no glimpse of him through the shadows, nor was there any sound to betray his location.

Winnie walked forward, gripping her cell phone ever tighter, determined to never let it drop from her hands again. She didn't trust her pockets with such an important item. She wanted to feel that safety net in her hand and know that she could have the police on the line within a matter of seconds. Or, better still, her Mommy.

When she reached the spot on the street where her mysterious stranger had been standing, she turned in the direction of the woods and tried her best to find him in the shadows of the trees.

Maybe he's just shy, she thought to herself, *but then again, shy people usually wear clothes in public.*

There had been no attack. Nobody had tried to chase Winnie and drag her into the night. There had been no closure of any kind, and it was eating away at her.

Why would he run? Why would he not come toward her? Could he have been the victim of some crime? Perhaps he had been as scared of her as she had been of him. Maybe he needed her help, or even just a piece of clothing to wrap around himself.

She hesitated for a second or two, running through the possibilities in her head and wondering what her favorite movie and television characters would do in a situation such as this. Surely, no super sleuth would allow this situation to go uninvestigated. Without a doubt, any reputable action hero would not simply walk away from potential danger. Assuredly, any ace reporter would question the obvious impact that the entertainment industry has had on the decision-making process of today's youth.

Realizing that what she was about to do would not be considered wise by anyone, Winnie shrugged off her future critics and entered the woods in pursuit of her mysterious stranger.

24

Tami was many things to many different people. She was popular at school, without anyone—to her knowledge—hating her for it. She was a favored student amongst the teachers, because she read the lessons carefully and tried her best to understand what she was meant to learn. If she didn't understand, she could smile and fake her way through a conversation with the best of them.

To her parents, Tami was a little girl; sweet, and innocent. She loved to curl up on the couch with her mother and watch a girlie movie on a rainy Saturday afternoon. She enjoyed going to the batting cage with her father more than she would have thought.

To Winnie, Tami was the queen of all bitches. The traitor. The one who could lose someone who may as well have been a sister, and still manage to go on with her life.

In all honesty, she didn't know what she was to herself. She was not a liar. She didn't put on acts and make believe that she was something that she was not. She was everything that people thought she was and yet, there was something inside of her that she never showed the world. It was a part of herself that even she didn't entirely know or understand, because she had done everything in her power to avoid looking into that corner of her soul. Something told her that if she ever accepted this part of herself, nothing would ever be the same. No more parties. No more fun.

She could dabble and poke around, but committing to what she felt in her heart would have made her an outcast in the eyes of everyone she knew.

She was not a perfect little angel; that much, Tami knew. She could date boys and go to parties and have fun without feeling as though she needed to join a nunnery afterward. She once sat on a park bench and watched a car get stolen, and while she felt guilty about not leaping into action for weeks after that car theft, she knew that by sitting by and watching it happen, she was contributing to the downfall of civilization.

She was quite the rebel, but that was not the part of her that remained hidden. Her hidden self would remain locked away until some random moment when it would spring out of her and she could deny it no longer. Until then, life went on. She had a party to get to.

The location of the party was not sent out in the invitations. Its location was encrypted *within* the invitation, though not very well. A series of numbers appeared on fliers that were plastered around the school. These numbers were the coordinates for the party's location. It was as simple as typing them into any cell phone with GPS capability.

It seemed like a lot of work to go through, in Tami's opinion. Surely the teachers were smart enough to put the puzzle together if the students could do it. The target demographic for the party wasn't exactly the honor roll students and chess club champions. Still, it was fun and mysterious in a lame sort of way, and mystery heightens the appeal of any situation. Finding the answer becomes irresistible.

Of course, there are some answers that are better left unknown. Sometimes, the truth is even more painful.

Cindy's body had been discovered at the bottom of a steep drop-off, near the main road which led up the mountain. That was it. No logical reason for her death. No clues which led to a greater mystery. Nobody would ever know what happened in the seconds before her death. Cindy was simply dead and Tami had tried her best to accept that fact without allowing questions to burn into her soul. For others, never knowing what happened meant never having closure. Their wounds festered.

Tami wasn't paying as much attention as she probably should have been as she made her way to the party. After typing the coordinates into her phone's GPS, she let her mind wonder and simply turned when the emotionless voice told her to turn.

As she neared her destination, Tami looked at where she was, and it took her just a moment to identify the location through the mess of cars and plastic cups that were mindlessly tossed onto the ground.

In years past, the Blackout Ball had been held in the middle of the woods or in abandoned buildings, far away from prying eyes. It was a logical pattern, since the party was meant to remain a secret from parents, teachers and law enforcement officers.

This year, those who planned the party had decided to go with a different style. Rather than find a hidden party spot, they chose a location for its thrill factor. It was dark and spooky. It was a place where anything could happen. After all, cemeteries were the home of the greatest mystery that one could imagine. They were the home of death.

As she parked her car and calmly turned off the engine, Tami's palms grew sweaty. A chill ran down her spine. Her jaw tightened and her stomach turned.

Many emotions ran through Tami in that moment, canceling each other out and causing her to remain still. It was only a matter of time before one of those emotions managed to boil slightly hotter than all of the others and when that happened, there would be no rational thought. There would only be reaction.

Cindy McKeller was at rest not far from where Tami was parked. Music was blasting in the distance, and she knew that at that very moment, some drunken high school student was either dancing on the grave of her best friend, or getting laid on it.

With that thought, one of the emotions inside of her grew hotter and brighter than all of the others. As her eyes narrowed and her hands balled into fists, Tami remembered that she had a baseball bat stored just behind the passenger seat.

25

She held the steering wheel with one hand and her cell phone in the other. The phone was capable of providing her with turn by turn voice commands, but Marion felt more in control when she was holding onto the phone, looking at the little red dot which represented Winnie's location.

The dot had not moved much since Marion first acquired the signal from Winnie's phone. It remained steady on a road that Marion had never traveled, surrounded by trees and wilderness.

Her heart was telling her to hurry. Her gut was telling her that something about this night was not as it should be. Her brain was telling her that she had raised a stupid, stupid girl. What was Winnie thinking, walking down an unknown, isolated road in the middle of the night? Just recently, Marion had read reports of a young man's body being found on the side of the road. No identification. No family to notify. That boy would forever be remembered as a John Doe because of his foolish decision to wander into the unknown.

It was not like Marion to be so judgmental. She had spent years holding back her opinions, and over time she had nearly lost the ability to recognize those opinions herself.

A boy, probably just out of high school, found on the side of the road was a heartbreaking story. It was a troubling story. Yet, all Marion wanted to do was smack that boy across the face. All she could think about was his mother, sitting at home, holding out hope for his safe return.

Her grip on the cell phone tightened, accidentally pressing the *volume* button on the side of the phone. The beeping which grew louder and louder brought her focus back to the task at hand.

Winnie was not John Doe. She didn't know John Doe. She would probably never even know of that boy's existence. She was her own person; a beautiful, intelligent, angry, sad, stupid, stupid girl.

Marion took a deep breath in through her nose and slowly released it through her mouth. In through the nose. Out through the mouth. Over and over again. She did this because it was what she would tell a patient if they were winding themselves up the way that Marion was at that moment.

Did this method help to calm her down or relieve her anxiety? Not really. This is probably why more than one of her patients had

ended their session early, telling her that they did not feel that
this practice was sufficient for their particular personality types.

Of course, they did not use those words. Usually, they used only
two words as they walked out the door in a fit of anger.

Marion felt a sudden kinship with all those people that she
couldn't calm. Part of her had always blamed them, because they
weren't following the guidelines of emotional response as
dictated by the numerous text books and case studies that Marion
had read. Now, she wanted to gather those text books, light them
on fire and throw them at their crackpot authors.

Truly, she was experiencing an awakening. She would need to
be sure to write down her feelings as soon as she got home and all
was once again normal in the world.

Well, as normal as anything ever was anymore.

Allowing her mind to wander through its self-examination
helped her to calm down and regain her senses. She knew that it
was merely a detachment from the situation and not true
progress, but she was happy to allow it for the time being. After
all, she had a daughter to track down and she was getting closer
and closer to Winnie's location...

A location which hadn't changed at all for several minutes now.
Certainly, that wasn't normal. After all, who would stop in the
middle of nowhere like that?

Marion scrolled through the GPS options on her cell phone and
pressed the *refresh* button, just to ensure that her phone hadn't
gone through a dead spot and lost Winnie's signal without her

knowing it.

On her phone, the image of a satellite appeared, telling Marion that the phone was acquiring updated information. The image remained on the screen for far longer than it had the first time, which Marion found strange at first, and then troubling.

She waited for the image to be replaced by the little red dot, letting her know where Winnie was. She waited for reassurance that she was on the right path. She waited... and waited.

At last, the image of the satellite vanished, but there was no red dot. Instead, there was an error message, which read: *UNABLE TO LOCATE REQUESTED DEVICE.*

In through the nose. Out through the mouth.

26

"Stupid," Winnie told herself under her breath, as she hurried between trees and over barely visible rocks, "Stupid. Stupid."

She was fully aware of how bad an idea it was to go chasing after a mysterious stranger, through the woods, in the middle of the night. There was not one part of that idea that could even be twisted into something that might sound rational if she ever had to explain herself. Yet, she was compelled to solve the puzzle of the mysterious stranger. If she turned in the opposite direction and returned home, she would never have the proper context for his appearance. Without context, the memory might nag her for the rest of her life.

Of course, there was no assurance that pursuing him would lead to answers. Since entering the woods, Winnie hadn't seen or heard any hint of the stranger.

From time to time, she could have sworn that she saw a dark figure moving between the trees, but only from the corner of her eye. When she turned to see who or what this figure was, she saw nothing but shadows.

Finally realizing that blindly wandering through the woods would only lead to her getting lost, Winnie stopped moving. Still gripping her cell phone tightly, she looked all around her.

There was only a hint of moonlight which made its way through the trees. Darkness surrounded her. Up above, tree branches knocked together as a breeze caused them to sway. On the ground something scurried, but it was not large enough to be a human being. This was the sound of something small and fast.

Winnie wasn't afraid. She was aware of the risk that she was taking and the eeriness of being alone in the dark woods, but she didn't feel that instinctual need to turn from it. On the other hand, the need to find out who the stranger was and what he was doing out there was overwhelming.

As she searched the shadows for any sign of the stranger, she ran down a list of reasons why he might have been out there without clothing. She considered the possibility of a demented attacker, but the more she thought about it, the more she gravitated toward the idea that he was a victim. He was just as alone as she was. He could have been scared. He could have been running from someone who wanted to hurt him—someone that Winnie was quite possibly walking toward at that very moment.

She knew that she should have wanted to turn around and run home, but that urge simply wasn't there. All she wanted was to find the stranger. If he did need her help, she wished that he would let her provide it. She had her cell phone. She could call for help, if he needed her to.

He was the one who ran. That meant that he was scared.

Or, it meant that he was playing with his dinner.

Her search was proving fruitless. She had no idea where the stranger was. She had no idea why he was out there. She could invent reasons all night long, but she knew that with every second that passed, she was putting herself in more danger.

She turned and started to walk back to the street. Even if she was curious, no amount of mystery was worth becoming the thing she hated most about teenagers in movies. She was more intelligent than Hollywood would give her credit for. There was no way she was going to give them the pleasure of—

Another rustling came from behind her. This time, it was not the rustling of a small animal, but of something much bigger.

Winnie stopped walking and turned around, expecting to see her mysterious stranger standing behind her, back-lit by moonlight and perfectly framed between two trees, as many movies had programmed her to expect. Only, she did not find the mysterious stranger as she turned. Instead, she found herself looking into the strangely bright, yellow eyes of a rather large coyote.

To call herself *stupid* no longer seemed adequate. Instead, she stood still and allowed the coyote to look her up and down while trying her best not to make eye contact with it.

She could never remember the rules of eye contact with wild animals. Instinct told her that making eye contact and intimidating the creature would cause it to run off, so she chose to do the opposite. After all, her instinct appeared to be on the fritz that night.

Though the pain in her ankle had come and gone all night, it chose this moment to begin throbbing once again. With each throb, pain shot up her leg and down her foot. This, she thought, was fate's way of letting her know that she was every bit as stupid as she believed herself to be. Now, she was injured and alone in the dark woods, chasing a naked serial killer, face to face with a rabid coyote that would pounce at any moment and rip her apart. She would be eaten alive, and whatever remained of her body would not be found for years or possibly decades.

"Way to go, Faery," came the sound of her sister's voice in her head, so vivid that Winnie would have loved to believe that her sister's ghost had spoken to her, but she knew better than that. This was a memory. Fitting for the situation, but a memory nonetheless. Winnie was alone.

Slowly, without making any sudden movements that might spook the coyote, Winnie raised her cell phone and pressed a button to activate it. Allowing herself only a quick glance at its screen, so that she might dial a number and call for help, Winnie was delivered yet another blow from her arch nemesis, fate.

On the screen of the cell phone, Winnie saw the words *SIM CARD ERROR.* Her phone had been reduced from being a connection to the rest of the world, to being a small and lightweight object that could be thrown at the coyote in an attempt to piss it off—something which she thought would probably be a bad idea.

The coyote remained still. It didn't growl or show its fangs, as Winnie had expected. It seemed curious, but there was no sign of impending attack. This was not particularly comforting to Winnie. She expected that there were other coyotes nearby. Probably surrounding her, waiting to attack.

She was smarter than any dumb old coyote. She knew quite well what they were planning. She wouldn't be caught off guard by their trickery. She laughed at their silly plan... deep down inside.

Outwardly, she stood her ground because she knew that if she ran, the coyote's instinct would be to chase. She wondered what that would have been like. She wondered how it would feel to be chased or bitten by the coyote. She didn't want it to happen, but she couldn't help but wonder.

It seemed like hours that Winnie stood there, waiting for something to happen. For a moment, she thought that the coyote was just as curious about her, but then it licked it's lips and turned to walk away, as though it had something better to do than waste its night staring at some dumb chick who was wandering around the woods at night.

Winnie couldn't help but grin. It was as though she had jumped out of a plane and played a game of chicken with the ground below—and somehow, she had won.

Her heart was pounding in her chest. Her ankle was throbbing more painfully than ever. She was lost and alone, yet she loved that moment. For once, she was the victor.

As she celebrated her win over the coyote, she watched it slowly walk away. It wasn't scared, but it was leaving. That was good enough for her.

And then, it was dead.

From the shadows, the mysterious stranger pounced on the coyote and ripped its throat open with his teeth.

Moonlight captured the redness of the coyote blood that ran down the chin of the stranger, and onto his body. For the first time, Winnie saw the Y-shaped incision on the stranger's chest which had been sewn up, but still looked gruesome and painful.

Her grin was gone and her cell phone dropped to the ground. In the distance, behind the bloodied stranger, Winnie could have sworn that she saw the shadows move, but she did not take her eyes off of him.

When he looked at her, there was a hollowness to his eyes. She thought that it might have been caused by the darkness or the moonlight, but they seemed inhuman to her; almost metallic in the way that they reflected the light.

The stranger drank the blood of the coyote as Winnie stood, unable to move; unable to even look away from the horrible scene.

27

Once upon a time, long, long ago, Mark would return from work and be greeted by the sounds of a hectic home. Two teenage girls watching TV, talking on the phone, or fighting over something completely random. His wife tapping away at her computer keyboard or listening to recordings of therapy sessions. Vegetables being chopped. Water boiling. Talking. Laughing. Overpriced shoes rushing up and down the stairs.

When Mark walked through the front door of his home, he never expected to be greeted in the tradition of Ward Cleaver or Rob Petrie. His was not the type of wife that would kiss him on the cheek and ask him about his day while preparing his evening martini. His was the type of wife who would ask him about his day while the two of them hurried to get something resembling dinner on the table before they either had to go to bed, or had to rush out the door to investigate whatever strange happening might be taking place on any given day.

In recent months, even those hurried conversations had become more and more rare. He had withdrawn into his own world, trying to figure out how he could communicate with Cindy. Marion had withdrawn into her own mind, where Mark could only imagine she was mourning in her own way, which didn't seem to involve him at all. Neither of them discussed Cindy's death with each other. It was easier this way. At least some distance would keep them from truly examining what had happened, and perhaps they could keep from pointing fingers if they simply never discussed it.

Then there was Winnie. The girl who had once been sweet and cute, and a little chubby in the face as a baby, was now more distant than any of them. Mark barely caught a glimpse of Winnie anymore, as she rushed out the door or up to her bedroom. When he did see her, she looked at him with such hatred in her eyes that he could tell what she was thinking and feeling without her ever having to say a word.

She blamed him. The sweet little girl who would squeal with delight as he tossed her over his head, and whose nose he would kiss as he tucked her into bed now loathed him. The only child he had left, and she wanted nothing to do with him.

He gave Winnie her space. He made himself small when she was at home. He let her hate him from afar, because as long as he allowed this, he would be spared hearing her speak those thoughts out loud. He could handle knowing what she thought of him, but to hear her say it to his face would be too much for him to take.

He had failed his daughters. As their father, he was supposed to keep them safe. It was the one job he had that meant anything, and he dropped the ball.

He had spent a year thinking of ways that he could have changed what happened to Cindy. None of them were rational. All of them would have required psychic abilities that he did not possess, yet he continued to push himself. He needed to make things right somehow, and if that meant letting Cindy go, he would do that. It would be the hardest, most painful thing that he could imagine having to do, but he would do it. He just needed to know that she was at peace before he did.

When he tried to express these thoughts out loud to a friend, or even to himself, it sounded like a lot to ask for. For as long as man had walked the planet, death had been that mysterious curtain that everyone wanted to sneak a peek behind, but which nobody really could. The answers to what came next would remain unknown until each person died and finally got clued in on the big joke of it all. Mark imagined that when that day came and everything was made clear, it would all seem so obvious and stupid. Everyone would wonder why we had spent so many centuries fighting and squabbling over these things when the answers were staring us right in the face. Political differences wouldn't exist. Religious differences wouldn't exist. The only disagreements would be along the lines of which ice cream flavor was the best, because those differences were about personal taste and opinion, not true matters of right and wrong.

For the rest of eternity, we would live with a full view of what this universe was and what it all meant. This is how eternal peace would be possible. There would be beauty to it all that we couldn't possibly be expected to see until we were able to step back and take in that view.

Mark took comfort from the idea that Cindy could be clued in sooner than he would be. He enjoyed knowing that she would be someplace better, watching it all unfold and screaming at him to not make the mistakes that seemed so obvious from her perspective, just as she had screamed at the TV so many times while watching horror movies. Or, he needed to know that she was laughing at him.

He needed to know without a doubt that she wasn't one of those mindless spirits, doomed to repeat the same horrible event that caused her death, over and over, for all time. He had failed her in life, but he would not fail her in death.

This was the nagging thought that ran through his mind, day after day. It kept him from sleeping. It kept him from focusing on his work. It kept him from realizing that an empty house at this time of night was very unusual.

When he walked through the door, Mark stopped in the foyer and looked in every direction for some sign of why Warren would have drawn the house. He had secretly videotaped different rooms on different nights, without finding any sign of Cindy. He had placed audio recorders around the house, hoping to catch her voice on one of them, but each of them came back without a trace. He had spoken to her every single day since she died, and he had never experienced any moving objects, mysterious chills or even the easily discredited orbs in photographs that some of the lesser ghost investigators would swoon over.

Why then? Why would Warren draw a picture of this house and tell Mark that it would mean something in his search for her?

"Hello?" Mark called for Cindy, but vaguely enough so that anyone who might be home could answer without finding him too suspicious.

There was no reply. The house remained silent.

"Cindy?" he inquired, in barely a whisper. He didn't want to sound crazy, but at the same time, he wanted to yell her name. He wanted for her to hear him, no matter where she was in the house.

He closed his eyes and muttered her name again, "Cindy?"

When he opened his eyes, they were beginning to tear. His chest was tightening. He needed for this to work. He needed for it to be *that* night. It was killing him to not know that she was at peace.

"Cindy?" This time louder. He was beginning not to care if the whole house heard him, or the whole neighborhood, "Cindy!"

He balled his fists, not in rage, but in desperation. His

fingernails dug into his palms, but couldn't bring themselves to be so dramatic as to draw blood.

It would have been too simple, he supposed, for his search to end there. Why anything would have changed simply because of Warren's sketch, he didn't know, but it would have been so convenient. All he needed was a small sign. The smell of flowers, or an object that wasn't quite where it was supposed to be.

Nothing.

It was painfully silent in the house. So much so that Mark would have almost preferred to hear Winnie yell at him to shut up, but there was nothing. Lights were on in the house, but nobody seemed to be home.

It was unusual for the house to be empty at this time of night. Mark tried to remember whether or not he had seen Marion's car in the driveway, but he hadn't paid enough attention to notice as he came home.

He made his way into the kitchen, looking for signs of dinner having been eaten, or a note telling him that Marion had taken Winnie out to eat.

As he entered the kitchen, he saw no plates in the sink or plastic containers holding leftovers. The oven wasn't keeping anything warm. There was no note. It was as though his family had vanished.

His mind flashed to the story of Roanoke Island and the colony that had disappeared, never to be heard from again. Part of him worried that it had happened again, but only within the walls of his own home. Part of him felt the eyes of cruel fate staring at his back, waiting to strike once again and take away even more of the people that he loved.

It was irrational. It was nonsensical. Odds were that the colonists of Roanoke Island integrated with some American Indian tribe and simply forgot to leave a note, telling the rest of the world where they were heading off to.

Mark forced that feeling to leave him, as a boy would force away the fear of a monster living in his closet.

He turned and prepared to walk out of the kitchen, on his way to search the internet for some clue as to what Warren had drawn in those other pictures.

As he moved toward the doorway, something caught his eye. Sitting on the counter, he found an audio recorder. It was the same recorder that he had left at Cindy's grave.

28

There were times when all she wanted in the world was her Daddy. Times when she felt as though she was six years old and all she wanted was to be picked up and carried through the world, being held close. She missed that feeling of true safety. She missed her ultimate protector. Most of all, she missed the days when she could believe in such things.

Her father wasn't infallible. He wasn't a superhero who could withstand any danger and prevent bad things from happening. He was just as vulnerable as any other person, and since Cindy died, Winnie had suspected that his armor had grown even weaker. Still, in that particular moment, as she stood alone in the woods, watching the mysterious stranger ripping into the coyote that she had briefly felt threatened by, all she wanted in the world was her

Dad.

Winnie couldn't see the eyes of the stranger any longer. She couldn't see the teeth or the expression on his face. All she saw was the curve of his back as he hunched over the coyote, and the moonlight highlighting the muscles in his arms as he held the animal close.

She took a step backward, closing her eyes and waiting for the incredibly loud sound of a twig breaking. In the movies, there was always a twig to break. When she heard no such snap, her panicked mind allowed her the slightest sense of victory. One step down and only a thousand more to go before she was clear of danger.

With that step, she once again chastised herself. She had always believed herself to be of, at the very least, average intelligence. Certainly not below average. Possibly well above the average, at certain moments. So, how she managed to convince herself to chase the mysterious nudist into the woods was something that now baffled her. How could someone of even the slightest bit of intelligence have been so stupid as to think this was a good idea?

Another step backward, and still there was no snapping of a twig. There was another sigh of relief, another declaration of stupidity for having gotten into this mess, and another step back.

The cycle repeated.

She was beginning to feel as though the fragile balance of fate was turning in her favor. It was risky for her to feel even the slightest bit of relief. She knew that if she let her guard down, she could be attacked and torn to shreds, just as the coyote had been. She couldn't afford to be stupid any longer.

She opened her eyes, and her attention was immediately drawn to the dead animal on the ground. Its blood appeared black in the darkness. Its fur was soaked in it. Somehow, the predator that Winnie had feared only moments earlier now seemed like a poor, injured puppy. The sight of it no longer frightened her, it broke her heart.

Her eyes moved away from the coyote, toward the stranger who was still crouching beside it. His hands, chest and face were covered in its blood. His eyes were masked by tree shadows, but he was looking directly at Winnie; that much she knew. Her plans of a stealthy escape had not gone as smoothly as she had believed.

Upon realizing that his eyes were on her, Winnie gasped and that breath became trapped in her lungs. She stopped and remained as still as possible, as though this stranger were some animal that wouldn't react unless she made a sudden movement.

The stranger's stare was as unwavering as her own. Each of them was waiting for the other to make the first move. Winnie considered running, but she didn't want to turn her back to the stranger. At the same time, she hardly wanted to spend the night, stuck in the woods with this person. It was an impossible decision for her to make, and she wasn't completely certain that her body would respond even if she did command it to run.

The stranger cocked his head ever so slightly, revealing a level of curiosity that Winnie hadn't expected. With this new angle, the glimmer in his eyes changed. They no longer seemed dark and cold. The dim light of the moon revealed depth in his eyes, unlike anything she had ever seen or could put into words. They were like windows into a dark abyss.

Winnie looked to the coyote once again, and then back to the stranger. Her mind would not provide her with a proper course of action for a situation such as this. She could run or fight, but neither of these options seemed right to her.

His eyes were beautiful. The fact that he had killed a coyote and torn it apart with his bare hands and teeth did not escape her, but there was something about him that piqued her curiosity. She cocked her head slightly, and realized that she was showing the same interest in him that he had shown in her only moments before. She was beginning to suspect that maybe he had killed the coyote in order to protect her.

"So..." she began, with a small voice and no idea what to say next. She finally decided on, "Who are you?"

It seemed like a reasonable question to ask, and a simple enough answer for him to give. Yet, he didn't. He remained silent, staring at her.

"What's your name?" she asked.

Still, there was no answer.

"Why are you... y'know... naked?"

When he didn't answer her this time, Winnie began to suspect that maybe he couldn't respond. She thought that he could have been unable to speak for some reason, or couldn't understand her. Being a foreigner might explain his odd behavior.

"Do you speak English?"

Nothing.

"Do you need help?"

Again, the mysterious stranger said nothing. This time however, he stood up.

The coyote's blood that covered him looked even more gruesome when he stood, yet the expression on his face was not animalistic or evil. It was a blank expression, with some hint of puzzlement. At least, this was how Winnie perceived it. He seemed innocent in a way, and completely frightening at the same time.

Winnie noticed that he was wounded... In addition to the huge stitched-up incision that she had spotted earlier. These other wounds were precise and uniform. They looked like puncture marks on his arms and legs. It appeared to Winnie as though someone had tortured him. She would have expected such nasty wounds to be red and swollen—scabbed, if not bleeding—yet they weren't. They were clean holes in his skin.

"Are you hurt?"

She was beginning to wonder why she insisted on asking questions that she knew would not be answered. He either chose not to speak, or he could not speak. Perhaps he didn't wish to lose the element of mystery that kept her from knowing whether he was friend or foe. That could be taken to mean that he was as scared of her as she was of him. Then again, it could mean that he was lulling her into a false sense of security so that he could rip her apart with his bare hands.

Given what she'd witnessed with the coyote, she really didn't have any sense of security, false or not.

She wondered how long they could stand there, not speaking or moving. She wondered how long he would insist on keeping his motives hidden from her. She wondered how long she could keep her eyes from wandering.

As soon as that thought occurred to her, Winnie could think of little else, but she forced her eyes to look at the stranger's face and nothing else.

There was a rustling in the woods behind Winnie. In her mind she saw coyotes gathering, waiting to exact vengeance for their fallen brother. Since she stood between the source of that sound and the man who had killed the coyote, she did not find that thought very comforting. She wanted to turn and see what had made the noise, but to do so would mean taking her eyes off of the stranger. It would mean giving him an opportunity to attack.

She saw his eyes scan the woods behind her, though his expression did not change. If he had seen a pack of coyotes, he wasn't letting on.

Having seen him look past her made Winnie even more uncomfortable about the rustling from behind. There could be a thousand reasons for such a noise, but the stranger had more information than she did and she didn't like that. He could see any oncoming threat before she did. He could signal his allies to attack her while she was distracted. All she could see was him.

Without taking her eyes off of the stranger, Winnie angled herself, so that she could take a quick look without turning her back to him completely. While it didn't make a lot of sense, as the stranger could charge her just as easily from the side when she wasn't looking as he could from behind, it allowed her to at least *feel* as though she was taking some precaution.

She planned a quick look back and nothing more. Nothing that would give the stranger enough time to do any real damage. So, keeping an eye on the stranger, Winnie silently counted down from three.

3... 2... 1!

A quick, blurry look at the dark woods. She saw nothing behind her. Of course, she gained none of the comfort that would have come from actually being able to actually see the woods before she turned her attention back to the stranger. Instead, when she turned to face him once again, any sense of security that she had gained from her supposed precaution quickly drained away.

He was gone. Without a sound, he had vanished. All that remained was the bloody coyote body.

Just as Winnie had begun to believe that her night could not get more uncomfortable or awkward, a nervous churning began in her stomach. She knew that the mysterious stranger had not gone back to wherever he had come from. He was close. He was watching her. She could feel it.

She scanned the woods for any sign of the stranger. She took a step backward, hoping to find herself up against a tree, but there was no tree directly behind her. She was vulnerable. He could have been anywhere.

She kicked herself for having taken her eyes off of him, especially since she didn't even get a good look at what was behind her.

With that thought, Winnie felt a wave of clarity wash over her. It was as though she was watching herself from outside of her body. Not because of any sixth sense, but because she had seen this scenario play out so many times in the movies that she felt stupid for not realizing what would happen next as soon as the stranger had vanished.

In the movies, a character would slowly turn around and find themselves face to face with their knife-wielding killer. While Winnie could be pretty certain that the stranger had no knife, she knew that he was dangerous and she refused to become a stupid movie character.

Rather than turn slowly, Winnie spun around quickly, ready for whatever she would find.

It surprised her a little when she found herself facing nobody. All that she saw before her was the dark forest. No signs of her stranger. No signs of whatever had made the sound earlier. Nothing at all, which meant that her stranger didn't possess some supernatural ability to teleport around her. He was a mere mortal, just like her. He was just as vulnerable as she was, and she was sick of playing prey to this guy. She was sick of being the victim. She wanted the upper hand for once.

She turned around, determined to march off into the woods and find the mysterious stranger. She was going to solve the mystery once and for all, whether he wanted it to be solved or not.

This was a great plan that would have found Winnie forcefully making her way through the woods, tracking her prey like a pro. It was an awesome image inside of her mind. Strong. Powerful.

It was also thrown out the window as soon as she turned and found herself face to face with the mysterious stranger.

No longer hidden by the shadows of night, he stood close enough for her to see every detail of his face. The blood that covered it. The deep, reflective eyes. He was close enough so that she could smell his breath... except, she couldn't. As far as she could tell, he had no breath.

No breath. The blood. There was also that wound on his chest, which she had noticed earlier, but which she hadn't fully comprehended for whatever reason. *Y*-shaped. Surgical.

Autopsy.

The word came to her like the clanging of a loud bell, and reverberated through her in much the same way. She was looking into the eyes of a blood-covered, coyote killing, naked corpse.

As she tried to process this information and to allow it to make sense in her mind, each of the stranger's actions were beginning to fall into a bizarre sort of context that she had been trying her best to evade for so many years, watching her parents go about their quest for the supernatural.

She had laughed at the idea of ghosts. She didn't have a strong feeling one way or the other when it came to religion. She was not the type of person who would put her faith in things that she could neither see, nor touch. To her, the world was a cold, harsh reality. The dead were gone. Their bodies were rotting shells, and nothing more.

Now, for some reason, the only logic that her brain would allow her was the logic of the otherworldly. She had no doubt in her mind that the boy who stood before her was dead. What she didn't know was exactly what that meant. Was he a vampire? A ghost? A zombie? Was he a creature composed of bits and pieces of many people, sewn together in order to make one monster?

While these and many other questions raced through Winnie's head, the primary matter at hand did not escape her. Whatever this guy was and wherever he came from were secondary to the fact that she had seen him rip apart a living creature, and he was now standing so close to her that she could have counted the stitches on his chest.

She looked him squarely in the eye, waiting for whatever came next. She wanted to close her eyes and look away. She wanted to pretend that she was a little girl again, and the monster terrified her to the core of her being. She could feel that fear, deep inside of her, screaming to get out. But she was no longer that little girl, afraid of death. She lived with it every day of her life. Now, she was looking into the eyes of this mysterious stranger and she wondered what it would feel like to have him ravage her body. She could practically feel him inside of her, grabbing her still-beating heart and ripping it from her chest.

The stranger returned her look. The depths within those eyes might have seemed beautiful to her, if they hadn't been connected to a corpse. They had a quality to them that she couldn't quite understand, but which was almost hypnotic. She saw herself in his eyes, and the world that stretched out behind her. Had she looked into these eyes in another time and place, she could have gotten lost in them for hours.

She pulled herself out of his gaze, cursing herself for being pulled into his evil, dead stare. Obviously, this was all a part of his monster shtick. His eyes must have been meant to incapacitate his prey, so that he could snap their necks or rip open their faces. Winnie was too smart to be caught in such a trap.

Now the dimples, on the other hand, were probably there before he died.

Slowly, he began to lift his hand. Winnie was hesitant to look down, for fear of being distracted at a vital moment when she would need to fight off an attack. Did he have a weapon? Was he planning to grab her? She simply didn't know, and without knowing, how could she possibly react?

She didn't move. She didn't look to his hand. Instead, she found herself meeting his gaze once again, hoping that her expression was one of strength and not merely a mindless stare. She tried to imagine herself as one of those strong female role models that she'd grown up with on TV and in movies. She imagined herself as a weapon in and of herself. Sarah Connor meets Cheetara. There was not a corpse alive that could take her down.

She assured herself of this strength over and over again. She was woman. Power personified.

The stranger's hand continued to rise, but Winnie refused to give into the urge to look. She remained calm, keeping her glare solid.

His expression was blank. His eyes were deep, but empty. They betrayed none of his intent.

At last, he raised his hand high enough so that what he held was nearly touching her face, and she deduced what it was. A rock. A smelly rock. A smelly, red rock. About the size of—

Oh, God, she thought, *it's a heart.*

Repulsed by the thought of the coyote's heart being held so close to her face, Winnie could feel the contents of her stomach making a mad dash for her throat.

Out of reflex, she jumped backwards with a gasp. As she did this, her left foot landed on a smooth rock, covered in wet and slippery leaves. Losing her balance, Winnie squealed and threw out her arms, desperate to latch onto anything that she could grab.

Her hands found nothing but air at first, and then they slipped across the bloody, stitched-up chest of the dead man who stood before her. When she finally managed to grasp onto something, she found herself continuing to fall backwards, now holding the heart of the coyote in her hand.

She hit the ground hard and her head smacked into something solid. A flash of light cut through her vision and then blurred. Despite her best efforts to remain conscious, Winnie felt herself slipping away.

The stranger took a step toward her and watched her from above as she blinked in and out. He, and the woods around him were a blur of dark colors and dim light. No matter how hard she tried to remain awake, her eyes were demanding otherwise. Her limbs were refusing orders to move. Whatever the stranger was planning to do with her, she was helpless to stop him.

29

When Winnie's GPS signal was dropped, Marion felt as though she had lost her daughter in the middle of an ocean. Winnie was no longer a red dot with an exact location, she was a speck of dust on the globe.

Marion was gripping the steering wheel tightly as she drove down the street. It seemed as though there should have been more light from the street lamps, but everything seemed to grow darker by the second.

The darkness made a perfect movie screen, onto which she projected images from her past. Pictures of Winnie as a baby, squirming and giggling, were mixed in with slow motion video of the day that Cindy died. The video had no sound, because Marion couldn't remember anything said that day. As soon as she was told of Cindy's death, the world slowed down and voices became like long, frustrating moans.

She figured that it was perfectly reasonable for her to be superimposing the day that Cindy died with her current situation, even though she didn't believe that Winnie was dead. She knew that teenagers were prone to acts of rebellion, used to assert their independence. Winnie was most likely at a party or a movie. Her mind was simply focusing on the worst possible outcome due to fear.

Except, the last known location was not near any theater. It was a long and empty road, lined by trees, and only a scattering of houses which Winnie would be lucky to find in the event of an emergency.

Marion continued to assure herself that Winnie was not Cindy, and that one daughter's tragic death did not mean that the same thing would happen to the other. People went out into the world all the time and didn't turn up dead. Not everyone was the victim of a hit and run. In fact, very few pedestrians were killed by cars in the area. If Marion were to take into account the fact that a young man had been killed in a similar fashion only days earlier, and he had been the first since Cindy—who was the first since another girl, hit in the late 1990's—she would have to conclude that the chances of Winnie being hit and killed by a car were very low.

Unless the boy had been killed on purpose. If he was merely the first in a string of similar killings, there could be no way of knowing what Winnie's odds were. In fact, the same killer could have been responsible for Cindy's death as well. For all Marion knew, this could have been the pattern of a serial killer who was yet to be discovered.

She was beginning to test the limits of her own imagination. The odds of her family finding themselves trapped in some sort of crazy homicidal plot was about the same as aliens landing in their backyard and asking for brisket. Sure, it *could* happen. It just wasn't *likely* to happen.

As she drove, she kept her eye on the last known location of Winnie's cell phone. While Marion's phone no longer had the red dot on it, she remembered the general location of that dot and had called it up in her navigation program. Now she watched that map as though it were a live video feed of that street and Winnie could walk into view at any moment.

Marion was full of illogical, completely irrational thoughts on that night. It was something that she made a note of and planned to revisit as soon as she had a moment of free time to use for self-diagnosis.

Streets full of houses and shops gave way to trees and isolation. Soon, there was nobody. In the event of an emergency, Winnie would have been hard pressed to reach help. She could have been alone, on the side of the road, broken and bleeding, and nobody in the world would have the slightest hint.

The more that Marion worried about Winnie, the less alone she began to feel herself. There was a small voice which had managed to grow inside of Marion's head after years of hunting for ghosts in dark and quiet houses. This voice was the inkling of fear that could make her feel as though she was being watched. It told her that someone was standing directly behind her. It made the slightest wind outside sound like the voice of a dead man, yelling at her to get out of whatever rundown old building she was investigating.

Lesser investigators would have added these feelings to the list of evidence that they gathered. They would listen to hours of audio recordings and swear on their mothers' graves that the normal hiss of low quality recording was the voice of a spirit. The sound of a shoe on the floor became a threat of violence. Most investigators dealt in paranoia rather than hard evidence. For some, it was a desperate attempt at proving something deeply personal for themselves. For others, it was a way of profiting off of whatever audience they were playing to that night. Either way, this type of evidence was, in Marion's expert opinion, a load of crap.

That voice accompanied her on every investigation, and seemed to be with her as she searched for her daughter. Marion listened to the fear, but she did not allow it to rule her. Fear was natural and healthy, when kept in its proper place. When allowed to take over, fear would lead to irrational behavior. Instead, Marion remained in control of her fear as she pulled over to the side of the dark, secluded road and got out of her warm, safe car.

She stood beside her car, with the engine still running and the headlights lighting the road directly ahead of her. Winnie was nowhere to be seen.

Marion walked to the edge of the pavement and looked into the woods. There was no sound. No movement. No crumpled body in a ditch.

"Winnie?" she said, at a normal volume level, rather than a full scream.

Unless Winnie happened to be standing in the darkness within a couple of feet of Marion, there was little chance that she had heard her mother's voice.

"Winnie?" Marion said again, this time with a little bit more urgency.

There was no response. Marion wasn't surprised. Aside from the fact that Winnie had probably moved on long ago, Marion wasn't even sure that this was the exact location where Winnie's GPS signal had been dropped. She only guessed the location based on what she could remember.

The fact remained, Winnie was not dead on the side of the road, as far as Marion could tell. This was a small victory, but didn't help to soothe Marion's nerves. She wanted her daughter in her own hands, and she wanted her now. She wanted to grab that girl by the arm and drag her back to the car, by force. She wanted to drive Winnie home, nail her window shut, and ground her until she was old enough to run for President.

Normally, Marion's style of parenting would have been more along the lines of asking Winnie to come back home so that they could have a calm discussion about her sneaking out of the house, while they ate a warm meal and burned the scented candles that Marion always found to have a calming effect on her patients.

This was one of those rare times when the line between patient and daughter was very clear. Marion wanted to lock Winnie in her room and throw away the key. She wanted to sentence Winnie to three years of community service. She wanted to scream.

She turned to face the other side of the street. As she did this, something strange caught Marion's attention. As her eyes passed by the headlight beams, Marion could have sworn that she saw something dart across the street. She didn't get a very good look at it, but from what she could tell, it looked like one of the shadow figures that she had heard about so often in the world of paranormal investigation. She had only experienced those shadows once herself—In a dark room. Out of the corner of her eye. Not exactly solid proof of the supernatural.

If she ran home and told Mark about what she had seen, he would have chalked her up as yet another loon in the community of supernatural investigators. She wanted to shrug it off herself, but there was something about the shadow that she couldn't ignore.

It could have been an animal. It was small and fast, but it made no sound. There was no rustling of the leaves on the side of the road, or the clicking of claws on the pavement. It would also be out of character for a dog or a coyote to choose that particular spot for crossing. The running car and bright headlights would normally intimidate an animal. Sure, they might rush into the street and find themselves in front of a moving car by mistake, but a parked car was another story.

Marion was left to consider the possibility that she was either seeing things, or there was a rabid animal running around, out of its mind and entirely unpredictable. Those were her rational options, and yet neither of them felt like the truth. There was a weight to the shadow that she couldn't explain. Whether or not she could retell this story or claim that she had experienced a paranormal encounter, Marion felt that what she had seen was more than a dog on the street.

The scientist within her was tempted to pull out her camera and night vision goggles. The therapist in her was tempted to sit down and write in her journal about the experience while it was still fresh in her mind. Neither of these were as strong as the mother in her, wanting to find her daughter, right—the hell—now.

"Winnie!" she yelled, turning to the woods and once again trying to search between the trees.

All she heard was the engine of her own car. All she saw was the darkness.

30

Bat swinging. Bones breaking. Blood splattering across the graves. Girls screaming. Boys attempting to calm her down. Music pounding in unison with her own heart.

Tami gripped the handle of the baseball bat tightly as she imagined what would happen if she allowed herself to open the car door and step outside. She was furious. She was hurt. She was disgusted.

From inside her car, she could see people arriving for the party. They were laughing and drinking, even before they reached the cemetery. Tami hadn't been able to pull herself out of the car, because she knew what would happen if she did. She would see her best friend—her *sister's* grave, covered in beer bottles.

For a year, she had perfected the craft of self-control. She refused to allow her world to fall apart because of what happened to Cindy. She refused to let life end, because it would be an insult to everything that Cindy was. She wasn't a girl who would want her friends and family to suffer. She would have wanted them to throw a party at her grave.

Her family. *Her* friends. Not a bunch of drunken, sex-crazed teenagers, getting off on the fact that they were dancing on the grave of a dead chick.

After Cindy's death, one question ran through Tami's mind, over and over again: *What now?* She didn't know what she was supposed to do. She didn't know how she was supposed to act. She didn't know if Cindy's family would want to see her, or if stopping by the house would only make matters worse for them. She didn't know how her grief fit into the scheme of things. What right did she have to claim even a small part of their pain? She was lost.

What Tami decided on was life. She decided to live with every ounce of her being. This didn't mean that she was jumping out of airplanes or sleeping around with every guy she met, but it meant that she wouldn't let sadness or fear stand in her way. Cindy hadn't known how short her life would be, but Tami could no longer ignore the fact that she was dying. Be it a day, or a month, or fifty years, she was on her way out of the world. Now, she needed to figure out what she wanted her final thoughts to be, and all she knew for sure was that she didn't want those thoughts to include the words *should have.*

Instinct told her to shut down. She was scared of life. She was scared of facing each day without her partner in crime—Without her best friend around to tell her that her current crush of the week was a loser. She was worried that she would end up in a constant cycle of mistakes without someone to give her a reality check when she needed it.

As she sat in the car, she found herself in one of those moments when a best friend's advice would have been useful. She wanted to make her way through that party, leaving no teenager in attendance without a bruise or a bloody nose. The feeling of rage surging through her was powerful, but not overwhelming.

She loosened her grip on the bat, because she refused to give into her emotions. She wanted to walk through life with eyes open, and going on a rampage with a baseball bat hardly seemed the sort of action that one would take with a clear and level head.

The palm of her hand was numb from having gripped the baseball bat so tightly. Her rage gave way to a more pure and focused anger. Tami unbuckled her seat belt and stepped out of her car.

"Tami! You have to try this... thing. What was it?" said the voice of a girl from behind, drunk and faceless because Tami didn't care to identify her.

"Jell-O shot," replied the equally drunken voice of the girl's boyfriend.

Tami ignored them and walked through the gates of the cemetery, noting the lock which had apparently been cut off by torch. That lack of subtlety made Tami's anger even more powerful. To simply bust the lock with a hammer or cut it with a saw would have been bad enough. To cut through it with fire, and burn their way into the cemetery seemed especially evil to her.

Inside the cemetery, she was accustomed to finding peace and calm. She would normally feel as though the world had melted away and she was the last person on the planet. Tami never believed that she needed to sit at Cindy's grave in order to talk with her, but being there gave her focus when the world began to blur. It was a sanctuary.

Music blared now. It was the horrible beat of popular—but annoying—dance tunes. The shallow, soulless music which Tami may have bounced around to on a normal day, but which now seemed pointless and grating.

Fires had been built to light the party, and around those fires, half naked teenagers danced to the beat of a synthetic drum. They drank and laughed while standing on the graves of strangers. They threw their cans and cups onto the ground, and Tami could all but see the contents seeping into the dirt where bodies were laid to rest.

Countless couples—and even a few triples—kissed and groped and peeled off their layers, tossing their clothes onto cross-shaped headstones.

Earlier in the night, before she knew where the party was being thrown, Tami had been primed for fun. Had this party been held at an abandoned warehouse or an ice rink, she would have grabbed a cup and joined the fun. She was not a prude. She could grope with the best of them. But in that place, she found the sight of the party repulsive. The figures which danced in the light of the fire were not friends and classmates any longer, they were monsters.

As she stood in the middle of the party, several drunken teenagers offered her drinks and drugs. Some hit on her. Some bumped into her because they were incapable of seeing straight. Tami ignored them all and reached into her pocket. From it, she retrieved her cell phone and dialed 9-1-1.

"9-1-1, what's your emergency?" came the voice of the operator on the other end.

"There's a party going on in the Rose Hill Cemetery," Tami told the woman, in a calm and collected tone, "They're destroying the place."

Before the operator could say anything else, Tami hung up the phone and waited for the police to arrive. She wanted to watch the partiers scatter like cockroaches when the lights came on.

Having done the responsible thing and avoided violence, Tami took pride in her self-control. A lesser person would have reacted in a far less mature manner.

She turned and finally took a look at Cindy's grave. On it, she found three unfamiliar teenagers, smoking pot and posing for goofy pictures with the headstone.

"Cynthia McKeller!" one of the stoned boys giggled, with the sort of giggle that Tami only seemed to hear from potheads,

"Check it out."

The boy used his lighter to burn the edge of a stick, and used that charred stick to alter the name on the headstone.

"McKiller!" the boy giggled, "Because she's dead!"

His friends laughed along with his lame joke, which nobody seemed to find offensive in the least as they gulped down booze from plastic cups, spilling half of their drinks on their own shirts.

Tami walked to the grave and stood over the group. She looked down at them and smiled.

"You guys!" she said with great enthusiasm, "That is *so* funny! Can I see your lighter?"

She strived for maturity. She did not always achieve this goal.

The boy handed Tami his lighter. She lit it, and watched the flame burn for a moment before looking to the teenagers once again. She inhaled deeply. The air stank of whiskey.

"What are you drinking?" she asked them, "Is that whiskey?"

The boy who handed her the lighter nodded and said, "Mickey stole it from his dad's house. Want some?"

Tami smiled and gestured toward the boy's shirt, "It looks like it might stain. Your shirt's soaked in it."

"I'm a little wasted."

"You're also a little flammable," she told him. "I could light you up right now. And I will, if you don't grab your drinks and your weed and get your asses out of here. Now."

Tami wasn't used to threatening people. She was a nice girl, who preferred to be loved by all who met her. She always tried her best to be polite and courteous. The fact that she had managed to threaten anyone surprised her. That she managed to do it with a straight face gave her a rush.

The kids that sat on Cindy's grave didn't move. They stared at Tami as though she was wearing a clown costume. The reaction was not what Tami had hoped for, and it made her even more furious. The nerve of these people, to sit on her friend's grave, getting high and drinking whiskey made her want to scream. The fact that they didn't even have the decency to feel threatened by her made her want to follow through on her threat.

"Listen," she said, with a stern face, putting out the lighter, "I know the girl whose grave you're sitting on. She was my best friend."

The teenagers froze for a moment, staring at Tami, and then began to stand.

The teenager who had handed Tami his lighter looked her in the eyes and said, "Dude, I'm sorry. Yeah, we'll clear out."

Tami was thrown off by the effectiveness of simply explaining herself to them. She wasn't sure how to react to their rather agreeable response, except to give back their lighter.

The teenagers cleared away from Cindy's grave, leaving Tami alone there. She sat down, as she had a hundred times before, and leaned against the headstone.

"That was so weird," she told Cindy, and couldn't help but laugh.

31

Whether or not Winnie ever lost consciousness, she wasn't really sure. Her eyes closed, but she tried her best to open them, fighting the desire to drift off. There was an urgency to her wanting to stay awake, but she couldn't quite remember what it was.

There should have been more pain. She was aware of the fact that she'd fallen and that her head had hit something hard, but her arms felt too heavy to raise, so she couldn't examine herself or see if there was serious damage done. All she knew was that she was tired, and the world was a Dali painting. It seemed in motion, with her perception ever-shifting. One moment, she was flooded by swirls and blurs and the next, she was spinning and everything else looked normal.

There was a rustling sound nearby, which Winnie thought might be the ocean, but only for a fleeting moment. After she regained some of her senses, she remembered the stranger who had torn the heart from the poor, helpless coyote that had once threatened her life. She remembered the stranger holding up the heart, and how this had caused her to fall.

Where the stranger was now and what he was planning to do next was of grave concern to Winnie, and yet she couldn't bring herself to move. It felt as though she was not fully connected with her body anymore. It was heavy and weighed her down, but it was not part of her. It was merely dead weight. In that moment, she was very aware of the line between herself and the shell that she used to walk this world.

The thought of her mysterious stranger ripping into her chest and removing her still-beating heart crossed her mind once again, but she lacked the ability to react. She was outside of the situation, if only for a moment or two, watching it play out in front of her.

The stranger was not alive. This came back to her, along with the memory of the stitches on his chest, and the incision that they held shut. She remembered the holes in his arms and legs. She remembered his eyes.

Her finger twitched, and a wave of nausea rushed over her, shaking the world around her and bringing the spinning to a sudden halt. She was no longer outside of herself. She was present and aware, and could feel the throbbing pain in her head, which she managed to put her hand to at last.

She was surprised when she found no blood gushing from her scalp. For all of the trouble this fall had caused her, she had expected more. She expected blood and infection. She expected defeat. She expected the mysterious stranger to drag her into a cave where he would skin her alive and boil her bones for soup.

All of this pain and expectation funneled through her and escaped her mouth as a single word, "Ouch."

There was another rustling sound. This time, Winnie sat up to figure out where the stranger was. With every inch that she raised her head, the intensity of its throbbing grew, but she had no choice. There was a dead man walking in the woods and she could not risk turning her back on him.

When she saw the stranger, it was through a blur of motion which nearly made her sick. That turn of her head was like a roller coaster ride, but she was able to figure out where he was and what he was doing.

The stranger stood nearby, in front of a tree. He watched her, but he didn't seem menacing. He watched her with a glint in his eye that she might have mistaken for innocent curiosity, though she acknowledged that she may have suffered a greater blow to the head than she first thought. After all, very few zombie movies involved cute, innocent zombies, looking out for the well-being of the film's starlet. At the same time, Winnie had seen many movies which involved cute vampires who brooded and sulked rather than pillage and feast on the blood of the innocent. If she could believe in a vampire with crazy hair and impeccable taste in clothes, then why not a boyish zombie?

The stranger lifted his hand to his mouth and took a bite of what Winnie at first assumed was an apple, but which she quickly realized was the heart of the coyote. As if her probable concussion weren't enough to make her sick, she now had this image stuck in her head.

The stranger chewed on his mouthful of coyote heart, and blood ran down his chin, dripping to the ground by his feet. He didn't move toward Winnie, either to attack or to help her get up. He simply watched and ate, as though she were putting on a play for his benefit.

Winnie rolled over onto her stomach and her head once again began to spin. She could have sworn that all of the blood in her body was inside of her skull, and that it was swishing around each time she turned.

She mustered the strength that she needed to push herself off of the ground and to her feet. How long she could remain on her feet, she wasn't quite sure. Her head was whirling and pounding like a dryer full of bricks. Her wounded ankle still hurt, but it was the least of her concerns for the moment.

The stranger, standing and watching, was annoying her. At the very least, he could try to kill her while she was dazed. She would understand that. She did not understand his standing there, watching. His lack of menace was far more creepy to her than any attack could have been. On top of that, corpse or not, it was just rude of him to stare without any hint of concern.

He took another bite of his bleeding heart.

"You're disgusting," she told him, "I just want you to know that."

Winnie closed her eyes, trying to realign whatever gears were out of place in her head. Every once in a while, as she went about her normal life, Winnie would look down at her hand or catch her reflection in a window. She would wiggle her fingers or blink her eyes, and she would feel disconnected from the thing that she controlled. The reflection was not her. In those moments, everything felt so mechanical that she viewed her body as no more a part of herself than she would a car. Since Cindy's death, Winnie had been having those moments more and more often, but never quite as strongly as she did that night in the woods.

Her body was broken and out of whack. She could think and feel just fine, but her body was not responding as it should. Her eyes weren't focusing where she told them to focus. Her movement was not as smooth as she would have liked. She pushed and struggled to regain the normal connection between mind and body, but her body was lagging.

She felt like a zombie.

This feeling couldn't last. She needed to pull herself together and resume the bizarre adventure that the night had provided for her. She refused to have the story end with her telling people that she bumped her head and had to take a nap, so the dead guy found someone cooler to stalk.

When Winnie tried to walk toward a fallen tree so that she could sit down, she felt every pound of her body's weight pulling against her. It wanted to go down, but she refused to give in to its demands.

"Listen to me, you stupid piece of crap body. You will not win. I am in control. I own you. So shut the hell up and do what I say," she insisted aloud, plopping down on the fallen tree.

As she sat, she glanced up and saw the mysterious stranger, still standing as he had been before.

"Oh, I wasn't talking to you," Winnie smirked, feeling oddly jovial in this strange and potentially dangerous situation.

It was interesting how closely she resembled her old self at certain moments, when alone. She could laugh. She could joke. She could even be goofy, if she happened to be tired enough when *"Don't You (Forget About Me)"* came on the radio. When someone else entered the room, Winnie changed. She became angry at every person, no matter what they said or did. The more they cared about her, or tried to say the right thing, the more angry she became. She hated this version of herself. She didn't enjoy being bitter. She did not consider herself a hateful person, and yet there was this monster inside of her, waiting to pounce whenever it saw a potential victim.

The mysterious stranger took another bite of his coyote heart. Winnie could hear the sound of it as he chewed, but didn't dare look. Her mind had been filled with enough disgusting imagery for one night.

"Seriously dude, consider going vegan," she quipped. The lighthearted tone of her voice sounded alien to her.

Eyes closed and taking deep breaths, Winnie's gears were beginning to realign. Her head wasn't spinning as much as before, and her hands were beginning to feel less like excess baggage and more like the finely tuned robot limbs that she knew and loved.

She opened her eyes and looked at her mysterious stranger. To her relief, he no longer looked like a flesh-colored blur. As her head began to clear, all of her questions about him came racing back, but she didn't bother asking them. She knew that the stranger wouldn't answer.

She watched him as he watched her, and she tried to figure out what her next course of action would be. His being there placed a responsibility on her shoulders. She couldn't go home, hop into bed and call it a night. She needed to find a way of dealing with him. She needed to figure out why he was there and what he wanted.

Without notice, the stranger dropped his half-eaten heart and turned away from Winnie. He started to walk into the shadows of the night. It was as if he could sense that she had resolved to see this mystery through to its end, and was now daring her to follow.

She didn't follow him right away. Before she could get to her feet, Winnie stopped herself and shook her head, wondering if she had suffered more brain damage than she had initially thought. She wasn't, after all, an idiot. She knew how stupid it would be to follow a zombie deeper into the woods, on a path to God-knows-where. It would be insane. Normal girls don't chase dead guys around all night.

But he was getting farther and farther away, and taking any chance for answers right along with him. She couldn't let him leave. She needed to find out where he was going. She needed to go with him.

Whether or not it was the right thing to do, Winnie got to her feet and walked after the stranger, making sure to remain at least ten feet behind, just to be safe.

She smiled at that thought. *Safe* was a joke.

32

Mark sat in his office chair with the audio recorder plugged into his computer, staring at the monitor in front of him as it displayed the recording that was playing. Aside from that computer monitor, the room was dark. Mark preferred to keep distractions to a minimum when examining evidence, and by keeping the lights turned off, he could remain focused on what was right in front of him.

The display of the recording looked like that of a heart monitor, hooked up to a person who was either extremely nervous, or suffering through electrocution. At times, the line on the screen would remain calm and almost steady, but with each sound that came over the speakers, the line went crazy.

Unfortunately, his recording had been compromised by Winnie, who had decided to visit her sister's grave during his investigation. This made the examination of the recording difficult, because the sound of a ghostly voice in a recording could be very subtle. In many cases, a spirit who is unable to make their own voice heard might manipulate another sound, such as a breeze or an airplane, and use that altered sound as their voice in communicating with the living world. It could take an investigator years to learn how to properly listen for those sounds, and even then it is an art form that many never master. Some investigators make fools of themselves, grasping at digital artifacts or the sounds of their own footsteps.

Mark was always careful not to jump at the first sign of a voice. He was his own worst critic when it came to accepting his findings, and always insisted on looking for a solid explanation for whatever voices he might think he heard. He liked a clean working environment, free of outside noise whenever possible. This is why he sighed and shook his head upon hearing Winnie's voice on the recorder. She had contaminated his recording.

At the same time, her being there provided an interesting opportunity. If Cindy never chose to speak to her father, perhaps she would attempt to communicate with her sister. So, Mark listened to the silence between Winnie's words, and tried to picture the scene around the grave so that he could account for any other sounds on the recording.

When Winnie spoke, Mark took the opportunity to take a sip of coffee, or a bite of a quickly-made sandwich. When she went silent, he froze, and stared at the screen, waiting for any anomalous sound or fluctuation of the line on his monitor.

Each time he froze, he was like a child, listening to hear Santa's footsteps on the roof on Christmas Eve. He never assumed that there would be no voice. No matter how much time passed without hearing any hint of a message from Cindy, Mark expected something to turn up. Each time the wind blew, he wanted to believe that her voice was hidden in that sound, and that he had finally struck gold. But he couldn't manage to convince himself of any such treasure. Each time he got his hopes up, they quickly dissolved and vanished with the sound of the wind. Each time, his office seemed darker and his house felt just a little more empty.

Ever since he had first learned of Cindy's death, Mark had been in a state of limbo. He had expected to be struck by the realization of her death at some point, and to have it drive through him like a knife. That realization never came. On an intellectual level, he didn't deny that she was gone. There was no way to ignore that fact. However, on an emotional level, something was missing. There was no closure. There was no finality to it. He *knew* that she was dead, but he didn't *feel* that she was dead.

Every time he walked through the door, he expected to see her. Every time he walked past her bedroom, he expected to smell that horribly overpriced shampoo of hers.

Each time he sat down at a computer to examine audio recordings from Cindy's grave, or her school, or her bedroom,

Mark was reassured of the logic in continuing his hunt. Though he hadn't found any evidence to support his beliefs, he knew that Cindy was not gone. She couldn't be.

The recording ended, and Mark had heard no sign of Cindy. He wished that Winnie had left it alone and had allowed it to continue running, rather than bring it home. He assumed that she thought he'd dropped it or forgotten it somehow. Nobody knew that he was looking for Cindy, so she couldn't know that he meant to leave it there. She probably thought that she was being helpful by bringing it home.

There was anger, deep inside of him. It was a fuming, raging anger. He had no desire to scream or punish Winnie, but he was irritated that she had ruined his recording, tainted his evidence, and now forced him to start all over again.

It was buried deep. He barely recognized it as anger at all, but he knew it was there, and tried his best to ignore it. Winnie wasn't his concern now, Cindy was. Cindy needed him to help her. Winnie was alive and well. She could take care of herself.

33

Tami stretched across Cindy's grave and stared at the stars up above as the party raged on around her. She knew that the police were on their way, and she was just waiting for them to get there. She had no intention of running, as everyone around her was undoubtedly about to.

"Do you remember that time when we were in first grade and Mrs. Lundy wore that bright orange skirt and everyone in class was laughing about her looking like a pumpkin?" Tami asked.

She didn't expect a response. She wasn't even sure why she was talking, since she sincerely hoped that Cindy wasn't spending eternity tied to her grave. She just felt like talking about these things, and there was nobody else in the world who wanted to hear it, so she often found herself speaking to Cindy.

"What was the name of that kid who gave her the nickname? The one who always got dragged down to the office by the ear? And do you think that was child abuse, by the way?" Tami stopped talking and shook her head. "Okay, now I'm actually asking questions. I'm losing it for sure."

She was distracted by the sound of a police siren in the distance. Though the music was still pounding away at the party, the siren to cut through the noise and everyone at the party perked up as they heard it.

The music stopped. The loud conversations halted.

"Dude, five-oh!" one of the boys called, and the crowd began to scurry.

There was a chance that one of those people was going to run right over Tami without a second thought. She was on the ground and didn't hurry to move as the rest of the partiers ran for their cars. She knew the risk, but she didn't care. Instead, she looked up at the stars.

"Bundy! Chris Bundy. That's why I always connect him to Mrs. Lundy. It rhymes," Tami smiled and snapped her fingers as the memory came back to her.

The sirens didn't stay on for long. To Tami, it sounded as though the police were sounding their sirens just enough to give warning to the partiers, so that they would clear out by the time the police showed up.

Partying in the cemetery was trespassing. Breaking the lock probably bumped it up to breaking and entering. Trashing the place was vandalism. Underage drinking. Drugs. Tami was sure that there were any number of parking violations and disturbing the peace... But kids will be kids, as they say. The police most likely wanted to avoid the sort of paperwork that would go into arresting the hundred or so minors who were committing those crimes.

She wondered if anyone knew that it was her who called the police. If so, she wondered if any of them had figured out why. Would any of them remember that one of their own was buried in that place? Would they care?

She was starting to sound like Winnie, and she had to smile at that thought.

Most of the other kids had already run off by the time Tami decided to drag herself to her feet. She calmly brushed off her pants and looked around at the cemetery. It was a mess.

She shook her head, hating to see the place in such a horrible state, dishonoring those who were at rest there. It was normally so peaceful; so beautiful. Whether she believed that those dead people cared about the party or not was irrelevant. What had been done to them disgusted her.

As she walked back to her car, she continued to assess the mess. If only cups and bottles had been the worst of it, she would have been thankful. The condom wrappers and the underwear that was draped over one of the headstones turned her stomach.

"I can't believe that these are the people I hang out with," she said, not even knowing whether she was talking to herself or to

Cindy at this point.

She reached the gates as other cars were speeding off. Kids were hooting and hollering as they left. Music began to blast from car stereos. Dust was kicked up.

"I guess the party is moving," Tami muttered. "I wonder if I'll get the invite."

By the time she reached her own car, the area was empty, save for the one or two stragglers who were stumbling down the road on foot, far too drunk to drive.

When she saw her car, she no longer had to wonder whether the other kids knew that she was the one who called the cops. Her windshield had the word *RAT* written across it, in bright red lipstick. On each window there were crudely drawn pictures of what she assumed were supposed to be penises, and a variety of offensive—though misspelled—messages scribbled in different shades of red. Tami cringed as she saw those images. She could just imagine what her father would say if he ever saw what was on his little girl's car.

"So much for my invitation," she said to herself as she got into the car. "At least I didn't leave my window open for once."

She pulled away from the cemetery just as a police car was pulling in. Without even thinking about it, she waved to the officer behind the wheel as she passed.

Tami was not fleeing, but waiting. As soon as she found a suitable area, she pulled off of the road and behind a cluster of trees. In that spot, she was hidden from any car that was driving to or from the cemetery.

She turned off the engine and headlights, and waited in silence.

From the corner of her eye, Tami could have sworn that she saw something move. She turned and looked for one of those stumbling stragglers or an angry teenager who was coming at her, armed with super shiny lip gloss. Instead, she saw nothing. All she could make out from that spot were trees and shadows.

Tami remained perfectly silent as she waited. The odds of anyone being able to hear her, even if she chose to call a friend and chat on the phone, were slim to none. Yet, she breathed quietly and calmly. She made not a sound.

The shadows swayed as a breeze blew through the trees. As that breeze made its way through the grass, it looked as though there was a monster beneath the ground, speeding away from the party so that it would not be caught by the cops.

When those shadows took on a new life and the light in the area turned from a pale blue to a bright yellow, Tami was caught off guard. She gasped, but remained still.

All of the writing on all of her windows became more defined as the world outside her window lit up. The police car was leaving the area. Though she could not see the car very well, she knew that they would be looking for teenagers and she quietly prayed that they would not spot her car. She could not be shooed away from the area—not yet.

The lights passed her by and continued down the road which led away from the cemetery. Once it was gone, Tami remained still. She did not want to start her engine or turn on her headlights until she was absolutely certain that the police were not coming back.

She wound up waiting much longer than she probably needed to, never feeling quite comfortable with the idea of revealing her location. Yet, with each minute that passed, Tami began to feel more and more vulnerable. Though she saw nobody around her, she felt as though she was being watched. She tried to shake off that feeling, but couldn't. At any moment, she expected to turn around and find a creepy old man in worn clothing and a grin on his face, peering in at her through one of her obscene windows.

"There's no such thing as creepy old men," she told herself, closing her eyes. "There's no such thing as creepy old men."

Finally, she turned her key and started the engine. As her headlights came on, the shadows in front of her darted off, just as the teenagers at the Blackout Ball had done not too long ago.

Tami slowly and carefully pulled her car out of its hiding spot and back onto the road. She did not drive away from the cemetery. Instead, she drove toward it.

When she arrived, the place was empty. Not so much as one straggler remained, yet the gate was still swinging freely and she could see the garbage on the ground beyond it.

She parked her car and looked out at the cemetery. Part of her just wanted to go home to her nice warm bed, but the part of her which held the most resolve was the one which caused her to shut off her engine and get out of the car.

Tami walked to her trunk and pulled out a box of garbage bags and a pair of gardening gloves which she was very thankful for, considering the types of mess that she might find in the aftermath of a raging high school party.

Walking toward the gate, she braced herself for the work that she had ahead of her. She took a deep breath.

"Okay," Tami said, to herself or possibly to the dead. "Let's do this... Quickly and without much hassle."

She dropped the box on the ground, pulled one bag from it and went to work. She would not stop until the place once again resembled the peaceful sanctuary that it was meant to be. She would not allow Cindy's family to witness what those inconsiderate children had done.

In that moment, Tami realized that no matter how hard she might try, she would never be one of those kids again. She would never be able to party without thought or care. She would never be able to identify with anyone who would behave in such a way. Whether she liked it or not, Cindy's death had changed her. Not in quite the same way as it had changed Winnie, but it had changed her nonetheless. She was alive, and that fact alone meant something to her that most teenagers could never understand.

She began to hum *This Old Man* as she worked. It helped her to keep her pace up and she found herself feeling strangely at peace out there by herself, in a cemetery, cleaning up garbage in the middle of the night. Everyone else had fled without a second thought. Tami would not have dreamt of being anywhere else in that moment.

As she worked, she kept her eyes on the ground, but from the corner of her eye, she could have sworn that she saw something dark moving nearby. When she turned to look, however, she found nothing but the night.

34

Winnie kept her eyes on the stranger as he moved through the woods. He moved without hesitation, as though he was on a predetermined path. He did not stop to double check his heading. He did not slow down to avoid stepping on pine cones or rocks. He did not even turn to see if he was being followed.

He had no fear, as far as she could tell. No doubt. He didn't worry about what was ahead of him, or what was behind. He just kept moving.

As she tracked the mysterious stranger, she hid herself behind trees and in shadows, just in case he hadn't noticed her. She took not one step without considering where it was that she was setting her foot down. She knew the risk that she was taking and that any sane person would have turned around long ago, but she couldn't bring herself to turn around. She couldn't go back.

The deeper into the woods they walked, the denser the trees became. Moonlight was being blocked by the branches high above and the world around Winnie was becoming harder to see. Yet while she was bathed in shadows, the stranger seemed to glow ever-so-slightly as rare hints of light reflected off of his pale skin. She couldn't take her eyes off of him.

He stopped walking and began to shift his weight. Winnie could see the muscles in his legs tightening as he turned toward her, and she hurried to take cover behind a tree. As she hid herself, she closed her eyes. Though she told herself that she was listening for the stranger's footsteps moving closer, the only sound that she could hear was that of her own breathing. It echoed through her head as she breathed in and out, and as she listened, she heard the sound of her own fear. Her heart was pounding in her chest. Her hands were covering her mouth. No matter how much she tried to convince herself that her pursuit of the stranger was calculated and her staying hidden was a way of keeping the upper hand, she could not manage to believe it. She was scared, both of the stranger and of what awaited her if she turned back. She wasn't taking cover and keeping the upper hand, she was hiding. From the moment she woke up in the morning until the time she went to sleep at night, she was always hiding.

It hadn't always been like this. As she stood there behind the

tree, listening to the sound of her own breathing, she
remembered what it was like when she was younger. She
remembered standing at the top of a hill when she was a little girl,
with the sunlight shining through her closed eyelids and the wind
in her hair.

Cindy was standing next to her on that hill, telling her to keep
her eyes closed and do everything that she told her to do. Of
course, being the younger and more naive sister, Winnie trusted
Cindy without question. When Cindy told her to take a step
forward, she took a step. When Cindy told her to run, she ran.
Blindly.

Winnie remembered the feeling of that day, running across a
field and feeling each bump in the ground as she went, but Cindy
told her that the coast was clear and Winnie never questioned
that fact.

Even knowing that nothing bad came from that experiment in
trust, Winnie felt nervous for her younger self as she replayed
that memory in her head. The older her knew that nobody could
ever really be trusted. She wasn't even sure that she could trust
herself. After all, she had managed to convince herself that
jumping from a second-story window was a good idea, and
looking back on that decision with an aching ankle, she was
beginning to think that it was not her smartest moment.

And now she was in the woods, following a stranger, but only
from a distance. The second he showed any sign of acknowledging
her presence, she hid behind a tree with her eyes closed. The

more she thought about that fact, the more she wondered why—if she was so concerned with his finding her—she was willing to close her eyes and leave herself defenseless.

Maybe she was waiting for Cindy to tell her which way to walk. Maybe she was waiting for the stranger to seek her out and take away her ability to decide her own fate.

Her breathing was slowing down and she could hear the world around her once again. She listened for the sound of footsteps moving her way, but she heard nothing more than the scurrying of some small animal, moving in the opposite direction.

She opened her eyes. She found herself staring at the tree in front of her, but it was progress. She was tired of hiding. She was tired of waiting. The stranger walked without care. He walked without shame. He walked freely through the night, either randomly or toward some destination that she was unaware of. It didn't matter. She wanted to walk the way he walked—Or, to walk a much more clothed version of the way he walked. She was tired of the back and forth in her own head. She was tired of being frozen by indecision. She was tired of waiting for someone to lead her. She didn't want to follow the stranger anymore, she wanted to pursue him.

Slowly, Winnie began to build her nerve. She tried to talk herself into moving from her hiding spot, knowing that the stranger could have already resumed his trek through the woods while she was cowering behind the tree.

Deep breath, she told herself. *On the count of three.*

She took her deep breath and quietly counted to three, placing her hands on the tree's trunk and preparing to move. Once she was done counting, Winnie pushed off of the tree and stepped out from behind it, looking toward the spot where she had last seen the stranger. At last, she was done hiding, and he... was nowhere to be found.

"No," she said, quietly to herself, not even realizing that she was saying it.

She moved forward, slowly at first, but picking up her pace as she made her way to the spot where the stranger had last been seen.

"No, no, no," she repeated to herself over and over again, scanning the woods for any sign of moonlight reflecting off of pale skin and rippling abs.

She turned around and looked in the direction from which she had come, thinking that maybe he had moved toward her without her knowing it, but there was nothing.

"Hello?!" she called into the woods, knowing that it might not have been the best idea to call out to the stranger who had ripped the heart out of that coyote, but she didn't care.

There was no response. She wasn't sure whether or not she had expected a response, considering the fact that the stranger hardly seemed like the talkative type, but calling out for him was for her own sake. She was declaring that she was done hiding. She was done pretending to be the victim in a bad horror movie.

As she stood in the spot where she had last seen the stranger, she saw no sign of him. If she wanted to track him and find out where he was going, she would have to be smart. She would have to stop thinking like the prey and begin thinking like the hunter.

Winnie knelt down and examined the ground where the stranger had been standing. She saw leaves which looked as though someone had been standing on them and she placed her fingers on these leaves, nodding to herself as she tried to figure out which direction these footprints led in, but soon began shaking her head as she came to the realization that Hollywood's course in tracking never extended beyond the main character discovering the footprints and rushing off in pursuit of their target. She had no idea how to track the mysterious stranger based on squished leaves or broken branches. He was gone. As far as she could tell, he had vanished into thin air—a notion which would have sounded completely insane on any other night. Now, it was up to Winnie to decide what she was going to do next.

With no trail left for her to follow, she could have turned around and walked back to the road. In her retellings of the story, the mysterious stranger would disappear, never to be seen again. It would send chills up the spine of anyone she told. It was a good story, but she couldn't bring herself to turn around. She needed to find him. She needed to see who he was and where he was going.

She took a step forward, still with no idea where she was going. Just as she had walked down the dark, unfamiliar road earlier that night, she now walked through the woods.

In her mind, she could almost hear the news reports about her own disappearance. She imagined that it would take her parents a while to realize that she was gone. Once they did, they would probably roll their eyes and curse her name, because they would have to deal with all sorts of phone calls and paperwork.

She stopped herself mid-thought, wondering how she could think of her parents as such heartless monsters. The people she imagined were nothing like the parents that she had grown up with.

Then again, neither were the people that she lived with after Cindy's death. She didn't see them as evil, but they were far from normal. Nothing about her life seemed normal to her anymore. She was as much a stranger to herself as they were.

She kept moving through the woods, more determined than ever to find the mysterious stranger and discover where he was going—more determined than ever to understand the path that she was on. Until she had those answers, there was no way for her to go back home.

35

Marion stood on the edge of the woods, looking into the darkness. She didn't know what she was going to do. Winnie could have been in those woods, wandering and lost. She could be cold and scared, unable to find her way out.

To Marion, the woods became like a force of evil, capable of suffocating her daughter. She pictured Winnie trapped by branches which caught her clothing and scratched at her skin. She could all but hear Winnie screaming for help in those dark woods, but there was nothing she could do about it.

She considered rushing in to save Winnie, but she didn't know how. She didn't know where to enter the woods or which direction to walk once she did. She tried yelling to Winnie, but there was no answer. She tried calling Winnie's cell phone, but her call was put straight through to voicemail.

Marion took a step back and placed her hand on her aching head. The stress was beginning to get to her. She wanted to cry, but she forced herself to refrain. She would release her emotions at some other time. Right now, she just wanted to find her daughter.

"Cindy!" she called into the woods, before catching herself. She'd called the wrong name. She couldn't believe it, but she had actually called the wrong name.

Over the years, she had called the girls by the wrong name many times. On more than one occasion, she had even called one of them by the name of the family dog. It wasn't a mistake that she would have felt guilty about at any other time, but as she stood next to those woods and worried for Winnie's life, she could not believe that she had called Cindy's name.

Tears filled her eyes. She couldn't stop them. Sobs rose in her throat, but she managed to choke them down, remaining silent as she put her hands on her knees and hunched over. Her tears fell onto the pavement. Her hands were shaking.

That feeling was beginning to come over her once again; the feeling of sand slipping between her fingers and her being powerless to stop it. She wanted to claw and cling to Winnie more than anything in the world, but she was powerless. Her daughter was out there alone, and Marion could do nothing but stand on the side of the road and cry.

She refused to accept that. She took a deep breath and forced herself to stop crying. She wiped away the tears on her face as she straightened herself up. She had allowed enough crying for one night and now it was time to get back to the business of finding her daughter. If she could manage to bring Winnie home safely, she could then proceed to kill the girl herself. Until then, she needed to remain calm and to think this through rationally.

Taking another deep breath, Marion turned away from the woods. There was no way that Winnie would just wander into the woods blindly. She hadn't raised a fool, after all. Marion had to realize that her fear of Winnie being lost in the woods was born from her own fears, not her daughter's stupidity. She had to have more confidence than that in Winnie.

Marion looked down the road. Moonlight shined down upon the pavement up ahead but the world seemed to end as the street curved and everything in the distance faded into black.

She turned and looked in the direction from which she came. While the darkness seemed to pour over the edges of the road in that direction as well, it seemed somehow less intimidating to her, since she knew what lay beyond that darkness.

Going back was not an option. She hadn't seen Winnie on her way out to that spot, so she had no reason to believe that she would find her if she turned around and went back. Her only option was to push forward and to hope for some sign of her daughter.

Pulling her cell phone from her pocket, Marion once again refreshed the GPS map. She held her breath and waited.

It seemed to take forever for the map to reload. When the updated information finally came up, there was still no sign of Winnie. All she got on her screen was the same error message as before.

Marion exhaled. She was disappointed, but she remained calm and tried to think of where Winnie might have been. She asked herself if there was a friend who lived down this street, or a spot where the kids liked to hang out. All that she gained from this was the realization that she was terribly unhip and out of touch, because she had no answer for either question.

She walked back to her car and climbed inside, never taking her eyes off of the woods. She slowly pulled back onto the street and began to move down it, fully expecting to see Winnie around every corner or behind one of the many trees that her headlights lit up as she went along. Unfortunately, she did not see Winnie. The street was empty and dark.

There was no need for Marion to pick up her speed as she went down the road. There were no cars for as far as the eye could see. She was so far away from the town's busiest streets and there were so few homes in the area that there must not have been much use for this road at all, for anyone who didn't live down it.

Marion was accustomed to creepy feelings and dark places. She was usually unaffected by them after so many years of pushing herself to her limit. Yet, there was something about this particular road and that particular night that felt somehow wrong. There was something in the air which she might have described as a scent, but there was nothing to smell. It wasn't a scent at all really, but she couldn't quite put her finger on which sense was being triggered.

Setting aside this strange feeling and chalking it up to panic and stress, Marion drove on, scanning the road and the woods as she went. Hoping. Praying.

After driving for several minutes at an incredibly slow speed, Marion caught sight of something in the distance. At first, it was merely a glimmer of light which she thought could have been something inside of her car, reflecting off of the windshield. Yet, as she drove on, she saw this light again.

The light was from a distant home, hidden deep in the woods to her left. The light appeared and disappeared as Marion moved down the road and trees obstructed it from view.

She couldn't take her eyes off of it. Though she doubted that Winnie would be in any random house along the street, Marion was captivated by the light from that house, which seemed so isolated from the rest of the town that it might as well have been the last house on the planet.

When she reached the driveway which led down to the house, Marion pulled to the side of the road and stopped her car.

She told herself that it was not likely that Winnie would be down there, but if something had happened and Winnie needed to find help, that house could have been the only option available to her.

In some ways, it made sense. In other ways, it seemed like a stretch. There was no denying that Marion was desperate.

Marion stared at that light for several seconds, trying to decide whether or not she wanted to drive toward it. She pulled her cell phone from her pocket and thought about calling Mark and asking him for help in locating Winnie, but something stopped her. In the back of her mind, she pictured Mark screaming at her for losing another one of their children. She imagined him hating her.

It was irrational. She knew this on some level, but the voice in the back of her mind did not back down to reason. She put her cell phone back in her pocket and rubbed her temples.

After considering her options for another minute or two, Marion turned the steering wheel and pulled her car into the driveway of the secluded house.

36

Mark sat in Cindy's room, staring at the pictures that Warren had drawn. He had listened to a portion of the audio recordings that were made at Cindy's grave and he found nothing. He uploaded the audio files to his computer and ran them through several filters. The files were then transferred to his cell phone, where he would be able to listen to them wherever he went.

Now, he looked at the sketch of his own home and wondered what it could mean. None of the tests that had been run on his home over the previous year had resulted in any sign of Cindy, yet his home was one piece of the puzzle that would lead him to her —assuming that Warren could be believed.

The room was not untouched. Though Cindy's bed and furniture remained as they had been during her life and many of her schoolbooks and knickknacks hadn't been moved, her closet was now empty. Brown cardboard boxes were scattered across her floor and bed. They meant to donate her clothes to charity, but neither Mark nor Marion could ever seem to bring themselves to do it.

They offered Winnie and Tami whatever they wanted from Cindy's closet, but the only thing that Winnie had decided to hold onto was a tie-dyed t-shirt that she and Cindy had made together, years before. Tami chose an antique cross that she'd given to Cindy as a birthday present. Neither of them wanted to walk around town wearing Cindy's clothes, though they had often done so while Cindy was alive.

It was strange for Mark to sit in that room. The boxes did not make him feel as though Cindy was dead and her belongings were being disposed of. Instead, he felt like a normal father whose normal, living daughter was leaving home. For an entire year, the room drew this feeling from him. He was stuck in an unending transition from one chapter of his life to something else which he couldn't quite see just yet.

Her schoolbooks were sitting on the desk on the other side of the room. When Mark saw them, he thought that maybe they would provide him with a clue—maybe he would find a note or a doodle that would send him toward the next piece of the puzzle.

He walked to the desk and grabbed one of her notebooks from

the stack. He opened it and flipped past pages of math homework and drawings of spider-webs, all of which he had seen a hundred times before. He hoped that this time he would see something that he had missed before. Maybe he would find the name of a boy that she was in love with and he could do something with that information, because she might choose to latch onto that emotion after death and follow her boyfriend instead of her family. At the very least, he could ask the boy if he'd heard any sounds or had any strange dreams about Cindy. But there were no names or initials. There was nothing to see in that notebook that he hadn't seen before.

On one page, Cindy had written the phrase, *Winnie's a bitch*. Those words were crossed out and any disagreement between the girls had undoubtedly been resolved before Cindy died, but when Mark saw that line, he could almost hear his girls arguing. He put his fingers over those words, as though touching them would connect him to Cindy in the moment when she wrote them. But he felt nothing. As always, she wasn't there.

He flipped through more books and turned on Cindy's cell phone so that he could check her call log, but nothing stood out. There were no mysterious numbers or names. He scanned through some of her old emails and while this did make him feel like the worst, most untrustworthy father in the world, he found nothing that he would consider a clue. Though he did see one or two items that he would have gotten upset about if he had read those emails before his daughter's death, they now seemed so innocent and normal.

With a sense of hopelessness rushing over him, Mark stopped looking through Cindy's belongings and put them back where he had found them. It might have seemed strange to anyone else, but he felt like she would be mad at him if he didn't put them back exactly where they were when he first came into the room.

He gave Cindy's room one last look, wishing that he would spot something that he hadn't seen before. A flashing sign that gave him the exact location where she could be found and communicated with would have been great, but he would have settled for even the slightest hint of a clue. Instead, he found nothing. Everything was as it had always been. There were no new messages. No new significance to be taken from anything that she owned. Everything was just exactly as it had always been.

Mark could feel himself growing more and more annoyed. He had those clues from Warren and they seemed like they should be important and meaningful, but he was too blind to see how. He could feel that something had changed in the air and he was so close to seeing what was out there, yet it was just beyond his ability to understand.

He walked out of the room, turning off the light and closing the door behind him. He did not want to be angry, but he was. He was angry at everyone and everything and he could feel that anger getting ready to explode.

As Mark walked down the hallway, toward the stairs, he felt a cool breeze touch his cheek. It washed over him, stopping him in his path. He closed his eyes, isolating that feeling and examining every aspect of it. Hoping.

For years, he had read reports of ghostly encounters. Those who claimed to be touched by a ghost often described that touch as a cool breeze, but somehow more potent. It didn't run *over* them, it ran *through* them.

Mark opened his eyes. Hope quickly washed away and was replaced by reality. Just as he had encountered numerous times before, this cool breeze did not fit the ghostly description. It was just a breeze.

He turned toward Winnie's room and saw that the door was slightly open. Through it, he could see her window, also open.

"Son of a bitch," he muttered to himself as he started to walk toward the room. "It's the middle of October and she leaves her window open."

He walked through Winnie's room and shut the window without a second thought.

As he left the room, Mark clenched his jaw tightly, trying his best to contain his frustration. There were times when Winnie could be so thoughtless that he couldn't understand her at all. He tried to make allowances for her grief, but there was only so much that he was willing to tolerate.

And where was Marion? Where was she when their daughter was leaving windows open? Why didn't she ever put her foot down and tell their girl that enough was enough?

The night was wearing on him. He knew that if he saw either

his wife or daughter in that particular moment, he would have snapped. It was a good thing that they weren't there, because he would feel horrible about it later, but there was something inside of him that was screaming. He felt an almost physical pain that had been gnawing away in his stomach for a year, but on this night it was becoming far more distinct.

His daughter needed him. He knew it and he could feel it, but he could do nothing about it except ball his fists and grit his teeth.

He felt the drawings in his hand as his fists tightened. Mark had forgotten that he was still holding them, and as he reached the bottom of the stairs he looked through them one more time.

"What does it mean?" he asked himself.

He flipped through each picture, studying them for some hidden meaning. He considered the possibility that they might contain some code that he hadn't noticed before, but the pictures were not detailed enough for something like that. If there was something to be seen, he would have seen it by then.

His hands began to tense up and cramp. He found himself throwing the pictures to the ground without even realizing it.

Mark couldn't think straight. Where one thought trailed off, another picked up. Where that one hit a dead end, another thought swirled around it. His head hurt. It wasn't a physical pain exactly, but the conflict of thoughts in his head made it hard for him to focus.

He needed to do something. He needed to get away from that house and that life and clear his mind before he drove himself crazy. Of course, this was assuming that he hadn't gone crazy already.

The next picture that he wanted to explore was the cemetery. It was an easy place to begin, since he knew where it was. The other images were a mystery to him, which he would have to figure out as he went along. The grave—on the other hand—he was familiar with. He had been there many times and had researched the area, with nothing to show for all his effort. He wanted to know why it could suddenly be of importance to his investigation. He also wanted to know why there was a cup next to the grave in the picture that Warren had drawn. What did it mean?

He grabbed the pictures and his jacket and hurried out the door. Normally, he would have left a note for Marion and Winnie, but he figured that he could call them from the road and let them know that he would be home late.

As he closed and locked the front door, Mark felt clear-minded. It was moments like those which he lived for. To some, a stiff drink might have been an adequate escape, but Mark's addiction was the pursuit of answers. As long as he kept moving and had some glimmer of hope, he would be fine. As long as he didn't have to stop and think about what his world had become, he could avoid a complete collapse.

The night was cool and the air was fresh. Simply being outside of his house made Mark feel as though he could breathe once again. The hunt for answers was on, and he was certain that he would find what he was looking for. He could feel it in his bones.

37

There was a cluster of large rocks in the woods, covered with leaves and moss. Beneath them—or between—there could have been any number of animals living, but Winnie climbed to the tallest of these rocks and stood looking at the world around her.

She couldn't see far, but what she could see was that there were no houses nearby. No stores. She could hear no cars. She could see no people. In that spot, there were no e-mails or text messages. There was only her—and possibly a naked stranger, though she hadn't seen him for some time.

In that moment, she could have been anyone and she could have been living in any time. None of it mattered. The world, as far as she could tell, was empty and dark. Somehow, this comforted her more than her own bedroom, in her own house, with her parents nearby.

She stood tall on those rocks, expecting her feet to slip out from under her at any moment, but not caring. It was peaceful. Out there, she could think and feel without anyone trying to figure out which stage of grief she was in. The rage that she often found bubbling inside of her was lessened. In those woods, she resented nothing. The trees had lived long before she or Cindy, and they would quite possibly be there long after she was gone.

Winnie closed her eyes and allowed the air to wash over her. As her hands hung by her sides, she turned them outward so that she could feel the coolness on her palms.

In the distance, she could hear the leaves being blown by a breeze that hadn't yet reached her. As this breeze moved closer and closer, Winnie waited for it to rush over her face. It seemed to take its time getting to her. With her eyes closed, her mind created an image of this breeze. The image looked like a serpent made of mist. It slithered through the treetops, moving back and forth rather than straight toward her. It drew nearer.

Winnie heard the trees above her shaking—in her mind, hissing—as the breeze reached them. A moment later, it enveloped her, blowing her hair away from her face. She breathed deeply, filling her lungs with the essence of that time of year which she loved most.

Winter would be there far too soon for her taste. She lived for this in-between place, where the world around her seemed to be stretching and bending, unwilling to commit to either hot or cold. She loved it. To her, nothing seemed more alive or more real than it did in the middle of a cold fall.

As the breeze passed and continued to slither through the trees behind her, Winnie opened her eyes and remained still. She was in no hurry to get anywhere of importance. She'd lost the trail of the mysterious stranger and was now free to do or be whatever she wanted, wherever she wanted.

The moonlight was playing tricks with the shadows of the trees. On the ground, they moved back and forth, seeming to wrap themselves around each other and pull themselves apart. From the corners of her eyes, it looked as though they were running in every direction, circling her.

She turned to study the movement and assured herself that there was nothing to run from. There were no such things as ghosts.

As that thought came to Winnie, she couldn't help but chuckle. She was not one to obsess over the supernatural, but it was becoming increasingly difficult for her to ignore. Considering the fact that she had been lured into the woods by a genuine zombie, she would have to reconsider her parents' quest for answers. They might be insane and obsessed, but at the very least they might have a point.

Zombie.

The word made its way through her mind once again, but did not sit right with her. She had seen his wounds and the emptiness in his eyes, but she was beginning to doubt her memory and the conclusions that she'd come to. Surely, this could not have been a dead man walking. Her parents and their wacky notions had gotten to her and clouded her judgment.

More likely, this man was an escaped hospital patient. Perhaps he was on medication that gave him the empty, highly reflective eyes, and he'd torn the hospital gown off because he didn't want to be seen roaming through town in a dress.

Maybe he was a victim. The drug theory still held up in this scenario, and his wounds could have come from his captors who had done things to him that Winnie didn't even want to think about.

Logic and reason were washing over the conclusions that she had drawn upon seeing that mysterious stranger up close. Her brain was beginning to rewrite the memories that she had of him.

With this new reasoning, she began to feel a sense of guilt over letting him wander off. Surely, he needed help. He hadn't attacked her. If anything, he had saved her from a coyote. Ripping the heart from that coyote and eating it right in front of her could have—in theory—been a sign that he was malnourished or... something.

She scanned the woods once again. This time, she was not paying attention to the shadows or the wind. She was only looking for the stranger.

It didn't take long for her to spot him in the distance. He seemed to glow as the moonlight hit his pale skin. He stood out amongst the shadows and the trees, and he was facing her; staring at her from a distance.

He didn't move. He did not react to Winnie seeing him, but she could tell that he saw her too. For all she knew, he had been waiting for her to find him. He could have been staring at her for as long as she had been on the rocks. It should have given her the creeps, but it didn't.

The two of them remained still and looked at each other, as though each of them was waiting for the other to make the first move. She half expected to see him rush toward her. She pictured herself running through the woods and being tackled by him. She pictured the struggle; her grasping at dead leaves on the ground as she tried to find a weapon to fight him off. She imagined herself screaming as he plunged his fist through her chest and ripped out her still-beating heart, and wondered if the last thing she ever saw would be him taking a bite of that heart.

Yet, she didn't move. She stayed calm and allowed those images to pass.

The stranger was the first to move. As he shifted his weight, Winnie could feel herself preparing to run in the opposite direction. But he didn't move toward her. Instead, he turned and began to walk away, deeper into the woods. Out of view and possibly out of her life.

She was running before she could understand what was happening. Her keen instinct for survival had turned into a stupid need for answers.

Winnie pushed branches out of her way as she hurried through the woods, jumping over rocks and fallen trees. She felt her lungs beginning to burn, but she could not take her eyes off of the spot where she had last seen the stranger, out of fear of losing his trail.

When she reached that spot where he had been standing, she stopped. Placing her hands on her knees and catching her breath, Winnie looked through the woods for some sign of him, but she could not find one. Just as he had before, the stranger seemed to vanish into thin air.

She began to walk, keeping her eyes on the ground at first, looking for any clues as to where he might have gone. His trail ended not far from where she had last seen him. Though teleportation was not one of the powers of a zombie, according to every legend she had ever heard, she was beginning to suspect that he could appear and disappear at will. With that thought being taken into careful consideration, Winnie also had to take into account the fact that she was not a hunter. It was far more likely that she just sucked at tracking things.

Another breeze blew past her. As it grew in intensity, leaves from high above her began to rain down, catching both the light and the shadows as they fell. Winnie couldn't help but marvel at the beauty of this moment as the world seemed to slow down around her and for just a second she was filled with a sense of calm. As she watched this, Winnie once again caught sight of her mysterious stranger. While still at a distance, he was closer than he had been before.

Between them, the leaves continued to fall. The dance of light and shadow.

She did not run toward him, though she wanted to. Instead, she put one hand up, telling him to hold still.

"Wait. Please," she said, in a voice far too low for him to hear. She increased her volume as she continued. "I'm not going to hurt you. I can help."

He must have heard her, but he didn't respond. He did not so much as move a muscle in reaction to her words. He simply stared.

"Who are you?" she asked, holding back the question of whether he was living or dead, because she thought that it might be in poor taste to ask someone that question, having just met them.

He didn't respond to her question.

Winnie took a step forward, once again assuring him, "I want to help you."

She took another step; slowly and carefully. She felt that any move she made could have sent him running off, so she walked as though she were on eggshells.

"It's okay," she assured him. "I'm a friend."

There was no telling whether or not he heard her. He did not respond to her voice or to her movement. While he was looking directly at Winnie, she felt as though he didn't quite see her there.

She felt as if she were making progress, though she had no clue what she planned to do when she actually caught up with the stranger. In that moment, her only goal was to get closer to him. After that was accomplished she would figure out her next move.

She took another step toward him.

He turned his head and looked into the woods to his right. Winnie couldn't tell if he was reacting to a noise that she hadn't heard or if he had merely sensed something in that direction, but she stopped moving.

"Calm," she said in a soothing voice. "It's okay."

The stranger took a step toward whatever it was that he was looking at, and Winnie knew that she was about to lose him.

He ran. In a blur he was gone and Winnie reacted out of nothing more than instinct as she chased after him.

She ran through the woods at full speed, ignoring the growing ache in her ankle as it twisted and shifted on the uneven ground. She refused to allow herself to be slowed down by something as stupid as an injury. Pain meant nothing to her.

38

Tami couldn't believe how much of a mess could be made by a group of teenagers in such a short amount of time. She could only imagine what the place would have looked like if she had allowed things to go on longer.

It must have been late, but Tami didn't check her watch or her cell phone to find out the exact time. She didn't want to know how much sleep she was missing any more than she wanted to stand back and take another scan of the mess. It didn't matter how much was left, as long as there was still work to do.

The breeze was growing colder as she went along. The night progressed, and darkness seemed to envelop everything. Tami loved a good, sunny day. She loved feeling the sun on her face. She loved wearing sunglasses. Even during the winter, she seemed more tolerant of the cold when the sun was out.

As she stood in the cemetery with the bag of garbage in hand, everything around her was bathed in blue and black. The world was quiet. It was hollow.

From the corner of her eye, she saw something move. It wasn't the first time that it had happened, but it never failed to catch her attention. Each time she saw this thing, she picked up her head and scanned the area, hoping to figure out what it was that she was seeing. Time and again, she found nothing.

The shadows were playing games with her imagination. Each time a breeze blew through a tree, the shadows moved and they appeared—from the corner of her eye—the same as any person would have. She tried her best to ignore those shadows, but instinct demanded that when she saw something move, she must stop to see what it was.

So far, all she found was her time being wasted by an overactive imagination.

She turned back to her work as another breeze blew by. Her hair was swept across her face and over her eyes. The coldness of that breeze cut through her clothes, chilling her to the bone.

Still holding onto the garbage bag, Tami put one hand under her arm and pulled the glove off of it. She brushed the hair out of her face and tucked it behind her ear, knowing that it would only fall loose once again.

"I should have tied my hair back," she said, still unable to tell whether she was talking to Cindy or to herself. She didn't know if it mattered. Either way, she was probably insane.

She put her glove back on and grabbed a plastic cup off of the ground. As she stuffed this cup into her bag, she could have sworn that she saw that thing out of the corner of her eye. It was dark, and low; like a dog, perhaps. She didn't hear this thing, but she could have sworn that she saw it.

Of course, when she looked to see what had run past her, she found nothing. Again, the night was playing tricks with her eyes.

Another breeze blew past her and her hair fell over her eyes. She wanted to cry. More than that, she wanted that night to be over with. She wanted to go home to the safety and comfort of her own bedroom.

Pressing on, she once again began to hum *This Old Man* as she picked up plastic cups, beer bottles and other assorted and disgusting pieces of garbage. There had to be better songs for her to keep herself occupied with. Something fun and peppy would have helped to keep her energy up, but somehow the songs that managed to get stuck in her head never seemed to be the songs that she would like to have on a constant loop. On this night, her mental playlist was comprised of a single children's song.

She could hear another breeze making its way across the cemetery. She could hear the rustling of the leaves and the garbage blowing across the ground. She knew that it was only a matter of seconds before her hair was going to be blown over her eyes again, but she kept working. The sooner she got the job done, the sooner she would be back in her car, pulling her hair back and turning on the heat.

As she worked, she anticipated the chill of the breeze that would undoubtedly work its way through her clothing and to her skin. She prepared herself for the chill, hoping that it wouldn't come as such a shock to her system if she told her arms and legs to ready themselves.

She was ready for it. She was whining about it before it even reached her. She was fully prepared for the cycle of breezes to continue. Yet, it didn't. She could hear the breeze, but Tami didn't feel it. Though she waited, the chill never came.

She looked around the area. Not one leaf seemed to be blowing. Not one cup was moving. Still, the sound of that breeze continued.

"What the hell?" she said under her breath.

The lack of movement did not frighten her; it puzzled her. She knew that there had to be some sort of explanation, so she didn't immediately panic. Instead, she marveled. Until she figured out the cause of sound without associated movement, there was a strange sense of wonder and mystery to that moment.

Her mind began working on the puzzle. There must have been a breeze somewhere—Perhaps in another area of the cemetery. Maybe a dust devil. She wasn't sure how they were formed because she slept through that class, but it made sense that there could be some sort of wind burst in one spot and not another.

From the corner of her eye, she saw that movement again. Fast and low, like an animal racing across the cemetery. She turned, but saw nothing.

"Hello?" she called out, though she didn't really expect an answer.

If this was some sort of prank that was being played on her by classmates out for revenge, she would be impressed by their sudden knack for subtlety, the time that they were putting into it and their ability to remain quiet.

No, this wasn't anyone she knew. This was something else.

She saw the shadow thing move from the corner of her eye, this time on the other side. She turned, but nothing was there.

A predatory animal might hide from her until it was ready to pounce, but surely it would have seized its opportunity by then.

"Hello?" she called once again, this time hoping that she would get a response and hear the hearty laughter of teenagers who had succeeded in making a fool of her.

Her hair moved across her eyes, and she quickly brushed it out of the way, tucking it behind her ear. She did not want to miss a chance to identify whatever it was that she was seeing, especially if she had to make a run for it.

It took her a few seconds to realize that there hadn't been a breeze when her hair moved over her eyes. No sound of a breeze. No coolness. The air around her was—for the moment—still.

She dropped the garbage bag and pulled off her gloves, taking a step backward and feeling a surge of adrenaline as she realized that something was near her. Something so close that it had gently moved her own hair over her eyes.

"Who's there?" she asked with a voice now shaking and uncertain.

Oh, how she would have loved to believe that she was imagining things. She was tired and standing in the middle of a dark cemetery by herself. Surely, there was enough material here for her mind to go wild, but this was not her imagination. Her imagination could not create distinct sounds or move things.

Deciding that she would allow the groundskeeper to finish the job of cleaning the cemetery, Tami took a step toward the gates which would lead her back to her car. As she took this one small step, there was a shift in the ground before her. She stopped and waited to see if it happened again.

As she tried to wrap her mind around a situation that was making no sense to her, she realized that the ground had not moved at all. It was a layer of shadows on the ground which had recoiled in response to her movement.

It was hard to see this layer. It was the sort of shadow that would come with moonlight shining through thin clouds, just barely casting a shadow on the ground. Yet, there were not many clouds in the sky, and none that covered the moon.

Tami knew that she had to be seeing things. She was allowing her own mind to play tricks on her and there were no shadows or sounds that could not be explained with enough time and thought. She knew that there had to be a logical and reasonable explanation, even if she didn't immediately know what that explanation was.

She tried to think about how long it had taken the police to show up after her call to them, earlier in the night—how long it would take them to come back.

The cemetery was normally such a calm and soothing place for her to be. It was quiet and peaceful. Now, all of those things which she normally loved about the place seemed to highlight the fact that she was very much alone. If she did find herself in danger of some sort, there would be nobody there to help her.

She took another uneasy step toward her car and once again, the ground seemed to shift in front of her. She froze, trying to hold as still as possible, half expecting the ground to lunge toward her if she dared to make the wrong move.

Tami felt the sting of tears forming in her eyes and heard the shakiness of her own shallow breathing. She would have liked to believe that in a scary situation, she would take charge and kick ass, but sadly this was not the case. She was scared; *really* scared. This type of thing was not supposed to happen in the real world. It wasn't supposed to happen to *her*.

As she closed her eyes, the tears that had been forming rolled down her cheeks. She didn't wipe them away, for fear of making any move at all. She stood there with her eyes closed, vulnerable to attack, but she needed to gather her thoughts and she could not do that if she was staring at the shadows on the ground.

"Oh, God..." she said to herself. "Jesus, help me. Please. Get me out of here. Please, God."

The sound of the phantom breeze had died down. Now, there

was silence.

Tami could have sworn that she felt the wind blowing her jacket, but she felt none of the actual wind itself. She felt none of its coolness. The air was still—dead. The penetrating silence was more frightening to her than anything else that she could have imagined. A growl or a moan would have scared her less, because at least then she would have had something real to respond to.

She opened her eyes.

Run! she told herself, sternly but silently. *Damnit,* **RUN!**

Her brain was giving her body an order that it didn't respond to right away. She didn't know why, but she couldn't bring herself to move for what seemed like an eternity. At long last, her legs kicked into gear. She turned herself around and ran away from the front gate where she was parked; away from the shifting shadows, and away from where anything that was watching her would expect her to run.

There was another gate on the far end of the cemetery, which allowed visitors to easily reach the graves of those who were buried toward the rear of the cemetery. If Tami could make it to that gate, and manage to hop over it, she could cut through a short stretch of woods, across a field beyond those woods, and reach the road that led to her high school.

She had a plan, which made her feel better for only a second or two. As she ran through the cemetery, she caught a glimpse of something in the distance. It was not the same shifting of the ground that she had seen before. This was the darting creature that she had seen from the corner of her eye, only this time it had crossed directly in front of her. There was no denying it. There was no escaping it.

39

Marion pulled her car down the driveway slowly and carefully. It was covered in weeds and rocks, with sudden dips that her car could undoubtedly withstand, but which made her uneasy.

As she made her way, the road behind her faded from view. The world now seemed to consist of nothing more than woods and an incredibly old, rundown house.

She never would have driven down this driveway on any normal night. If given the choice, she would have turned around and carefully made her way back to the road and to a more familiar part of town. Her fear was entirely irrational, she knew. Her response to the house was born from years of horror stories and urban legends, telling her that small houses in the woods were the home of inbred cannibals, violent fundamentalists and evil witches. She knew better than to put her faith in such ignorant stereotypes.

Still, the knot in her stomach grew tighter with each passing inch of driveway.

As she approached the house, she could see a car parked in front of it. The trunk of this car was wide open, which struck Marion as odd. More than that, as she parked her car in front of the house, she noticed that its front door was open as well.

Maybe whoever lived there had just gone grocery shopping. Maybe they were packing their car for a trip. There could have been a hundred perfectly rational explanations for why the trunk and front door would be left open, but something about that place felt wrong to her.

She sat, staring at the home for a moment or two, wondering how wise it would be for her to approach it. Everything about that place was telling her to turn and leave, but she couldn't bring herself to listen. Winnie was missing in this area. If she was in this house, then no horrors of the imagination would keep Marion from investigating.

She couldn't seem to convince herself to take off her seat belt and open the door, but she could hardly investigate the situation from the safety of her locked car.

Marion closed her eyes and pictured Winnie. In that moment any hesitation was gone. She unbuckled the seat belt and stepped out of the car.

As her foot touched the ground, Marion could hear a *squishing* sound. The ground was soft and muddy, though it hadn't rained for days. Normally, she would have done anything to avoid caking her shoes in the thick mud, but on this night she couldn't afford such concerns.

She closed her car door and pressed the button on her keychain to activate the alarm. It was more of a habit than a conscious action. Since the woods around her were silent, the sudden techno-chirp of the car alarm startled Marion. She flinched as she heard that noise, before realizing where it had come from. After that, she couldn't help but smile at her own skittishness.

"Very calm, Mare," she muttered to herself.

Once she had gathered herself, Marion began to walk toward the small, rundown house. As she approached it, she studied the structure of the building, taking in the historical nature of the house. It was old—though obviously renovated—and could have been beautiful, had it not been allowed to deteriorate. Now, the overgrown foliage and weather-worn wood made the home uninviting. What could have been a quaint, welcoming, rustic old house now provoked the imagination far too much to be anything less than creepy.

The part of Marion which sought to fix everyone and everything around her began to make a list of all the things that she could do to that home, to restore it to its former glory.

As she rounded the car that was parked in front of the house,

Marion peered into the trunk, half expecting to find Winnie, bound and gagged, struggling to get free. Of course, Winnie wasn't there. Such things rarely happened in the real world.

On the ground beneath the trunk, she spotted what looked like the markings of something being dragged through the mud and into the house. Of course, there were a number of explanations for this. People dragged things out of their trunk all the time. Yet, Marion's mind naturally thought the worst.

She shook off the images that came to mind and said to herself, "Calm down. This isn't a horror movie."

Marion slowly approached the door, ready to turn and run at any moment in spite of her determination to remain calm and collected. As she neared it, she heard something inside. It was faint at first, but grew more defined as she grew closer. As she stepped onto the front stoop of the house, she listened to the rhythmic *shh-shh-shh* sound which repeated itself over and over again.

"Hello?" she called through the door.

The noise stopped. Now, she heard nothing.

Inside the home, she could see dust and cobwebs. She could see clutter, but nothing so extreme that it would set off any alarms. The furniture was old and worn. The floors were in need of refinishing.

She stopped herself from being too nosey and called once again, "Hello?"

This time, she heard another noise. It was the sound of

something being dropped to the floor, followed by footsteps. The steps were loud and fast, but Marion saw nobody within the home. She waited for someone to appear at the door, but nobody came.

"I'm looking for my daughter," Marion explained. "I was wondering if you've seen her tonight."

More hurried footsteps, followed by a *thump*. Marion would have walked away, except the thump sounded like that of something soft but heavy hitting the floor—a person, perhaps.

"Are you okay in there?" Marion called into the house.

She turned and looked to see if the road was visible from where she was standing, and if any cars were passing. If she could see some piece of the outside world, Marion thought that she would feel more confident in her position there. Unfortunately, all she saw was darkness.

She knocked on the front door and she took a step forward, into the home. Her heart began to pound in her chest and she found herself moving more slowly and carefully than she would on any normal night.

"My name is Marion," she said as she entered the house. "Are you okay? Do you need help?"

Marion didn't want to walk any deeper into the home. She wanted to check the house off of her list of places to look for Winnie, hurry back to her car, and go home. In a perfect world, she would have found Winnie sitting in the kitchen, eating warm chocolate chip cookies and complaining about her broken cell phone.

But she knew all too well that this was not a perfect world. Bad things happen when you neither expect them nor prefer them. Someone in that house could have needed help and she could never live with herself if she turned her back on that possibility.

She moved in a little bit farther, calling, "Are you in here? Are you okay?"

After she was several feet into the home, she stopped pretending as though she was simply leaning in for a quick peek and she straightened up. She did not close the door behind her as she moved into the house. It made her feel somewhat safer to keep it open.

From where she was, Marion could see the main living area of the home, the dining area and the kitchen. The walls had plaster peeling off of them. The ceiling had water stains. The windows were dirty. There was no pretending that the house was beautiful to look at, but the potential for beauty was there.

She saw nobody. Though she would have preferred to spot whoever was in the house while remaining near the front door, she had no such luck.

"It's wrong..." came a whisper, just loud enough to give Marion the creeps. She could not tell where it came from, or even whether the whisper was from a man or a woman.

"Hello?" she called again, this time hearing the shakiness of her own voice.

There was no response.

As she walked deeper into the house, Marion looked down to the floor, where she saw the drag marks from outside, continued in mud across the hardwood. She followed these marks slowly, gripping her keys tightly and preparing herself to use them as a weapon, should the need arise.

"It's wrong..." came the whisper again, trailing off toward the end. This person was not talking to Marion, but to themself. It was not a statement, but a fragment of a thought that would be continued in this person's own head.

"My name is Marion," Marion repeated.

She heard something slam against the floor, and this time she knew which direction the noise was coming from. She looked toward the dining area, where she saw a large rectangular table. She saw no person at first, but continued to walk.

As she got closer to the table, she saw something on the floor next to it. Initially, she thought that it might have been a cloth bag or a stack of crumpled laundry, but Marion soon realized that she was looking at a person, curled up on the floor beside the table. It appeared to be a female, though Marion couldn't be certain right away.

The woman slammed their hand on the floor once again and cried, "No. No. No. No."

The woman's clothes were ragged and her hair unkempt. She was barefoot, but Marion could make out little else about this woman, as the woman kept her back turned. It was hard to tell whether or not she was aware of Marion's presence at all.

"Are you okay?" Marion asked, in a soft and soothing tone—her therapist voice.

"It's wrong," the woman muttered again. She picked up a brush and began to scrub the floor with it.

Marion wasn't sure what was wrong with the woman. She could have been sick, or she might have simply been ignoring Marion. It was the tone of her voice that caught Marion's attention the most. She wasn't merely upset, she seemed somehow *damaged*.

Marion looked to the drag marks on the floor once again and wondered if perhaps the woman herself had been locked in the trunk. It would make sense for the woman to be disoriented if she had freed herself or had been pulled into the house by an attacker.

Looking back toward the front door, Marion half expected to see a madman with an ax, waiting to take her hostage as well. She saw nobody, but that did not ease her mind at all. Whatever was going on, Marion needed to help this woman.

She no longer hesitated. Marion needed to act quickly. She hurried to the woman who was scrubbing the wood floor and bent down closer to her.

"It's okay. I'm here to help you," Marion said, in a low but confident tone.

In the back of her mind, there was random series of thoughts. That part of Marion that was drawn to the paranormal began to consider whether or not Winnie's GPS signal had been real at all. Perhaps some force beyond her ability to understand had brought

Marion to that stretch of road and to that woman for a reason. Stranger things had happened—reportedly.

Gently, so as to not startle the already broken woman too much, Marion placed a hand on the woman's shoulder and said, "It's okay now. Whatever happened, it's over."

In a blur of movement, the woman dropped her brush and grabbed Marion's wrist, squeezing it tightly. Marion winced in pain as the woman slowly turned her head and looked her in the eyes.

Marion couldn't help but gasp when she saw the woman's face. It wasn't her physical appearance which startled Marion; the woman might have been beautiful under the proper circumstances. Instead, what caught Marion off guard was the look in her eyes. It was not merely cold and hateful, but possessed an emptiness unlike anything Marion had ever witnessed before. It was as though there was a void where the normal spark of human life was meant to be and all that remained was an echo.

"Oh, it's not over," the woman said to Marion. "It's far from over."

40

Winnie ran. She ran faster than she had ever run before, just to keep the mysterious stranger in sight. He always managed to stay ahead of her, yet he never seemed to hurry. She lost track of him from time to time, but always spotted him in the distance. Whenever she thought that she might finally catch up to him, he would step behind a tree or a rock and he she would lose track of him once again.

Her problem was that it was dark and the shadows in the woods hid things from her. If calling out to him would have helped, Winnie would have worn her voice out. But she knew better.

As she ran, Winnie wondered where the stranger could be

going. He seemed to walk with purpose and determination—as much as one possibly could while remaining dead. Each time he stopped, it seemed like he was waiting for her to catch up, the way Cindy used to wait for her when they were young children, running home from school. Somewhere along the way, she had begun to think that he wanted her to follow. But why?

She wasn't focusing. She wasn't paying attention to where she was going, because she had stopped caring about finding her way home before this foot chase had begun. As she ran, she kept her eyes on the stranger whenever possible, but her mind was not as sharp as it should have been. This is why Winnie nearly ran off a cliff.

She tried to stop herself short, but the momentum was pushing her body forward in spite of her planted feet. She was too close to the edge and the slightest stumble could send her over.

She bent her legs and allowed her feet to slide out from under her as she fell backward and hit the ground. She felt her feet slipping over the edge and she twisted in an effort to grab onto whatever she could find that would keep her from falling over.

The ground was dry and loose. It slipped out from under her as she fell, making it that much harder for her to stop, but she fought the momentum and won.

She was gasping for air. She couldn't tell if her racing heart was the result of her running through the woods or the adrenaline of nearly running off of a cliff, but her hands were shaking. Her legs felt numb and weak. Her mind was racing with *what-ifs*, taking her down many roads which led to many fates—all of which were bloody and painful.

"Whoa," she said to herself, allowing her head to fall back onto the ground and ignoring the small rock that was digging into her thigh.

In that moment, Winnie didn't care about the mysterious stranger. He was gone from her mind as her brain attempted to catch up to her body and process what had just happened. Her legs dangling off the side of the cliff prevented Winnie from feeling entirely safe, but she needed to stop and think before she tried to get up. She needed to regain her focus, or risk making a deadly mistake.

As the panic began to subside, Winnie found herself laughing at the situation. After the fact, nearly dying was a rush. It did not make her feel more alive, as many adrenaline junkies claim when they hurl themselves out of airplanes. Instead, nearly dying made Winnie feel closer to death. While her heart was returning to its normal speed, she felt closer to Cindy than she had in a long time.

After nearly falling off a cliff, she knew what Cindy must have felt in those final moments. She knew the instinctual reaction, rather than the conscious reaction, that must have kicked in and how the world became a blur. She had spent a year wondering what must have gone through Cindy's mind as she died, and now she had a pretty good idea: Nothing.

The difference between her and her sister was that nothing carried her through to the great beyond. Winnie had her taste of that blur before death and she had been so close to seeing what came next, but now she was back on solid ground. Life went on. She had been pulled away from that border, just before she got her chance to see beyond it.

Laughter gave way to tears. Winnie didn't know what she thought or felt exactly, she just knew that she was so close to something; so close to making sense of a world that had become gibberish to her since her sister died.

Everything felt wrong. No matter what she did, she felt wrong. She felt guilty for living, but scared of dying. She felt angry at others for moving on, but jealous of their ability to do it. She loved her sister and wanted her back, but hated Cindy for ruining her life.

Everything was wrong. Everything was messy and frustrating. She just wanted it to be over. She wanted to find a way out of that mess, either by moving on or passing on. She just wanted something to make sense.

She wiped the tears from her eyes and pulled herself away from the cliff. As she sat up and prepared to get to her feet, Winnie felt a hand on her shoulder.

Startled, Winnie gasped and turned to see who was touching her. In that split second, she wondered if her mother or father could have tracked her down in the woods, or if Tami had followed her.

Instead of finding any of those people, Winnie found herself looking at the stranger. He was squatting next to her, hand on her shoulder, and staring at her. Part of her wanted to scream and pull away from him, but she didn't. She didn't move. She didn't even breathe at first.

She couldn't read his expression. It was blank, but there was something else to it. Not concern, exactly. It seemed more like he was waiting for her to get up before he could resume his own journey through the woods.

He took his hand off of her shoulder and held it out as he stood, offering to help her up. She couldn't believe it. After all of that chasing and running and uncertainty, there he was. All of him. And while she was sure that at some point, she would be able to look up and meet his gaze, for the moment she just hoped that it at least *looked* like she was staring at his hand.

She was frozen; stuck staring at him inappropriately and unable to pull her eyes away no matter how hard she tried. Winnie had pictured this moment many times in her life, yet somehow she always imagined that it would involve a vampire, not a zombie.

Finally, she blinked and turned her head away.

Her breath returned to her as she debated whether or not it would be a good idea for her to take his hand. Surely, the kids at school would make fun of her when the news reported on her having been eaten alive by a zombie after she willingly let it grab her. Yet, she didn't want to pull away.

She felt as though she was standing at a threshold. If she stopped herself from looking across that threshold, would she be able to live with herself? If she allowed this opportunity to pass without fully exploring it, would she always wonder?

Winnie took the stranger's hand. As she got to her feet, the stranger looked down at her hand. He raised it and stared at it, as though studying if for some great and important reason.

He looked into her eyes. Still, she could not even begin to understand what he was thinking or doing. Part of her was waiting for him to rip into her chest and pull out her heart.

Obviously, she was not getting over that coyote incident anytime soon.

He looked down to her hand once again and raised it higher. He lowered his head and moved her hand toward his mouth. She expected him to sink his teeth into her and rip out a chunk that he could snack on.

Instead, the stranger turned her hand over, exposing her palm and he gently kissed it.

For just a moment, Winnie felt that this mysterious stranger was displaying a tender side. Regardless of the fact that he was naked and unashamed, he came across as somewhat old fashioned when he kissed her on the hand like that.

And then reality struck. He was cold with death. His eyes were inhuman. She had seen him eat a heart. He had been autopsied. Nothing about him seemed natural. In that moment, his kissing her became far more creepy than any attempt at killing her could have been.

She pulled her hand back and the stranger raised his eyes to her. He stared at her, without a hint of anger, confusion or sadness. She wondered if he felt some emotional response to her pulling back, or if he was even capable of feeling anything at all.

The stranger turned and began to walk, resuming his path toward wherever it was that he was going. He made no attempt to grab her or force her to go with him. He was not acting like a monster.

Winnie stood for a moment, conflicted. Logic and curiosity were at odds. She wondered what she should do, but knew the answer to that question very well. The true question that needed to be answered was whether or not she would follow him in spite of what she should do.

She began to walk. At first, she stayed behind him. She kept a distance, trying to convince herself that he was nothing more than a curiosity to her. Yet, as she went along, Winnie found herself picking up just enough speed to walk beside the mysterious stranger.

For his part, the stranger did not vanish into the shadows. He did not race off when she wasn't looking. He allowed Winnie to walk beside him as he led the way toward wherever it was that they were going.

41

Tami paused as she reached a section of the cemetery which was more open and clear. Up ahead, she could see the rear gate and knew that if she could just make it out of the cemetery, there would be nothing to stand in the way of her getting someplace safe and public.

Of course, there would be a long way to go before she was *completely* safe. There were woods to run through, and a field. If she was caught before she found other people, she would be utterly alone. No road that someone might travel. Nobody to hear her scream.

As she stood there, staring at the gate, she wondered if she was making the wrong decision. Of all the times to second guess herself, this was perhaps the worst, but she couldn't afford to be wrong. She couldn't simply react to what was happening. She had to think rationally.

Tami turned around and looked across the cemetery for the shadows which had been stalking her. She was far from where the party had been held now; far from the trash and from her car.

There did not seem to be a good place to turn or a proper direction to run. She didn't know how to plan for something which should not be happening in the first place. She was being chased by nothing more than shadows—it was insane.

As she looked across the cemetery, she tried to see if those shadows were still on her trail, but this was an impossible task to accomplish. The night was full of shadows. The moon was shining bright in the sky, making every tree and every headstone into a shelter for her attacker. Every blade of grass had a shadow; every cloud in the sky. There was no escaping.

She didn't cry. This was a point of great pride for Tami. She could have easily broken down and given up. She could have collapsed onto the ground and allowed whatever this thing was to wash over her, but she didn't.

None of the shadows in front of her seemed to move in any way that struck Tami as unnatural or wrong. This did not mean that she was safe, but it meant that she could at least think things through.

Of course, thinking through her situation in that moment led her to believe that she was being completely irrational. She was literally scared of her own shadow.

The more she thought about it, the crazier she felt. Surely, she had been imagining things. Shadows moved because the trees moved. Hair fell over her eyes all the time.

She tried her best to stop believing in what was happening to her. She told herself over and over again that she was losing her mind, but she could not shake the feeling that something was wrong. The air itself seemed wrong to her. She could feel something about that night that wasn't as it should have been and while she could not explain this feeling in any sensible fashion, she could not convince herself that she was wrong about those shadows.

Tami reached into her pocket and wrapped her hand around her cell phone. She needed to call someone—anyone. She needed to hear another human voice, if only to know that she had not fallen into some alternate universe where she was doomed to suffer alone.

As she pulled her cell phone from her pocket and began to move her eyes down to it, she saw the shadows on the ground shift in front of her. The shadows between the blades of grass appeared to move, though the grass itself remained untouched and unchanged.

Tami froze and stared at the ground, waiting. But there was no further movement. She wondered if what she saw could have been the blur of motion that she usually overlooked as her eyes moved from one spot to another, but that did not ease her concerns.

Slowly, she raised the phone, just enough to unlock its screen and prepare to dial. As she did this, she saw something move from the corner of her eye. She turned to see what this thing was, but as usual, she saw nothing. No charging animal. No ghostly figure, coming to drag her into the underworld.

She found herself wishing that she did see some horrible creature. Part of her wanted to be attacked by something real and tangible, if it meant that the shadow puppets would go away.

Tami looked down to her phone and pressed the button which brought her list of contacts to the screen. Once she did this, she looked up and scanned the area for shadows. She saw nothing in front of her, but the sudden realization that she had completely neglected the world behind her struck her hard. She could practically feel the eyes of some unseen thing watching her. She imagined shadowy hands creeping up her back.

She spun around and looked for any of these shadows, but she saw nothing—of course she saw nothing.

Tami turned back to her phone and looked at the list of names, wondering who to call. Her parents? A friend? How could she explain to any of them what she was experiencing? Her parents were more likely to yell at her for being at a party in the cemetery than they were to entertain the idea that she was being stalked by shadows.

She found herself scrolling down to Winnie's name. Though Winnie seemed to hate her with every fiber of her being, she was the one person in the world that Tami wanted to call in that moment. Hers was the voice that Tami wanted to hear, because if anyone knew how dark and cruel the world could be, it would be Winnie.

Pressing the button and putting the phone to her ear, Tami began to move. She didn't run, because she was so confused about what to do that she could not think of where to run. She did not head for the rear gate, because the woods scared her. She didn't go toward the front gate, because it seemed obvious, which meant that it would be dangerous.

She turned to her side and she began to walk at a quick pace, waiting for Winnie to answer. She wasn't walking toward anything in particular. She simply wanted to stop feeling like an easy target.

Winnie's phone rang, and Tami held her breath. It rang again, and she could imagine Winnie seeing her name on the caller ID and ignoring it. It rang again, and only then did Tami feel a tear fall down her cheek. She had managed to hold them back for so long, and she hated herself for allowing that tear, but she couldn't help it.

"Pick up," she said into the phone. "Please. Please. Please pick up."

"This is Winnie. Leave a message," came the recorded message on Winnie's voicemail.

Tami sucked air deeply, wanting to give in to the sobs, but holding them at bay.

Beep.

"Winnie, it's me. Please call me back. Please. I'm scared.

There's... Something's after me. Shadows," Tami said. "God, I sound crazy, I know. I know you hate me. I... Please call me. I'm at the cemetery. Tell them to look there."

Tami hung up the phone. It took her a moment to realize that she had just told Winnie where to have people look for her body.

She felt something move across her pant leg. Looking down, she saw nothing, but she *heard* something. It sounded like someone exhaling right next to her ear, though she felt none of the warmth that would come from someone's breath. The air did not move at all.

Tami ran. She still had no idea where she was going or what she planned to do, but she ran because she would not allow this thing—whatever it was—to take her without a fight. If some evil wanted to drag her into Hell, she would not help it along by being weak and pathetic.

As she ran, Tami thought that she saw something from the corner of her eye. Low and fast, it seemed to move across the cemetery, keeping up with her as she ran. She did not bother to look. She knew that she would see nothing, and if she took her eyes off of the uneven land in front of her, she ran the risk of tripping over a small hill, or running into a headstone.

She was closer to the front gate than she was to the rear, though she was not on a direct course for that exit. As she ran, her breathing was heavy. It sounded too loud to her. She worried that the sound would lead her pursuer right to her, but she couldn't help it.

She clung to the cell phone in her hand, unable to dial another number because she could not look to her contacts list. She could only hope that Winnie would get her message and call her back.

Winnie might have been angry with Tami—maybe even hated her—but she would not ignore a message like the one that Tami had left. Tami was counting on Winnie and gripped the phone with all the strength that she could without breaking it. She would not risk dropping that phone. If she did drop it, there would be no stopping to pick it up. She planned to run until she could run no more.

In the distance, a low rumble began to rise. Tami didn't know what it was, but she did not believe that anything could surprise her at that point. If the ground opened up and a dragon flew out, spitting fire in every direction, Tami would quite possibly shrug it off. She might even thank it for lighting up the area and getting rid of the shadows.

The rumbling became more distinct and recognizable as the seconds passed, until Tami finally knew what it was. She knew that someone was coming. A car was driving toward the cemetery. Perhaps the police officer was coming back to make sure that the party did not pick up again. Perhaps some relative of a deceased person had heard about the party and came to clean things up; or maybe it was the caretaker. It didn't matter who it was. All that mattered was that someone was coming and Tami had a chance to save herself.

She looked toward the front gate. It was farther away than she would have liked, but she could see headlights approaching. Not slowing for even a moment, Tami changed her course and ran for her life.

42

Mark could have driven to the cemetery blindfolded. He went there often, though he did not usually sit by his daughter's grave, talking to her about all of the details of his life. Instead, he went there to think of ways that he might communicate with her—*really* communicate.

In the year since Cindy's death, Mark hadn't stopped to mourn like most parents. He didn't believe that her death was the end of their time together. She had simply moved on to some new leg of the journey, cutting in line ahead of Mark and Marion. It wasn't right, and part of him resented her for that, but he did not pretend for a moment that she had ceased to exist.

Mourning for Cindy was something that he was not willing to do. Though, if she had simply moved out of the house, to some far off place where he would not have been able see her for years or decades, he surely would have grieved. But this was different.

It had become something of a routine, slipping into the cemetery after it had been locked up for the night. Mark could hop the fence with ease. He was still young enough to pull off such tricks, though he could feel his knees beginning to weaken more and more with each visit.

As he approached the cemetery, he wasn't thinking about where he was going or how he would be getting in. He was thinking about those pictures that Warren had drawn for him. He was thinking about how he would track down those places that he did not recognize.

Because he wasn't paying attention, Mark nearly plowed right into the back of another car that was parked outside of the cemetery. As his mind snapped out of its preoccupation and reacted to the sight of the car, Mark swerved out of the way and came to a stop just next to it without getting a very good look at the car itself.

As he stepped out of his car, Mark kept his engine running and his headlights on. He wanted to see who was at the cemetery and ask them why. Perhaps that answer was what Warren had intended for him to discover there.

He stood by his car and looked into the cemetery, but saw no sign of anyone else. His headlights did not light up the area as much as he would have liked. He had a narrow field of vision where his lights could reach, but everything outside of those beams seemed darker than they would have without any light at all. The cemetery was a pool of darkness and shadows.

Mark reached into his car and turned off the engine. As he did this, he looked through the passenger side window and took a better look at the car next to him. The crudely drawn images and offensive words caught his attention first. He cringed at the sight of them, before tilting his head and noting that a couple of the images were not at all anatomically accurate. As soon as he took the time to consider the car itself, he recognized it.

"Tami?" he muttered to himself as he grabbed a flashlight and exited his car once again, this time closing the door behind him.

He turned on the flashlight and shined it toward the main gate of the cemetery as he walked. From a distance, he could see the chains dangling and the gate itself swaying slightly in the gentle breeze.

When he reached the gate, he stopped to look more closely at the cut chain. He held it in his hand and studied the cut, realizing that it had been cut with a torch rather than bolt cutters.

He pushed the gate open and walked into the cemetery, shining his flashlight toward Cindy's grave. It only made sense that Tami would have been there, but he didn't see her. What he did see was the mess of cups and bottles that had been scattered around the area.

Somehow, he'd had a hard time imagining Tami breaking in; much less with a torch. He knew that she never would have trashed the place either.

"Tami?" he called into the darkness, though not very loudly. For some reason, a cemetery seemed like an inappropriate place for yelling; like a library or a museum. It seemed like the type of place where one should be respectfully quiet and somber.

A scream broke through the silence. It was the scream of someone in danger, and that meant that *Tami* was in danger. The sound of that scream sent a chill running up his spine and squeezed his heart until he thought it would burst, but he didn't have time for hesitation. Without a second thought, Mark ran toward the scream.

"Tami!" he cried out, but the only response that he got was another scream.

He ran faster.

To his side, Mark thought that he saw something moving. It was low to the ground and moving quickly. He thought for a second or two that it might have been Tami, and that she had fallen, but when he stopped running and shined his light to investigate, he saw nothing.

"Somebody help me! Please!" came the sound of Tami's voice. She was crying.

"Tami!" he called back as his heart seemed to leap into his throat. The sound of that girl screaming for help was unbearable to him. He'd lost one child already and though Tami might not have been his flesh and blood, he had been there for every one of her birthdays and every one of her school plays. Blood or not, she was family to him.

In the distance, he saw movement. It was a dark, shadowy figure, running toward him. While the figure was far beyond the range of his flashlight, Mark could make out the form of Tami.

"Tami!" he called again as they grew closer to each other, though he still couldn't see her face or tell if she was hurt.

When Tami finally entered the beam of his flashlight, he saw terror in her eyes. She grabbed onto his arm and struggled to catch her breath, but she did not look at him. She looked in every direction but his, as though expecting someone to come after them.

"We have to get out of here," she told him.

Mark put his hands on Tami's shoulders in an attempt to get her to settle down and look at him as he asked, "What's happening? Did someone hurt you?"

She shook her head and swallowed hard, saying, "Everyone left. The police got rid of them. I tried to clean up and then..."

As she trailed off, she finally looked Mark in the eyes. It was as though she didn't want to finish what she was saying, but at the same time, she was scared of not telling him.

"Tami, it's okay. Just tell me what you're running from."

"Shadows."

As she let that word slip out of her mouth, Tami looked behind him once again. She smiled, though the panic in her eyes didn't fade. She was smiling at the absurdity of what she'd just said.

Mark couldn't help but look around the area himself as he tried to understand exactly what it was that she was saying.

"At first I just—I saw them out of the corner of my eye, and there was nothing there. Over and over again, the same thing kept happening. The corner of my eye, but nothing was there. But then the shadows started moving. I looked right at them and the shadows were moving. And there was something that... It touched me."

Mark had spent many years researching the paranormal. He believed in ghosts and demons. Monsters, he supposed, could exist in some form or another. He spent a good amount of his life dedicated to finding proof of such things, and he was there on that night to communicate with his daughter who had been dead for a year.

Despite all of this, when Mark heard what Tami was telling him, his paranormal interests flew out the window and he was simply the father of teenage girls.

"There was a party here tonight," Mark said. "Did you drink anything? Did you take anything?"

Tami looked at him as though he was on crack and shook her head. While the question was perfectly valid and he still thought that there was a chance that someone could have slipped a drug into her drink without her knowing it, there was something about the way she looked at him which made him feel like an idiot for asking.

"I know how this sounds," she told him. "I know it's crazy. I saw it, and even I think it sounds crazy. But I saw the shadows move. I felt... something."

Mark turned away from her, scanning the cemetery.

"One of the shadows was like this animal thing. It was short, but fast," Tami told him.

Mark remembered seeing something out of the corner of his eye. He had dismissed it as nothing more than a figment of his imagination, but he was beginning to rethink that call.

"Listen to me," he told her as he led her toward their cars. "We're going to get you out of here. You're going to get into your car and you're going to drive straight home. Do you understand?"

Tami nodded and asked, "What about you?"

Mark didn't answer that question. He was there that night for a reason. Warren wouldn't have drawn Cindy's grave if he wasn't supposed to be there. He thought the shadows might be another clue. Maybe they weren't hostile, as Tami said. Maybe the shadow was Cindy, unable to manifest in her familiar form.

For as long as Mark had been researching the paranormal, he had heard stories of shadow creatures. Different cultures had different legends, but they were one of the most consistent reports from investigators—only out of the corner of their eye or in the distance. The reports could not be counted as hard evidence, because human eyes played tricks in the darkness, but nearly every investigator had a report of seeing those shadows. Some had even managed to capture them on video, though the quality of those videos was usually too poor to be of any use.

His flashlight was aimed directly in front of them and his eyes were on the brightly lit ground as he walked. Tami was still searching the darkness for her pursuer and Mark's mind was racing with investigative procedures and ideas.

He saw something move through the light, which caused him to stop walking. It was brief and he hadn't been paying enough attention to what he was doing to be sure of anything, but he could have sworn that he saw a shadow on the outer edge of his light flinch as the light grew near.

As Tami stopped walking beside him, she asked, "Did you see it?"

"I'm not sure," Mark replied.

"But you believe me? You believe what I told you?"

"I believe that you think you saw something. And I have enough faith in your judgment to know that you wouldn't be this scared if you didn't believe what you saw."

"I have no idea what you just said, but thanks."

He started walking again, this time studying the shadows and the light more carefully. He wished that he'd had the forethought to grab his equipment from the trunk of his car before he entered the cemetery. He wanted to scan the area for electro-magnetic fluctuations and record for electronic voice phenomena. He wanted to set up cameras and search the area with his night vision goggles.

As he made a list of all of the things that he wanted to do with his investigation, Tami asked, "Is Winnie okay? I saw her earlier. Please tell me she's not out tonight."

"She's fine. She's with her mother," Mark replied, still running down that list and scanning the shadows on the edge of the light.

"Thank God," Tami sighed. "Good. We just need to get out of here. I don't know what this is, but—"

The shadows jumped back once again and this time Mark was paying full attention. He knew what he saw, but when he stopped walking he didn't want to panic Tami any more than she already was. If she was going to be driving home, he wanted her to have a clear mind.

"Take this," Mark said, handing Tami the flashlight. He wanted her to have the light so that when he told her to go to her car, she would not need him to go with her.

She caught on to his plan and gave him a questioning look.

"You're leaving too, right?" she asked him. "You're not staying here."

"It's okay. You know what I do. This is just another day on the job for me."

"This isn't some garbled voice on a cheap recorder."

"I know. And if I want answers, this is my best chance at getting them."

They didn't say anything else as they walked to the cemetery gate. Mark thought the matter settled as they approached their cars and he prepared to start his investigation, but Tami stopped walking as she neared her car. She shined the flashlight at the ground and stared at it for a moment before finally looking back to Mark.

"I can't leave," she said in a tone that was not forceful or scared. She was stating a basic and simple fact.

By the time she said this, Mark was standing by the trunk of his car, prepared to open it and remove his equipment once she was underway. He looked at her, hoping that she could not read the annoyance in his eyes. He wanted her to go; not only for her own safety but so that he could take care of his work without interruption.

"Tami, get in the car," he said, in a stern tone.

She looked toward the cemetery and then back to Mark, saying, "This place scares the crap out of me. I've seen things tonight that I will never be able to get out of my head. And don't get me wrong, I'd like nothing more than to drive away from here and never turn back. But do you really think I can do that?"

"I'm telling you to."

"I've been walking away for a year. I'm tired of turning around and seeing your family right where I left you."

"Leave."

"Not until you do."

"Tami, go home."

"You're not my father. This isn't your property. You don't get to tell me when to leave."

Mark wanted to grab Tami and force her into her car. He wanted to make sure that she was clear of this place before he moved on to his investigation, but she wouldn't budge and he couldn't make her listen if she didn't want to.

Her being there at the cemetery would change everything. He

couldn't investigate as aggressively as he had planned, because whatever was out there might pose a threat. He was more than willing to put his own life on the line in his pursuit of answers and closure, but he was not completely irresponsible. He couldn't risk Tami's life.

The funny part was that he hadn't realized just how willing to die he was until that very moment. He had never thought of himself as suicidal or even depressed, yet when he held his own life up and compared it to Tami's, he suddenly realized that he didn't care what happened to himself.

43

Marion looked at the woman who remained on the ground, scrubbing the floor with her brush. She wasn't sure exactly what to do or say. The woman was obviously very disturbed, but to what degree, Marion couldn't say.

"What do you mean when you say that it's far from over?" Marion asked, but the woman ignored her.

Marion's wrist still hurt from the woman's grip as she spoke those words. She rubbed her wrist and looked around the house, trying to figure out why this woman seemed so disturbed.

The air smelled foul. There was a large pot on the stove and whatever had been cooking in it was obviously not meant to be eaten. The air seemed thick, though the door was wide open and it was not humid outside. Just being in that house gave Marion a strange feeling. She regretted ever stepping inside.

"I'm looking for my daughter," Marion told the woman on the floor, hoping that by talking, she would draw the woman into a conversation. "She snuck out of her room."

The woman seemed to slow her scrubbing, just slightly. She had heard what Marion said and she reacted to it, though she said nothing and soon resumed her normal scrubbing speed.

"I know that it's normal for teenagers to sneak out of the house. Rebellion is healthy, to a degree. I'm just uneasy these days. It's a dangerous world out there."

The woman stopped scrubbing and pulled herself to her feet. She moved quickly toward Marion, causing Marion to back against the table. The woman then looked Marion in the eyes, studying her.

It was not easy to make Marion nervous. In her career, she often dealt with people who were angry and some who were even scary. She'd perfected her reaction to such people over the years, being sure not to look too weak or intimidated while remaining human and relatable.

This woman was different. It wasn't her attitude that caused Marion to shrink back, but the look in her eyes; the cold, empty look.

"Death," the woman said, right in Marion's face. "You reek of it."

"I don't know what you mean."

The woman smiled, but it was not a warm or happy smile. It was a mocking smile.

The woman turned away and walked toward the kitchen. She grabbed the pot off of the stove and placed it in the sink. As she ran water into the pot, the woman began to clean off the counters.

"My name is Marion. What's yours?"

"My name is acid on the tongues of all who speak it."

"Try me."

The woman shut off the water and turned to face Marion. She seemed to be sizing her up. Marion had seen this look many times in the past, but for some reason felt more exposed than usual as this woman looked her over.

"My name is Obell. And now I have a question for you."

"What's your question, Obell?"

Obell hesitated for a moment before asking. It was obvious that she was trying to figure out exactly how to phrase what she wanted to ask. When she finally spoke, each word was carefully pronounced. She asked, "When you look at the world, what do you see?"

All in all, it was a fairly tame question. Marion had been expecting some sort of lashing out. Some veiled threat or an inappropriate comment about Marion being a whore, which always seemed popular with her more disturbed patients for some reason.

She thought carefully about how she wanted to answer that question. She tried to imagine what Obell was hoping to hear in response, but she could not get a clear read on this woman. She could try to place her into any number of categories that she was familiar with, but there was something different about Obell, which Marion found unsettling.

"What do I see?" Marion repeated, buying herself just a second or two to think about her answer. "I see... potential."

Obell was silent. She stared at Marion as though she expected there to be more to the answer, but Marion did not offer anything else. She wanted to see what Obell made of that word.

Obell half-smiled and said, "You see potential? Where?"

"Everywhere."

"Potential for what?"

Marion hesitated again. This was an interesting fork in the road of their conversation. She would rather have Obell decide which direction to take their talk in, so she simply said, "What do you think?"

"I think you have no idea what you're talking about," Obell replied.

Obell turned and continued to clean off her counter as she said, "I think you know exactly what you see when you look around, but you don't want to see it. So, you pretend that it doesn't exist. You run from it. You hide."

Marion allowed Obell this assumption, though she did not agree with it. She believed that Obell was using Marion to voice her own thoughts, which Marion was interested in hearing.

Marion made a list in her mind, of all the various ways that Obell was not correct in her assumption. She saw darkness in the world on a regular basis, and she handled that just fine. She allowed the idea of the supernatural to exist and she pursued it, rather than run from it. She knew of pain and suffering. She knew loss. She did not run from any of it. She fully acknowledged it and processed it accordingly.

"What am I hiding from?" Marion asked, in that soft and comforting tone that she normally used at work.

Obell did not answer that question. She pretended that she did not hear Marion ask it at all, as she went about cleaning her kitchen.

Marion looked down to her watch. Though the time itself didn't matter to her, she didn't know how much time she wanted to spend in that house, talking with Obell. Winnie was still out there, somewhere. Marion didn't have time to chat with a random stranger in the middle of nowhere.

She looked around that house once again, asking herself why she had walked into it with so little hesitation. She was not one to walk into homes uninvited. She was not one to risk her life when a situation felt wrong to her, and nothing about this situation felt right.

She knew that she should walk out of that house. Winnie needed her. Yet, that heaviness in the air was puzzling her. It was not difficult to breathe. It was almost as though the heaviness was not in the air itself, but had more to do with the house and the situation.

"Are you in need of help?" Marion asked, wanting to end her visit as cleanly and quickly as possible. "Are you hurt?"

Again, Obell remained silent. She went about her work as though Marion was not even there. She showed no signs of listening to Marion, or caring about their conversation. She also showed no immediate sign of being a danger to herself or others, so Marion decided to leave the situation where it was and she began to walk toward the door.

Just as she was beginning to believe that she would leave that house and allow it to be nothing more than a strange event, occurring on a strange night, Obell spoke.

"Aren't you?" Obell asked, in nearly a whisper.

Marion paused, but kept her eyes on the door. She considered walking out the door in spite of Obell's words, but that inquisitive part of her would not allow her to do such a thing.

"Pardon?" she said, still facing the door.

"Are you not hurt?"

Marion turned around slowly, wondering what Obell was talking about and where this conversation could possibly lead. Obell was facing her, resting her arms on a small butcher block island in the kitchen.

Marion considered her words before speaking. When she did reply, she thought that her voice sounded far more defensive than she intended it to. "I don't know what you mean."

"You know exactly what I mean."

Marion did not respond. She allowed Obell to look at her and study her with those cold, hollow eyes. She waited patiently for Obell to explain herself. For a moment or two, Obell seemed more than willing to play this game. She did not speak or move. She showed no signs of wavering.

She had no smile on her face when she finally spoke, saying, "You're broken. You feel lost. Confused."

"Doesn't everyone?" Marion asked.

"I don't."

Marion took a step toward Obell, looking the woman squarely in the eyes. She was trying to read the person in front of her, but there was something about Obell that kept Marion from connecting to her in the same way that she had always connected to other people. Marion was both intrigued and disturbed by this.

"How do you feel?" Marion asked Obell, taking on a tone more suited to a therapist.

"Powerful," Obell replied. "I feel completely in control."

Marion nodded and looked down to the trail of mud on the floor, which ended at the brush that Obell had dropped as she moved into the kitchen. She told Obell, "I don't believe that."

"That, right there, is your problem."

"What?"

"You can't accept what you don't believe. Yet, what you believe is an illusion."

"I don't understand."

"What are you certain of right now, in this moment? What is there about your life that you can feel or touch?"

Marion didn't answer that question. She only looked at Obell with a puzzled expression, because she didn't know how else to respond. The question seemed nonsensical. Of course Marion couldn't touch or feel much of her own life while standing inside of a stranger's home.

"What do you see when you look at me?" Obell asked. "And if you say *potential*, I just might skin you alive."

Obell's lips curled upward, not quite into a smile but just enough to make Marion wonder whether or not that last sentence was meant as a joke.

Marion tried to think of a perfect response which would drive Obell into more discussion about herself, so that Marion could get a better understanding of the woman. That perfect answer didn't come to her.

She said, "I don't know what I see."

"You don't recognize it, do you?"

Marion hesitated for a moment before asking, "It?"

"That thing which makes you a person. That glimmer of life. That spark of humanity," Obell mused. "Do you see that thing in me?"

Truth be told, Marion didn't see much in Obell at all. Yet in her professional opinion, it was usually a bad idea to tell someone that you did not see a spark of humanity in them.

Obell went on, saying, "I'm not a person."

"What are you?"

"I'm so much more. I am powerful. I am immune to the weakness of human life. I have the ability to bend reality to my will," Obell explained, standing tall and taking great pride in herself. "I am a witch."

Marion nodded, rather unimpressed. This declaration might not have been common in her day job, but she was accustomed to hearing it in the paranormal field. This claim of being a witch caused her to switch gears from caring therapist to hardline skeptic. She crossed her arms.

Obell seemed amused by this. "You don't believe me. That's fine. But you can't ignore it forever."

"I'm not ignoring anything. I'm simply not willing to believe in something just because someone tells me to."

"I'm not asking you to believe me. What I meant to say was that you can't ignore the truth forever."

Obell seemed to be talking in circles, which was beginning to frustrate Marion. Still, she tried to show no sign of this frustration. "What truth?"

Turning around and resuming her chores, Obell spoke to Marion in a matter-of-fact tone. She said, "Everything you think you are is a lie. I look at you and I see the same illusion that had me fooled for so long. The world out there; the people. Eventually, you start to believe that you're one of them."

Marion didn't know what to make of that comment. Obell seemed to be placing her own issues and delusions on Marion. She was seeing things which weren't really there. Truly, she was in need of more help than Marion could offer.

"But I know the truth of what you are; deep down, where nobody can see it. You've hidden it. You might even believe that it's not there, but I can see it. Your eyes betray you."

"I don't know what you're talking about."

"You're like me," Obell told Marion as she dumped a handful of unused herbs and what looked like dirt into the garbage. "A creature outside of the world and never part of it. You look around you and all you see is weakness. All you want is control."

44

Winnie's pursuit of the mysterious stranger had somehow turned into a moonlit stroll through the woods. She was looking around at the trees and up to the stars. She was breathing in the cool night air. It all seemed so remarkably unremarkable.

She was limping on her injured ankle and as she went along, she noticed that the stranger was walking with a slight limp himself. She wondered if he was mimicking her movements for some reason, or if he had actually been hurt in some way.

Could a corpse be hurt? That was a question which was far beyond her ability to answer. She couldn't begin to calculate the odds of experiencing what she was experiencing on that night; to wander down a dark and unfamiliar road, only to stumble upon the undead, walking the earth in search of...something. To try to figure out any sort of logic for an already twisted world was not a task that she was willing to take on. At the end of the day, it didn't matter why he was limping.

The stranger kept his eyes forward and his pace steady. He didn't move around rocks or branches. Though his feet were bare and surely he must have sustained some sort of injury, his expression did not let on to any amount of pain. This made his limp even more puzzling to her.

Of course, he said nothing to her. Aside from the occasional interaction like what they had shared on the cliff, he paid her no attention at all. She was intrigued by him and curious to know more about where he came from and where he was going, but at the same time, this journey through the woods was beginning to bore her just a little bit.

"So," she said, though she wasn't sure that she expected him to respond in any way. "Do you know where we're going? Or is this just a random walk sort of thing?"

The stranger remained silent and kept his eyes forward. He showed no sign that he had heard her.

Winnie went back to looking at the trees and the moonlight. She kept her eyes peeled for any sign of coyotes or other dangerous wild animals, though she didn't expect to find any. Most animals would move away from humans, and the odds of her encountering two angry coyotes in the same night seemed slim.

On the other hand, the odds seemed to be thrown out the window on this particular night, so she couldn't dismiss any possibility. Perhaps coyotes were drawn to the scent of zombies in the woods. After all, her dead companion was—technically—rotting flesh.

Or was he? As the thought of rotting flesh occurred to Winnie, she realized that in spite of his rather dead condition, the mysterious stranger did not smell like a rotting corpse. Perhaps it was the coldness of the night preserving him like a morgue refrigerator, or some element of the supernatural force which had brought him to his feet.

She hadn't spent much time looking at the stranger up close. It seemed rude, considering his lack of clothing, but as she walked next to him, Winnie stole a glimpse at the stranger's arm. She observed what looked like puncture wounds from a needle, but this needle would have had to have been large and painful.

The wounds were not red and swollen. There was no blood, of course. They had likely been made after his death; possibly as part of the experiment or spell which woke him up.

Or maybe the wounds had been cleaned up after he was dead and that's why there was no blood. Winnie wasn't a medical examiner. She knew that whatever conclusions she came to would be her own gut instinct and little more.

She looked at his face. His expression was blank and he stared into the distance with unwavering eyes. Winnie's first thought was that his stare was as blank as his facial expression. She assumed that he was a mindless drone, wandering into the night toward whatever spot his instinct drew him to. She didn't give him the credit of complex thought or understanding of his situation.

Yet, he had shown signs of thought. He had attacked the coyote, seeming to respond to its stalking Winnie. He had made sure that she could follow him throughout the night. He kissed her hand in what had to have been the strangest moment of Winnie's entire life.

As she considered these things, Winnie had to wonder if perhaps the stranger was capable of thought. Perhaps there was a person inside of that dead body, buried deep down, where nobody was ever supposed to find him. She felt sorry for that person.

Given his looks, she imagined that he had been popular at whatever school he went to. He was muscular, so maybe he played sports or was an aspiring actor. She could imagine what he would look like if he smiled and she tried to decide whether he was the slow-but-lovable type or a brooding intellectual. There was a whole life to be lived, wherever he came from. There was a bedroom that now sat empty. There was a family, missing him. And maybe, somewhere deep inside, there was a part of him that missed them as well.

In spite of what he was and all that she had seen him do, Winnie felt bad for the mysterious stranger. As they walked side by side, she kept her eyes forward, but pulled her hand from her pocket and allowed it to drift toward him, until she felt her fingers brush against his and she hoped that he would take her hand.

It took just a moment for Winnie to realize that it was not the stranger's finger that she was touching.

Her body went numb as terror shot through her. She pulled her hand back, mortified beyond words and closing her eyes as tightly as she possibly could, as though the stranger would suddenly become bashful.

"Oh, God!" she cried, afraid to open her eyes. "I'm sorry. I'm so, so, so sorry. That was a mistake. A horrible, horrible mistake."

She opened her eyes and saw that the stranger had not slowed down. He was now ahead of her. She hurried to catch up.

"I mean... Not *horrible*. I'm sure you're very—Oh, God, what am I saying?"

She stopped talking and walked beside him for a second or two, allowing the moment to pass. He didn't seem to notice that anything out of the ordinary had happened at all which made her feel both relieved and more creeped out than ever, all at the same time.

She looked forward and nodded to herself, "Okay. So, we're pretending that never happened. Good plan."

She looked over to him with an awkward smile, and that was when she noticed those puncture marks again; the holes in his skin which looked as though someone had poked him with the most painful needle ever.

Winnie looked down to the stranger's hand this time, before she took it in her own and lifted it. The stranger didn't seem to mind. He didn't pull away from her. He simply continued on his way as though she hadn't touched him at all.

As she looked at his hand, she studied the holes where she theorized that someone had injected him with whatever potion or mixture of chemicals had brought him back to life. She winced, as though she could feel the pain of those injections, and came to the conclusion that whoever had inflicted those wounds on him had to be some sort of monster themselves.

She tried her best to keep from tripping over rocks and branches as she looked over his wounds, but stumbled more than once, causing the pain in her ankle to shoot through her leg.

She wasn't sure if the stranger could feel her touch. She was curious to see if he felt pain, as any normal person would in his situation. His feet must have been raw by this point, but she wasn't sure if he was incapable of feeling or simply didn't care.

Winnie moved her hand toward the wounds on the stranger's hand. She stopped herself before actually touching those wounds. Curiosity did not cancel out thoughts of disease and infection, and touching those wounds seemed like a bad idea. Instead, she allowed his arm to fall to his side once again and she turned her attention to the path ahead.

After a moment, she asked, "Do you feel?"

She looked at him, to see if he would respond with a facial expression, if not by speaking, but he did neither.

She continued, "Do you feel the pain of those wounds or is it just...gone?"

Still, there was no reaction from the stranger whatsoever. Winnie fell silent once again and she continued to walk with him.

She knew that she should have been scared. Nothing about this situation seemed wise or appropriate, but there was a strange sense of peace to it all. She couldn't put her finger on what might have given her that sense, but she was not scared.

"Well, if you're wondering, my ankle is killing me. I must have the mother of all bruises on my shoulder and it's getting a little cold out here," Winnie told him. She then looked in his direction and noted his lack of clothing before adding, "Not that I should be the one complaining about that."

Her attempt at humor did not seem to faze him at all. Eyes forward, pace steady. It was as though she wasn't there.

"I don't get it. You ignore me now, but I know that you're at least aware of me. I know that you've shown some interest in me. Not to say that you're *interested* in me. Though you did kiss my hand..." she trailed off. She didn't know what she was supposed to say or how she was supposed to act in a situation like this. Everything she knew about zombies told her that he was supposed to be trying to eat her brain. Nothing had prepared her for a nice stroll through the woods.

"I mean... Are you? Interested in me, I mean?" she asked. "Is this like a *King Kong* thing?"

His lack of response was somewhat frustrating, since she had a hundred different questions that she would have loved to ask him. But at the same time, she didn't really mind his silence.

She walked with him through those woods, without a clear idea of why she was walking with him. He didn't talk. He didn't ask her any questions. He didn't want to know how she was feeling or what she was thinking. He didn't insist on talking about his feelings about being dead and naked.

Normally, she would have probably been screaming at someone if they had spent this much time together, but he was making it very hard for her to get upset.

"I don't suppose you'd be willing to tell me how you died," she said to him. "Normally, I wouldn't even ask. It seems to be in poor taste when you first meet someone. Death has to be personal, right?"

There was another question that she wanted to ask him, but in spite of his completely blank expression and his unrelenting silence, the question seemed to get caught in her mouth before she could speak it.

She looked to the ground, at all of the dead leaves and the dead branches that had fallen. Somehow, she never noticed how death had completely surrounded her until just then. It was everywhere.

Taking a deep breath, she smelled the dead leaves, which had always been one of her favorite scents. It was the smell of fall; the smell of Halloween. It brought her back to her childhood, when she would dress up and go trick-or-treating with her entire family.

She could almost feel the weight of her pillow case, full of candy as she walked through the woods with the stranger.

Winnie couldn't help but smile, just slightly, as she said, "Can you imagine what the public service announcements would say about wandering off with a dead guy? I mean, they frown upon strangers of any sort, but you have to think that the walking dead would be, like, a big deal to them."

The humor seemed lost on the mysterious stranger. His eyes remained forward and not so much as a smirk crossed his lips.

The question still loomed in her head: What was it like to die—to *be* dead?

It seemed so senseless to Winnie. It was such a random thing to happen to a person who was so young. It was against the natural order of things, and no matter how hard she tried, she could not bring herself to be comfortable with that.

She looked at her dead friend and she wanted to make a case against death. She wanted to argue about how wrong it was and how cruel to those who survived. He was sure to agree with her, given his situation, but she couldn't bring herself to speak her mind for once.

Instead, Winnie continued to walk. She continued to step over and around the obstacles in her path and occasionally attempted to lead the mysterious stranger around those things which might damage him. Usually, he found a way to step on something equally harmful despite her best efforts.

45

Tami would have given anything to get into her car and drive away from the cemetery. She had no desire to track down whatever those shadows were and try to record voices off of them. Honestly, she didn't want to hear whatever it was that they had to say, because she was fairly certain that they wanted her dead.

She could practically feel her warm bed, which would smell like flowery fields, because it was laundry day and its sheets would be freshly washed. She could imagine climbing into her bed, with the blanket pulled close to her head. She could imagine sitting in that bed, with every light that she could manage to fit into her room turned on to their brightest settings. She had no intention of sitting in a dark room by herself in the near future.

Tami wanted to leave that place more than anything in the world, and never go back there. But as she stared at the ground near her car, she knew that she couldn't put that night behind her. As long as Mr. McKeller was staying there, she had to stay as well. If she left, she would feel horrible. If something happened to him, she would never be able to live with herself.

She racked her brain to find some logic that would change her mind, or some argument that would change his, but she could think of neither. Finally, she voiced her conclusion. She didn't like it, but she had no other choice.

"I can't leave," she said.

Mr. McKeller was standing by his car, waiting for her to leave and planning his investigation. He undoubtedly expected her to drive off and leave him alone. Maybe he wanted it that way. She didn't care.

When he looked at her after hearing her words, Tami could see a hint of annoyance in his eyes. He wanted to do this alone. She warned him of strange shadows stalking her and possibly trying to kill her, and he wanted to be there alone. She couldn't wrap her mind around that fact. All she knew was that it scared her.

When he spoke, he had that tone in his voice that she'd heard a hundred times before. It was that parental tone, which was normally directed toward Cindy or Winnie, but rarely Tami herself. "Tami, get in the car."

Her first instinct was to say *yessir*, get in her car and drive off.

He was an adult, after all, and she was just a kid. She had to gather every ounce of nerve that she could muster. She looked toward the cemetery, reminding herself why she wanted to leave so much and why she couldn't.

Looking back to Mr. McKeller, she said, "This place scares the crap out of me. I've seen things tonight that I will never be able to get out of my head. And don't get me wrong, I'd like nothing more than to drive away from here and never turn back. But do you really think I can do that?"

Her voice betrayed no intimidation. When she heard herself, Tami was surprised to hear a voice which sounded confident and mature. She was not the child that she had been when she last heard Mr. McKeller use that parental tone on his daughters. She had been through too much to ever be that child again.

"I'm telling you to."

"I've been walking away for a year. I'm tired of turning around and seeing your family right where I left you."

"Leave."

"Not until you do."

"Tami, go home."

"You're not my father. This isn't your property. You don't get to tell me when to leave."

She could see it in his eyes. He wanted her to leave; he wanted to *make* her leave. He wasn't angry, he was desperate. He looked tired and worn, and she began to wonder just what he was hoping to accomplish there that night. What was he hoping to find? She had to question how deeply he was willing to walk into that darkness in search of whatever it was that he was looking for.

Tami walked to his car and shined her flashlight at the trunk. She told him, "Let's go. If you want to go back in there and hunt down whatever that thing was, we'll do it together."

"It's dangerous," he replied.

She laughed. It was not something that she meant to do, but she couldn't hold back the laughter when she heard his comment.

"Seriously," she said to him, "you don't need to tell me that this is dangerous. Whatever that thing is, it's...aware. It knew exactly what it was doing."

"Did you get any sense of what it was or what it wanted?"

"Aside from wanting *me*? No."

Mr. McKeller unlocked his trunk and opened it. Tami had been expecting to see some video equipment and some audio recorders. She was surprised when she saw half a dozen night vision security cameras, three hand-held video recorders, eight digital audio recorders, two devices which looked like stud finders but which she doubted were stud finders, two large bottles of holy water, four silver crosses, and several bottles of what looked like oils and herbs, all stored in a custom-cut foam liner within his trunk.

The technology was impressive, but it was nothing that she was entirely caught off guard by. She lived in a world of technology and no amount of blinking lights would impress her anymore.

The crosses, holy water, oils and herbs, on the other hand, sent a chill running up her spine. She looked at Mr. McKeller.

"Do you hunt vampires?" she asked him, half-jokingly.

"No," he assured her. "Certain spirits can be more powerful than others. And not every call we get turns out to be a simple haunting."

"What else have you seen?"

Mr. McKeller seemed to read the worry in Tami's eyes. He told her, "You can still leave. It's not too late."

"I'm not leaving. I just want to know...What do you think this thing is?"

"I don't. I have a list in my head of all of the simple, normal things that it could be. An animal running by. The moonlight playing tricks."

"A crazy teenager," Tami nodded. "I'm rooting for that one at this point."

He reached into the trunk and grabbed one of the crosses. He held it in his hand and said, "I've only seen one. It was a long time ago, and now I just don't want to be unprepared."

She knew that he was talking about a demon without him saying the word itself. Once she knew, she didn't want him to use the word. She figured that if he never spoke it out loud, she could pretend that she was reading something into his words that wasn't there.

He held out the cross, offering it to her. Tami looked down at it for a moment, and then said, "No. Thanks."

She reached for a chain around her neck and pulled a cross necklace from under her shirt. It was a cross that Mr. McKeller recognized immediately, because it had once belonged to Cindy.

Tami expected Mr. McKeller to keep the other cross for himself, but when she turned down his offer, he placed it back where he found it. Something about his leaving the cross struck a nerve in Tami. That simple act told her that he was not the same man that he had once been. She couldn't help but wonder if he had changed more than she ever realized.

"We probably don't have time to set up all of the cameras and hook up the DVR to record all of the footage, so we'll take the hand-helds," he told her, removing one of the small hand-held video cameras from its holder and handing it to her. "There's a night vision button on it. That should help us see what's out there."

He took another camera for himself. He also grabbed three audio recorders before closing the trunk.

"We'll put one of the audio recorders near Cindy's grave, another at the entrance and I'll keep one on me. I might try talking to whatever's out there and it can reply on the recorder."

Tami nodded her understanding as she turned on the video camera and looked at the display screen to make sure that she was using it properly. As she did this, she nearly overlooked something strange that he had said. After she heard it, she looked back to him and asked, "Why are we putting a recorder at Cindy's grave?"

"Just in case," he replied, trying to sound reassuring. There was something about his tone that did not sit well with her.

He started to walk toward the cemetery gate, preparing an audio recorder as he walked. He began recording and said, "Cemetery investigation. October 18th. Mark and Tami recording. Recorder is being placed at cemetery entrance."

As they reached the gate, he placed the recorder on the stone wall which was about waist-high and supported the iron fence that surrounded the cemetery. After placing the recorder, Mr. McKeller turned on his own video camera and adjusted its settings. He continued to walk toward Cindy's grave.

Tami remained quiet as he went through the routine of setting up his equipment. She didn't want to ask too many questions or become too much of a burden. She assumed that he knew what he was doing, but none of it made any sense to her.

Once he was recording video with his camera, Mr. McKeller pulled another audio recorder from his pocket and repeated the same information into this recorder, changing only the location where the recorder was being placed.

Watching Mr. McKeller through the night vision of the video camera gave the situation something of a fictional feel for Tami. She had no desire to be in the cemetery, but at the same time, she was disconnected from the urgency of that moment. It was like watching one of those paranormal shows on TV.

Mr. McKeller placed the recorder on Cindy's grave and said nothing else for the recorder, or to Tami. He stood by the grave for a moment, reading the name and the dates which were etched into the stone. It seemed as though there was some part of him which still could not believe what he was reading.

After taking a moment, he turned and started to walk deeper into the cemetery, recording video as he went.

"Where did you see the shadows?" he asked Tami.

At first, she didn't respond. She was outside of the moment, observing.

"Tami?" he asked, turning to look at her.

It was then that she realized that he was speaking to her, and she was jolted back into that moment and that place. She looked away from the video recorder's screen and said, "I saw them all over the place. It started over there."

She pointed off to the side, where she first saw the shadows. Her half-filled garbage bag was still sitting on the ground. Mr. McKeller began to walk toward that spot. Tami hesitated before following, once again wondering if this was a good idea and once again coming to the conclusion that it probably wasn't.

Tami hurried to keep up with Mr. McKeller, not wanting to be left behind for even a moment. When she reached his side, she remained quiet, scanning the darkness with her eyes and then with the night vision.

When she saw nothing, her mind began to drift back to Cindy's grave and the recorder that was placed there. She once again wondered why he had placed it there. Rather than let this question linger in her head, she turned to Mr. McKeller and asked him, "Just in case?"

"Huh?" he replied, seeming to not understand the question.

"You said that we were placing a recorder at her grave 'just in case.'"

He turned and looked at Tami for just a moment, giving her the impression that he still did not want her there with him. He then said, "Oh... Just in case there's something out here. I have baseline recordings of the grave, so I can rule out some of the normal background noise."

He wanted her to take the answer and drop it. She could tell that from the matter-of-fact tone with which he had delivered the response. However, his reply only gave her more questions and it served to highlight his odd behavior.

"You record sounds there often?" she asked, knowing that he would not appreciate the question.

"Sometimes."

"Why?"

He wanted to tell her to shut up, but he didn't. He was too nice a person to be so blunt with her. She took advantage of that kindness, but she didn't care if he did snap. There was something wrong with the McKeller family and she was too invested to ignore that fact.

Mr. McKeller stopped and turned toward Tami. He seemed to be debating whether or not he should discuss this subject with her, but she was already onto him so there was little point in remaining quiet now.

"I just—I want to make sure she's okay. I need to make sure," he said.

"So you're trying to hunt down Cindy's ghost?"

As she asked that question, a chill ran across Tami's skin and into the back of her nose.

Mr. McKeller didn't answer that question. He looked to the ground, as though he didn't know what to say next.

"She's not here," Tami told him. "She's not in a cemetery. She's not wandering around town. Cindy is *gone*."

He looked back to her now, in a way that for a moment seemed like she had told him something that he didn't already know. Having someone tell him that his daughter was gone still cut him deeply.

Tami didn't enjoy being so blunt about a sensitive subject. She felt awkward even discussing Cindy with Mr. McKeller. She wondered if he hated her in that moment, but she couldn't afford to care.

"I know that I can't possibly understand what you're going through. She wasn't my daughter. She wasn't even really my family, I guess. So maybe you all have a right to tell me to shut up and go away, and if you really want me to, I will. But Cindy is not here anymore...and you shouldn't want her to be."

"You don't know that. She could be lost and scared."

"Or she could be at peace. And every day that you allow yourself to be brought down by this mission of yours is another day that you're turning her into something that she's not. She died, but she would want you to find some way to move on. She wouldn't want to be the reason for you to linger in the darkness for the rest of your life. You're turning her memory into your own personal monster."

"I just need to make sure. I just need to do everything that I know how to do, and if she still doesn't show up, then fine. I'll move on."

"When will that be?" Tami asked and then looked around the cemetery. "What are you doing here? What are you hoping to accomplish tonight? Because that thing out there sure as hell wasn't my best friend."

"But it's one step closer. It's something tangible that I can track down."

Tami shut off her video recorder and handed it to Mr. McKeller. She said, "That thing that was chasing me is not one step closer to Cindy. It's a mile in the other direction. And if you keep chasing those things—if you keep chasing the darkness, it will crawl inside of you and it will rot everything that it touches."

There was nothing left for her to say. She couldn't make him leave, and she was not willing to follow him down that path. Tami put her hands up to show that she was done with this search and she turned to walk out of the cemetery, leaving Mr. McKeller behind.

She had originally decided to follow him into that cemetery because she didn't want him to be alone with those shadows. She worried that he would be hurt and she couldn't allow that to happen, but as she spent more time with him and she saw how damaged he already was. She saw how unwilling he was to listen and she hoped that her words would mean more to him when stated bluntly and followed by an exit which served to punctuate those words. Staying would only serve to validate his actions, and she wouldn't do that.

All she could do for him at that point was pray that he would choose to follow her out of that graveyard, rather than follow those shadows all the way into the ground.

46

"When you look in the mirror, what do you see?" Obell asked Marion, still standing in the kitchen.

Marion didn't move toward Obell, despite the fact that they were having a conversation now. She wanted to keep space between herself and Obell. She had been grabbed by Obell before and she did not want to make that same mistake twice. She crossed her arms over her chest. She felt exposed with her back to the front door of the house, which remained open. Anyone could sneak up behind her, but she dared not take her eyes off of Obell.

"I see myself," Marion responded, offering no insight into her own mind.

Obell nodded her acceptance of that answer and said, "Do you know what I see when I look in the mirror? I see a beast. I see its cold, unrelenting stare. I see its worn flesh. Now, I didn't always see that beast. I didn't always know what it was that lived inside of me. I didn't realize the truth of my being for far too long."

"You're not a monster. You're a woman."

"You see what your eyes will allow you to see. Perception is the trick of this world. Perception is a demon that fools you into believing what isn't really there, trying to break you from the inside out."

Marion took a step closer to Obell, seeing a path which she could take this conversation down, but unsure whether or not she wanted to explore that path. She looked Obell in the eyes and she saw the beast that Obell wanted her to see, but she saw something else in there as well; something hidden deep beneath the surface.

"Tell me," Obell continued, "what did it make you see? What did it tempt you with? What did it take?"

"I don't know what you're talking about."

"Lying is an ugly trait, even for a beast."

"I'm not lying. I don't know what you're talking about."

Obell looked away from Marion, seeming to grow frustrated by her response. She turned, grabbed a ceramic bowl from her counter and threw it to the ground, letting out a scream as the bowl shattered into hundreds of pieces. With the breaking of the bowl, Obell seemed to gather her senses again.

She walked toward Marion, right through the sharp, jagged pieces of the broken bowl. Marion only now realized that Obell was barefoot. Her feet began to bleed as she walked, leaving a trail of blood on the wood floor.

Obell didn't seem to notice the pain or the blood at all. She walked around the island where she had been standing and stopped when there was no longer any solid object between herself and Marion.

Marion wasn't sure that she wanted to stay where she was. She wanted to leave the house, but she worried about turning her back to Obell. Instead, she took a few steps to her left, which put the corner of the kitchen table between the two women. It was not much of a shield, but it was something.

"When I was a child, I had no parents," Obell said. "I used to sit in the orphanage and wonder why my mommy and daddy didn't want me. I used to ask myself why nobody else wanted to take me home and raise me as their own, when so many of the other girls were adopted. What was wrong with me? Was it my skin? My hair? Was I not pretty enough or smart enough?"

"Those are common feelings."

"I was foolish. I didn't see what was right in front of me the whole time."

"What was that?"

"I *had* no parents! I wasn't left on the doorstep and abandoned. I wasn't born to some slutty teenager on prom night."

"Where did you come from?"

Obell smiled and raised her finger. She said, "That's the question, isn't it? I grew up feeling like an outsider. I was invisible to the world. Nobody saw me, just like they don't see you."

"People see me."

"Do they? Or do they see the image that you project? That's your power and you don't even realize it, but you know as well as I do that you're hiding something. The truth. The hate. The rage."

"Who do you hate, Obell?"

"I hate my enemy! I hate whatever it was that hid the truth from me," Obell replied. "There was another creature who could make people see what it wanted them to see. It made me question what I knew in my gut to be the truth."

"How?"

"It noticed me. It saw me and convinced me that I looked like everyone else; that I was a person, like everyone else. It tried to take my power from me. It tried to make me weak."

"How did it try to make you weak?"

"By loving me!" Obell screamed. "By *pretending* to love me. By cursing me and blinding me and..."

Marion waited for Obell to finish that sentence, but Obell didn't seem willing. So, Marion finished it for her, "By making you love it?"

"I can't love."

"But you did. Or, you thought you did?"

Obell looked down to the worn hardwood floor and tugged at her ragged clothing. She said, "It was a spell. A trick."

"To what end?"

"To take my power! What do you think it wanted? It wanted me to be weak. It wanted to make sure that I would never be able to destroy it. There's a war being waged, you know? Every witch, every beast, everything that isn't natural and human is fighting for dominance. And this thing wanted to make sure that I didn't win that war. It wanted to destroy me."

"How did it do that?"

Obell balled her hands into fists and started to pound them against her sides. She didn't look Marion in the eyes. She seemed to be pulling back, but Marion could feel a truth beginning to boil to the surface.

"Obell?" she pressed. "How did it try to destroy you?"

"How did it try to destroy you?"

"Nothing has come after me."

"Liar."

"Maybe I don't recognize it. Tell me what it did to you."

"The same thing it did to you," Obell replied. "It made me blind. Made me weak. Made me *feel*. It worked its way into me and grew and festered. It made me believe that I... It made me think that it was my child. But it wasn't. It was an illusion; a figment."

Marion was caught off guard by the mention of a child. She had to wonder what had happened to the child, if it existed at all. Obell was clearly not capable of raising a child in her condition.

"You have a child?" Marion asked.

"No. No, I thought I did, but that was a lie. That wasn't real."

"What happened to this...figment?"

Obell fell silent for a moment. She stopped pounding her sides with her fists and started shaking her head, as though casting out thoughts that she did not wish to have.

"Obell, answer my question."

"No," Obell said in a soft, almost whisper. "No. No. No. No. No."

Marion pressed Obell in a gentle tone, "Obell, where is your child?"

Obell looked up to Marion with nothing but pure hate in her eyes. Her mouth was curled into a snarl. Marion was frightened by the look that Obell was giving her. She once again became very aware of the fact that she was in a small house, in the middle of nowhere, and nobody would be passing by to help her anytime soon.

"I knew you weren't a person," Obell said, with rage in her voice. "The moment that you walked in here, I knew that you weren't one of them. You were a *thing*. I could smell it on you. I thought you were like me. I thought you were fooled like I was fooled."

"Obell, calm down," Marion said in a soft voice. She hoped that if she used Obell's own name often enough, she could remind Obell of her humanity, though this plan did not seem to be working. "We have a lot in common, you and I."

Marion didn't have a long list of things that she believed that she and Obell had in common. She did not identify with the woman at all, but she wanted Obell to believe that they shared a connection. She needed to talk Obell down.

"We are nothing alike," Obell shot back.

"I have a daughter," Marion blurted, hoping to connect as

mothers. "I had two...I lost one. She was killed in an accident."

"Lies!" Obell screamed.

"No. Her name was Cynthia—Cindy," Marion told Obell, feeling a lump forming in her throat, but trying her best to choke it down. "I loved her very much."

"I thought you were like me," Obell repeated.

"I am like you."

Obell shook her head and stomped her foot on the ground as hard as she could. She said, "I thought you were fooled, like I was fooled. I thought that you were a victim of the same projections."

"They're not projections, Obell. Your love and your pain are real."

"They're lies! But that's your game, isn't it? You're not like me. You're the thing that tried to fool me. You project images. You make people see what you want them to see, but you're not what you claim to be."

Marion didn't respond. She didn't know what she could possibly say in response to Obell's claims. She didn't know how to react to accusations of her being a demon or a monster.

Obell turned away from Marion, shaking her head and pounding her fists at her sides at the same time. She looked like she was fighting with herself. She began to mumble things to herself that Marion couldn't make out.

"Obell, concentrate. Focus on the voice inside of you that's telling you that what I'm saying is real. You're not a beast. You're not hollow, and you're not a witch. And as much power as you wish you had...You didn't have the power to save your child's life."

Obell froze. She had her back turned to Marion, but slowly turned herself around. She locked eyes with Marion, and Marion was instantly aware that she had said something very wrong.

They looked at each other for what seemed like minutes. Neither of them moved. Obell, because there was a fire building inside of her that could explode at any moment; and Marion, because she was afraid that any movement could set off that explosion.

Finally, Obell raced toward Marion as fast as she could, leaving a trail of blood on the floor behind her. As she neared Marion, she let out a shriek the likes of which Marion had never heard in person.

Marion threw her hands up, hoping to defend herself from the coming attack, but this defense was not enough.

47

She wondered what time it was and how long she had been walking through the woods. Winnie didn't care whether or not she made it home by dawn, but the night seemed unending; like the darkness of the world had finally won out and the sun would never be seen again.

Somewhere along the line, walking next to a dead person had lost its shock value. She no longer cared what he was or how he had gotten that way. The only thing that she wondered about was where he was going.

The stranger did not slow down or take a rest. He didn't stop to rub his feet or to get a drink of water. Winnie could have used a break, but she knew that if she stopped for even a moment, he could disappear once again, and she did not feel like chasing him through the woods at full speed.

At one point during their walk, Winnie checked the strangers wrist and neck for a pulse, just to make sure that he was really dead and that she didn't just make the whole thing up in her mind. There was no heartbeat. The stranger did not even seem to notice her checking.

"I don't suppose you have a name?" Winnie asked, though she did not expect an answer from the stranger. She knew better by this point.

She continued, "We could give you one. Maybe Dan or Scott... But you don't really look like one of those. You look more like a...I don't know—a dead guy. What do you name a dead guy? *K. Daver?*"

Winnie chuckled at her own joke, though the stranger did not seem amused by her sense of humor. She had to admit, he probably wouldn't have laughed, even if he did have a personality.

"Okay, no names. You can just keep on being dark and mysterious. It works for you," she told him.

She was rambling. This was not uncommon for her when she was tired, and made even worse by the fact that she was walking with someone who may or may not have been aware of her presence.

There was a noise overhead, which caught Winnie's attention. Leaves were rustling and branches were moving. She couldn't see what made that noise, but it was soon followed by the sound of something falling to the ground behind her and running off.

She looked through the woods, searching for whatever creature had made those noises, but didn't find it. Whatever it was, it was small and fast—most likely a squirrel.

Winnie's musings and distractions kept her from paying attention to where she and the mysterious stranger were walking. She allowed him to lead the way, not thinking about the path herself. She didn't notice when they climbed a hill and didn't pay much attention to the small river that was running past the base of that hill. It was only when the stranger stepped on a pile of wet leaves, lost his footing and fell down the hill that Winnie took notice of her surroundings.

She let out yelp as she watched the stranger twist and bend like a lifeless dummy as he made his way down the hill. He rolled over rocks and smacked his head against a tree, which caused Winnie to put her hand over her mouth.

Her heart began to race in her chest. Her mind, which had been lulled into a false sense of security during their walk, jumped into high gear and she tried to figure out what she could possibly do to help this situation. Gravity had taken over, and she could not prevent the stranger from falling even farther.

She watched, waiting for him to run into some object that would stop his fall, but nothing did.

"Oh no," she winced as she realized that he was headed for the river.

Winnie began to climb down the hill, desperately hurrying while trying to prevent herself from experiencing the sorts of painful contortions and head injuries that she had witnessed with the stranger.

She leaned back and allowed herself to slide down parts of the hill on her butt, maintaining control with her feet. This did not help her ankle at all, but she ignored the pain and pressed on.

Winnie had to watch her own footing as she went along, and couldn't afford to keep her eyes on the mysterious stranger, but when she heard a splash from below, she knew that the stranger had fallen into the water. She needed to get to him before it was too late—Before he died...or whatever it was that zombies did when they fell into water which was undoubtedly ice cold.

"I'm coming!" she called to him, still struggling to get down the hill without falling. "Oh, I hope you can swim."

By the time Winnie reached the bottom of the hill and stood by the edge of the river, she had lost track of the stranger. The river was not raging, but it was moving at a steady pace. Winnie knew that if she did not hurry and find the stranger, he would be dragged down river and who knew where he would end up then?

She could imagine him washing up in the backyard of some nice old lady's house, only to stand up and cause that nice lady to have a heart attack upon seeing a walking corpse. Most people were not as accepting of zombies as Winnie was. They would shoot first and ask questions later.

It wasn't clear to Winnie exactly why she was so concerned for the mysterious stranger, but she did care. He might not have been the most skilled conversationalist, but there was something about him that she found comforting. The less she tried to figure out what caused that feeling, the better. She did not even want to begin to contemplate the level of psychological issues that one would need to suffer from in order to form a meaningful connection with a horror movie castoff.

"Hello?" she called out, as she carefully began to follow the flow of the river. "Hello!" she called again, though she did not expect the stranger to answer her.

"Please don't be dead," she muttered to herself, before catching on to the fact that he already was.

She followed the river around a curve and scanned the water for as far as she could see. In the distance, she saw nothing; there was no sign of the mysterious stranger. Her eyes followed the river back toward her own location, and at first she did not see anything resembling a dead guy, but as she looked to the banks of the river, her eyes spotted something strange. It was not obviously the stranger, but there was a patch of *something* amongst a mess of sticks and trash which had been pushed to the side of the river and trapped behind a cluster of rocks.

This thing was pale and seemed to glow blue in the moonlight. Right away, her brain connected that glow with the flesh of the stranger. His naturally blue tone was made more unearthly by the shining of the moon.

She rushed toward the cluster of debris, still not entirely convinced that this was the stranger and not a piece of paper or tarp that someone had lost. She was prepared to be let down, but as she approached that area, the object began to take on the familiar form of the stranger. One arm was wrapped around the cluster of sticks, while the other floated lifelessly on the water. His legs were moving as though he was trying to walk, but Winnie couldn't tell whether he was doing this on his own or if the flowing of the water was pushing his legs back and forth.

He was face-down in the water, and as soon as Winnie saw this her heart sank. She realized that he was dead and that he probably hadn't been breathing for as long as she had known him, but something about seeing a lifeless body floating in the water caused an instinctual reaction in her.

She raced to get to him as fast as possible, and did not think twice about wading into the ice cold water of the river. She pushed her way through the sticks and garbage until she could finally get a grip on the stranger's arm with her right hand, and then she pulled. She pulled him close and finally grabbed him with her left hand. At last, her grip was strong enough to pull him the rest of the way to solid ground.

The mud near the bank of the river made it hard for Winnie to walk. With each step, her feet would sink into the mud beneath the water and she would need to pull them free before she could take another. As she got closer to land, her feet slipped through the mud and made it difficult for her to maintain the leverage that she needed to drag the stranger.

Once she was entirely out of the water herself, Winnie dragged the stranger onto solid ground and knelt beside him. He was still facing down, so she turned him over and looked for any sign that he was still a zombie and not merely a corpse.

His eyes were unmoving as they reflected the moonlight and the trees above. To Winnie, those eyes seemed like windows into some strange world of unknown creatures. She was stunned by how deeply the reflection carried in them.

"Are you still here?" she asked quietly, unsure whether she was talking to the same old stranger or just a kinda-gross corpse.

He did not answer. Winnie felt a sense of loss as she waited for him to move or show any sign that he had not left her. They weren't finished. They hadn't reached their destination. She needed to know where he was going; where *they* were going.

After waiting for what seemed like an eternity, Winnie saw the stranger twitch. His head jerked just slightly, followed by his limbs. She smiled as she realized what was happening.

The stranger's eyes found Winnie's. He stared at her as though he could see as deeply into the reflection in her eyes as she could see into his, but she knew better. His deep stare was really the gaze of a dead man, unfocused and distant because there was no life inside of him with which to focus those eyes.

Winnie smiled at him and said, "You're still here."

The stranger did not speak a response. Instead, he puckered his lips and kissed the air. This caused Winnie to laugh and she patted him on the cheek.

"Welcome back," she told him.

Suddenly, a chill came over her. For the first time, she felt the coldness of the water that she had been in. She felt the pain in her ankle. Her senses were coming back to her, and the smile on her face quickly faded.

48

Mark walked the cemetery alone after Tami was gone. He was glad to be alone. It was easier for him to work when he didn't have to think about anyone else. He didn't have to worry about their emotional well-being, or their physical safety.

If there was one thing that was proven by her being there, it was that the people closest to him would not understand him. They didn't get his need for answers. They couldn't understand why he had to make sure that Cindy was safe. Tami told him that Cindy wasn't around anymore, but she didn't *know* that. She couldn't promise him that his daughter was able to find peace.

He believed what Tami told him about the shadows. He could feel something in the air that wasn't right or normal. He felt a sense of desperation and fear growing within him, but he didn't know why. The only explanation he had was that his daughter was in danger, and he needed to find some way to communicate with her.

The cemetery was proving to be useless to him. While Tami's experience had been dramatic and impressive, Mark was seeing none of that. Since she left, there were no moving shadows. There were no phantom images on his video cameras. The cemetery didn't even give him the creeps, which he would have expected even on a good night. While the night itself felt wrong to him, the cemetery was empty.

Mark held an audio recorder in his hand and looked down to the red light which told him that it was recording. He said, "Is anyone here?"

He waited for several seconds, allowing whatever ghostly voices were in area to respond before he asked another question.

"What is your name?"

He paused again, allowing time for a response, though he heard nothing with his own ears.

Mark wanted to ask another question, but found himself hesitating. He could feel the muscles in his hand beginning to cramp as he held the recorder, but for some reason, he couldn't just say what he wanted to say.

Perhaps it was because there were too many questions. He would have loved to find Cindy and sit her down for a long interview. He would even settle for another ghost who could tell him whether or not she was still there.

In the past, even before Cindy died, Mark had a thirst for those answers. These days, it seemed like his questions all revolved around Cindy. Every supposedly haunted house that he went into presented a chance to get one step closer to understanding where she was.

He looked at the red light as though it was looking back. At long last, he spat out the only word that seemed to sum up all of his questions at once, "Cindy?"

Mark had done this a thousand times. He had asked questions and listened for the answers when he returned home. He had investigated dozens of houses over the years and he had been looking for Cindy for months. Yet on that night, he could feel something changing. He couldn't put his finger on what that was, but as he said her name, his eyes filled with tears and he looked up to the stars in the sky so that he could catch his breath.

After waiting for a minute or two, Mark turned off the recorder. He rewound the recording and played it back, listening for any sound which might be a voice responding to his questions.

Normally, this was done back at his house, on his computer. He had software that could filter the recording and boost even the faintest sign of a voice. In the cemetery, he only had his ears to rely on, but he held that recorder to his ear and closed his eyes, and he listened as carefully as he possibly could. He listened to the sound of his own voice asking the questions, and he held his breath during each space where he left silence in hopes of getting an answer.

All he heard was the constant hiss of the recorder, which was found on every recording that he made with it.

There were no voices. There was no response to his desperate attempt to communicate with Cindy. There was nothing but the hiss, which seemed to mock him for his attempt.

Mark shut off the recorder and put it into his pocket. He looked into the distance, trying to plan his next move. He didn't know what he was doing or where he was going anymore. He was tired.

He thought about the images that Warren had drawn for him. There were three which remained unexplored: The picture of a cliff, the picture of a small house in the woods and the final drawing, which was of a building that looked somewhat familiar but far too generic to be of any use.

If Warren was to be believed, each of those images would play a part in bringing him closer to Cindy. The question was, which of those images was he supposed to explore next? Since dropping them outside of Warren's home, Mark was no longer sure which order those pictures were meant to be in. Whichever he chose to pursue would simply be a guess.

He tried to think about the options rationally. The building would be difficult for him to narrow down. There were dozens of buildings which could more or less resemble the drawing.

The small house in the woods would be nearly impossible for him to find. He lived in a heavily wooded part of the state and would have to travel down each driveway in town in order to narrow the search; assuming the house was in his town at all.

The cliff became his best option. He had no idea where the cliff was, but of the three options, this would be the easiest to track down. Especially in an age where one could type a few words into a search engine and find the answer to any question.

He pulled his cell phone from his pocket and opened its web browser. He entered the words *'fathom county cliff'* and then pressed *enter*.

There were well over a thousand results. Most of these were for places with similar names, but in different states. He narrowed the results to his own area and searched again.

While several of the results described cliffs in his county, he could not easily narrow the search based on those descriptions. Instead, he looked at the image results and sifted through the pictures that people had posted online.

After wading through several pages of images, Mark came across an image which looked familiar to him. It wasn't that he had been there himself, but the view from the cliff and the shape of the rocks in the area looked like the image that Warren had drawn.

The description that was posted along with the image had not only a reference to the road taken in order to reach that cliff, but was geotagged with the exact coordinates of that cliff.

Mark smiled, "Gotcha."

He turned and hurried for the cemetery entrance, grabbing his audio recorders along the way.

As he got into his car and placed his phone in the cradle that he had suction-cupped to the windshield, Mark pressed a button which took the provided coordinates and produced turn-by-turn directions for him. Soon, he was on his way.

49

When Obell rushed toward Marion, Marion tried her best to get out of the way. She ran toward the door, but she was not quick enough. By the time she reached the threshold, Obell was grabbing her hair and pulling her back into the house.

Marion fell to the floor, slamming her head against the hardwood as she landed. Obell walked around her and slammed the door so hard that it popped open again without her noticing. Marion looked toward the door, now only barely open, and she tried to plot her escape.

She cursed herself for being in this situation. It was stupid of her to walk into that house, and even more stupid to engage Obell in conversation. She knew that Obell was unstable and that their location would prevent help from arriving quickly, even if Marion could manage to make an emergency call.

Marion was smarter than this. She knew how to handle herself in situations such as that, but she was not behaving like a therapist. She was allowing herself to be manipulated by situations. The walls which compartmentalized her thoughts and emotions were breaking down. Winnie was out there, somewhere. Even as Obell stood over her and Marion was trapped in that house, she found herself thinking about Winnie, worrying.

Something was wrong. The entire night was charged with a type of energy that she had never felt before. She couldn't explain it if anyone ever asked her to, but she just knew that something— or possibly *everything*—was not as it should have been. Everything seemed surreal. Colors seemed dull. Lines seemed blurred. Sounds seemed to grate on her every nerve.

She would have chalked all of this up to her head trauma, if only it had started when she was thrown to the ground.

"It's wrong," Obell said, standing over Marion, but not looking at Marion. She had a hand over her mouth and she was shaking her head. "It wasn't supposed to be like this. None of this was supposed to happen."

Marion didn't respond. She was no longer in the mood to discuss Obell's thoughts and feelings. She was only interested in finding some way to get herself to that front door and back to her car.

An image of Winnie flashed in Marion's mind. She pictured her daughter wandering into that house and being attacked by Obell. She had no reason to believe that any of these images were based in reality. There was no evidence to suggest that Winnie had been in the house, but Marion couldn't know that for sure. For all she knew, Winnie had been there before her, leaving the front door open. Winnie could have been attacked and dragged off to some other place.

Marion shook off that thought. She couldn't allow herself to be incapacitated by irrational fears. She could not force herself to stay in that place on the off chance that Winnie had found it first.

She looked toward the door and then back to Obell. Obell was pacing in small circles next to Marion, but paying Marion no attention.

Marion tried to inch her way toward the door, hoping that she could make a little bit of progress before Obell noticed her attempt. Unfortunately, she did not get far.

Obell placed a foot on Marion's chest and applied enough weight to it to make Marion uncomfortable. She then bent down over Marion and looked her in the eyes. Everything in Marion's training taught her that people like Obell were *troubled*, but everything in her gut was screaming *evil*.

"Stop moving!" Obell screamed, spitting in Marion's face as she did so. "I need to think. I need to figure out what went wrong and how I can fix it."

Marion stopped moving. She looked up at Obell and tried her best to remain still. She did not wish to provoke any sort of reaction from Obell. Given her position at that moment, it would have been difficult for her to defend herself from an attack.

Obell stepped back and looked down at Marion, appearing stressed and frustrated. She said, "I should be able to make you bend to my will. It was so easy before. And now—I don't know if it's you or me or...it. Something isn't right. Do you feel that? Do you get the sense that things are off somehow?"

Marion pulled herself into a sitting position, holding her aching head. She looked at Obell, wondering how far she would be able to get before being stopped.

As Marion began to stand, she got her answer. Obell raised a hand and said, "Stop. Just sit."

Marion stopped where she was and sat on the floor. She kept her hand on her head, but did not take her eyes off of Obell.

"Did I do that? Or did you?" Obell asked.

Marion had no clue what she was talking about. She didn't answer, but Obell must have read the confusion in her expression, because she went on to ask, "Did I make you stop or did you? I should be able to command you. I should be able to make you do whatever I want."

"I know it seems that way. We all wish that we could make people do or say whatever we want them to, but life doesn't work like that, Obell. Life is about people making choices and sometimes we're the ones who pay for tho—"

"Stop talking."

Marion stopped talking. Obell was staring at her with a look of intensity that told her that if she continued to press, Obell might once again resort to violence. She would need to be mindful of herself and not allow her own emotions to interfere with her ability to focus on Obell. If she wanted to escape, she would need to find a way to manage Obell, at least long enough to keep her distracted while Marion made a break for it.

As Obell looked at Marion, she seemed intensely puzzled. She began to bite her thumbnail as she tried to figure out what to do next. She shook her head just slightly as she seemed to find her inner voice to be disagreeable.

After careful consideration, Obell said to Marion, "Stand up."

Marion wasn't sure that she wanted to. She imagined that Obell's next command would be to walk outside, where Obell could kill her without getting blood all over the already-dirty floor and walls. She wasn't sure how far she could allow Obell to control the situation before she went too far.

Then again, there was not much that Marion could do to save herself from a seated position, so she stood.

"At the kitchen table...Take a seat," Obell ordered.

Marion looked to the table and to the chairs that were placed around it. She didn't want to sit down. Sitting was usually followed by being tied up and gagged. Marion couldn't allow the situation to reach that point.

When Obell saw Marion hesitating, she rushed to Marion and grabbed her by the hair. Though Marion tried to pull away and fight back, Obell would not allow it. She pulled Marion across the room, to the kitchen table and pushed her toward a chair.

Obell leaned in close to Marion and said, "Sit."

Marion saw her opportunity. While Obell was close, Marion reached up and grabbed her neck. Using every ounce of strength that she could muster, Marion pushed Obell's head onto the table and pinned it there.

Obell's arms flailed through the air, trying to grab onto Marion or anything which might help her break free. Marion grabbed one of Obell's arms and twisted it behind her back.

"Stop!" Marion yelled. "Enough of this."

"You show yourself at last, enemy."

"I am not your enemy."

"I find your argument to be unconvincing."

"You attacked me."

"You broke into my home."

"Your door was open."

"Your camouflaged yourself as a normal person. Why would you do that if you didn't plan on attacking me?"

"I *am* a normal person."

"Liar."

"You're a normal person too, Obell."

"Liar!"

Obell threw a kick in Marion's direction, causing Marion to move out of the way. In doing so, her grip on Obell loosened just enough for Obell to twist free. Marion stepped back, trying to put space between herself and Obell, but Obell countered each of

Marion's steps with one of her own.

Marion prayed that she didn't trip over anything as she moved. She watched her peripheral vision to find something which she could grab and use as a weapon if she needed to. She hated everything about that moment—the violence, the fear, the helplessness—but she would not allow herself to be killed. She needed to find Winnie.

From the corner of her eye, Marion spotted an object. She reached for it and found her hand over what felt like an ashtray, which she picked up. It was heavy; maybe marble. Regardless of what it was or the material which was used to make this object, it would make a good weapon. That was all that mattered to Marion at that moment.

Obell looked at Marion's hand and laughed. She said, "You plan on bludgeoning me to death in my own home?"

"I don't want to."

"You don't realize the power that I have. Death means nothing to me anymore. I am its master."

"None of us are death's master, Obell. It creeps up on us. It surprises us when we least expect it," Marion said. "That's what happened to your child, isn't it? The same thing that happened to mine."

"I never had a child."

"Yes, you did."

"It was a trick! It was a game. You and your kind play games. You enjoy messing with our minds, but I'm too strong."

"You loved your baby. I can see it. You try to hide it, but I can see it in you still. You're a mother."

"I am nothing."

"You held that child in your arms and for the first time in your life, you felt what it was to have a family. You were loved."

Obell balled her fists and gritted her teeth. She was growing more and more upset by the moment, but Marion knew that the only way to get past this mess in front of her was to go through it.

"Were you married?" Marion asked. "Did you find someone who saw you for what you were and who loved you for it?"

Obell smiled a hateful smile and said, "People are disposable."

"What happened to him?"

Obell didn't answer that question at all. She looked to Marion's feet as her mind drifted to some other place and some other time.

"Is he alive?" Marion pressed.

Still, Obell remained silent. Marion could see something in her eyes that she hadn't seen before. There was not just anger anymore, but something else: Pain. Obell kept her eyes directed downward.

"You were right about me," Marion told Obell, and Obell's eyes shot up to meet hers. "I'm not the person that I want people to think I am. I put on this act and pretend that I know how this all turns out. I hide what's inside of me, so nobody else will have to deal with it. So they can't see..."

Obell cocked her head just slightly and in a soft voice asked, "See what?"

Marion hesitated. She didn't want to say it out loud. She never wanted anyone to hear it. She had tried her best to ignore it herself for so long, but when she looked at Obell, she saw what she could so easily become.

"One year ago, my daughter Cindy was killed. On that day, Death came into my home. He's been there ever since, and none of us had the nerve to kick him out," Marion told Obell, feeling her grip on the heavy object in her hand loosening. "The truth is, when someone dies like that, there is a hole inside of you and it hurts. And if you try to sew up that hole, it just hurts more, so you let it fester. It grows. It devours you. And Death... After a while, he doesn't just live *around* you anymore. He lives *inside* of you; inside of that hole. Everything you are is defined by him—everything you feel. Suddenly, you didn't just lose one person anymore; you've lost everyone. You're alone. You're weak. You're scared. And you're desperate for it all to just be over."

50

For the first time in a long time, Winnie felt as though she was moving toward something. Even though she didn't know what that thing was, she could feel that there was significance to that night.

She was tired. Physically, she wanted to curl up and go to sleep —It was late after all. But there was a more profound fatigue inside of her. She was tired of everything that her world had become since Cindy died. She was tired of being angry. She was tired of being alone. Only now, she was neither of those things.

The mysterious stranger was not much of a talker. He barely acknowledged her existence, but she was not angry with him. She hadn't screamed at him or stormed away in a fit of rage. There was something oddly calming about walking with a guy who didn't ask her annoying questions about her feelings or her family or what she wanted for dinner.

The mysterious stranger never turned around to look at where he had been. He only moved forward, never stopping to think about which path he wanted to take. Either he knew exactly where he wanted to go, or he didn't care. Either way, Winnie wanted to be there with him when he finally stopped walking.

She was freezing now. Her clothes were soaking wet and clinging to her body. The stranger had dried off rather quickly, but then again, he was not burdened by such silly things as clothing and modesty.

Her teeth were chattering, which she would have found comedic if it had been anyone else, but she saw little humor in her own discomfort. She could not recall her teeth ever chattering like that before. In fact, the only time she could remember seeing it happen was in cartoons. She normally had the good sense to cover herself up before leaving the house on a cold night, so chattering teeth had never really been an issue.

The stranger seemed fine; no shivering or chattering. She couldn't see his breath when he exhaled... Probably because he didn't have any breath in the first place. Somehow that thought never grew old with her. The idea of never breathing and having no heart beating inside a person's chest seemed almost peaceful. She had never considered it before, but she now realized that people spent their entire lives struggling to exist. Their hearts never stopped struggling to pump blood. Their lungs never stopped struggling for air. Every second of every day was an uphill battle. The stranger didn't have that burden.

At first, she was put off by the idea of a dead guy walking around the woods, but after a while, she began to find the whole situation oddly intriguing. The *how* and *why* of the night may never be understood by her, but Winnie was enthralled by the oddity of it. There was an energy to the air that night which was not quite right. Whether this was good or bad, she didn't know.

However it turned out, Winnie felt that this was a night when anything could happen and she desperately needed for *something* to happen. She needed for her life to move in one direction or another, because standing still was not working for her anymore.

Her mind was a million miles away and Winnie was not paying as much attention to the path in front of her as she probably should have been, especially after the incident at the river. She did not see the road in front of her as she approached it. She did not realize that it was there until she and the stranger were standing in the middle of it.

When she saw where she was, Winnie stopped walking. The stranger turned and began to follow the road, but for a moment, she did not follow him.

Winnie looked around the area, for people or cars, or any sign that anyone was around. She knew this road. It was one of the main roads to and from her town, and during the day it was a road which people used quite a often. She didn't know how any of those people would react to seeing a naked zombie walking down the street in the middle of the night, but she couldn't imagine it going over well.

Fortunately, it was the middle of the night. Traffic was not as much of a concern at that hour. At most, there would be a few cars, and if she tried very hard, she could dare to hope that none of those cars would happen by for as long as she and the stranger were walking.

She watched as the stranger stepped beneath a yellow street light. Somehow, she had come to believe that the blue hue of his skin was caused by the moonlight and the darkness of the woods. She saw now that this was not the case. The stranger was the color that any corpse would be, no matter what lighting he happened to find himself in.

He did not care about the light. He did not care about traffic. The stranger kept walking as though he was still hidden by the trees.

Winnie hurried to catch up to him. As she rejoined him, she said, "Wait a minute."

He did not respond to her at all. She put a hand on his arm and stopped him. For a moment, he looked into the distance as though he didn't notice her even as she forced herself to be seen. She could feel annoyance building inside of her and knew that if that annoyance went unchecked, it would turn into anger. Fortunately for them both, he turned and looked at her before she lost control of herself. His eyes seemed to grow more metallic and less human as the night wore on. They were like mirrors, and she imagined that if she looked at just the right angle, she would be able to count the stars in their reflections.

The annoyance faded.

"Don't you think that we should stick to the woods?" she asked him. "I mean, you're not exactly dressed for company."

She didn't know why she expected him to respond to her in some way. When he made no effort to show that he was listening to her, she looked around the area again, knowing that someone could drive past them at any moment.

"Do you even know where you're going?" she asked. Still, he didn't answer. Despite that fact, Winnie got the impression that the stranger did know where he was going. She suspected that he had walked to that road on purpose.

She stepped back and let go of his arm. If he was determined to walk down a public road in his condition, she probably couldn't do anything to stop it.

He began to walk. His pace was as steady as ever. His focus remained straight ahead. There was not even a hint of consideration for Winnie's concern.

She watched him walk, but remained where she was. If she went with him, she would be connected to him. If someone decided to call for torches and pitchforks, she would be drawn into that showdown.

It wasn't that Winnie didn't want to see the situation through. She wanted to see wherever it was that he was heading. She had no thought of turning around and going home, because as chilly as she was out there, she normally found her home to be even colder.

Her concern was with how they would proceed. It was one thing for her to walk side by side with a zombie in the middle of the woods, but to walk with him on a road was something else entirely. He was a thing that should not be, and if she went with him, that was how people would see her.

She turned around and looked in the direction opposite the stranger. If she started walking, she could be home within an hour. She knew the way. She knew all of the twists and turns, and could see all of it in her mind. She could also see her parents' faces, looking at her with disdain. She could see Tami and her fellow partiers, having a blast and screaming obscenities to Winnie as they drove past her.

That road looked dark an ominous to her. It scared her.

Winnie turned around and looked toward the stranger once again. In that direction, there were lights. She didn't know where he was going or who would be waiting there.

She chose to follow the stranger. She walked away from what she knew and all that was familiar. She went with him because, of all of the people she had spoken to over the previous year, he was the one that she felt the most at peace with. With him, she felt as though she belonged.

As she joined him, Winnie said nothing. She did not look at him or take his hand. She simply followed him down the road.

51

Mark stood on the edge of the cliff, staring out at the world that was displayed before him. It was dark and cold. He imagined that most of the people who lived out there were fast asleep in their nice warm beds while he wandered through the night.

His GPS had led him to a road which was hidden in a heavily wooded part of town. He didn't remember knowing of this road before, but given the fact that it was in a part of town that he did not regularly travel and led nowhere that the main roads could not take him, he was not surprised by this. There must have been a hundred similar roads, just waiting to be discovered.

He could only go so far by car. Once the map on his cell phone told him where the best place the park would be, he stopped his car and finished the journey on foot. The roads were dark and creepy, but he was used to that sort of place. He'd spent years wandering through old buildings and dark woods in his off hours. He would not go so far as to say that he found them peaceful, but he was not scared off by them.

The woods smelled strange on that night. The smell of a rotting carcass hung heavy in the air and mixed with the fallen leaves to create a distinctly repulsive odor. The combination lingered in his nose long after he had moved away from whatever animal had died.

Finding the cliff wasn't hard. His cell phone led him directly to the right spot, with the only danger coming from his staring at the phone's screen more than he did the path in front of him. He allowed it to lead him without question, as though it would warn him of fallen branches or other obstacles.

Fortunately, he did not walk straight off the cliff. To do so would have been quite embarrassing for him, and perhaps even more so for his family.

As he walked out onto the cliff, he slipped his cell phone back into his pocket. He stood in silence, without any audio recorders or video cameras, just looking and feeling what that area had to offer. Honestly, he had no idea why he was there. He had no idea why Warren would draw a picture and lead him to a cliff that Cindy had probably never even heard of.

He could picture her there, looking out over the horizon. Either dead or alive, it didn't matter; she would find the view beautiful.

She might sit and do her homework there or write in her journal. She might simply allow her mind to wander as she gazed across the land below and imagined all of the lives which were being lived inside of every one of those houses.

Mark stopped himself, realizing that he was writing stories in his mind about the life that Cindy might have lived, if only she'd had the chance. It was crazy. He couldn't allow for his investigation to boil down to flights of fancy. He needed to be professional and scientific, or else he risked becoming the type of investigator that he made fun of—the type who relied on feelings and unspecified sixth senses as their evidence of the paranormal, rather than solid facts. After that, it was a slippery slope toward photographs of mysterious orbs, and he hated orb photography.

He allowed himself to stand on that cliff, waiting for something to occur to him that would put that place into perspective. He wanted it, but he just could not see it.

Though the world was glowing with moonlight, it seemed darker than it should rightly be to Mark. It was like a haze was hanging over the town below, but it wasn't a haze. It wasn't fog or clouds. He couldn't explain it.

He stared at the scenery, studying every detail in the hopes of making sense of Warren's drawing. He had no doubt that this was the right place, he just could not understand why.

Mark closed his eyes and allowed the cool night air to wash over him. He breathed deeply, trying to settle his mind and relax. He thought that he might be looking too closely; that perhaps this place was meant to be absorbed in some other way.

Or, he could have been too late to make sense of this place. The pictures were out of order. Whatever he was meant to see there could have come and gone by then, or could be delayed until after he understood the relevance of the other two drawings. The house and the building could provide him with the proper context with which to take in the cliff.

He was over-thinking.

Opening his eyes, Mark pulled an audio recorder from his pocket, turned it on, recorded his usual opening for an investigation file and placed the recorder on a nearby rock.

"Is there anyone here with me?" he asked.

As he gave the spirits time to answer, Mark looked around the area where he stood. He had spent so much time looking into the distance that he didn't stop to look at what was right in front of him.

He asked another question, "What is your name?"

The dirt around the cliff was disturbed. From the looks of things, it had been disturbed recently. There were two distinct sets of foot and handprints. One of these was from a barefooted person; male, from the looks of it. The other print was from a girl, judging from the size of the shoe. He could tell from the diamond pattern that the prints were made by a pair of Converse sneakers.

Winnie had the same brand of sneaker, so they were easy to identify.

"Why are you here?" he asked.

Judging from the disturbed dirt, there were a couple of possible scenarios that had played out near the cliff. Either someone had almost fallen off the cliff, or a couple of senseless kids had gone out to the cliff for some privacy and a good time. Since saving someone from falling off a cliff didn't normally involve taking off one's shoes, he suspected the latter of these two options to be the case.

"How did you die?"

Suddenly, he didn't want to know if Cindy had ever gone out to that cliff. If it was the place where kids went to grope each other, he did not need that mental image of his little girl running through his head.

He decided that someone had almost fallen off the cliff. At least then he wouldn't have to worry about his daughter being reckless and irresponsible.

Mark looked back to the audio recorder and asked, "Are you okay?"

It was the one question that he needed answered the most, if Cindy's spirit was lingering at that spot for some reason.

He couldn't stop staring at the recorder, as though he expected it to respond to him right then and there.

"I miss you," he said to it. He could feel the tingling in his nose that always accompanied the tears in his eyes.

Cindy would have loved that place. She would have loved that it was so hidden. She would have loved that it was quiet, and she could see so much of the world. She would love having a place where she could sit and think. She would play with the sleeves on her shirt, tugging them without even noticing it, as she often did when her mind wandered. She would plot and plan for the future, because she loved the possibility of it all.

Memories were not the same as having her there. They were painful when they popped into his head unexpectedly, and he had spent so much time trying not to think of them that he had nearly forgotten many of those little details that were now flooding his mind.

"I have tried so hard to find you. I have tried so hard to make sure that you're okay," he told the recorder. "I don't know what else to do. I don't know where else to look."

He turned away from the recorder and wiped the tears from his eyes. He took a deep breath and stared out into the distance once again. For some reason, the memory of taking his family on a trip to New York flashed through his mind. He remembered picking Cindy up when she was four years old and holding her as they looked out across the city from the top of the Empire State Building. She was scared of falling, and while he knew that she would be fine, he found himself holding her extra tight, just because he could.

"This isn't right. This isn't how things are supposed to be. I'm not supposed to be looking for the ghost of my dead daughter. I'm supposed to be taking pictures of you in your prom dress. I'm supposed to be intimidating your boyfriends. You're not supposed to—" he couldn't finish that sentence before the lump in his throat stopped him.

He waited for a moment, out of habit. He was used to giving spirits time to respond.

"I don't know where to go next. I don't know what the other pictures mean. I don't know what any of this has to do with you," he said. "I don't know anything anymore."

He wanted to sit down, but he fought the urge. If he sat, any energy that he had left in him would drain away and he would fall asleep. He may have needed sleep, but he didn't want it; not yet.

The view was beautiful. He imagined how it would look at sunset and he could imagine Cindy taking in that view. She would have loved it there, but he knew in his gut that she wasn't there with him in that moment. He would have felt something if she was close, but he felt just as empty and alone as he had felt for months.

"I love you, my baby girl," he said, with more tears falling down his cheek.

When they walked back inside of the Empire State Building, that little girl wanted to be free. She wanted to run around and look at the gift shop. He didn't want to let her go, but he knew that if he didn't, she would scream and kick. So, he gave her three quick kisses on the cheek and he set her down.

He turned away from the cliff and grabbed his recorder. After stopping the recording, he looked down at it. He stared at that recorder for several seconds, allowing his thumb to lightly move over the buttons. Finally, he allowed himself to press one button: *Delete.*

Cindy wasn't there. She was not at the cemetery. She was not at home. It had taken Mark a year, but as he stood on that cliff and looked out over the world, he found himself doing what he never could before. He said goodbye.

As he started to walk away from that cliff, the haze that seemed to cover the world pulled back.

Tami's words echoed in his head, telling him that he had been wandering in the darkness, looking for Cindy. She was right. He had fought against Cindy being dead for so long that any creature or monster that he could find would make him feel closer to her, and that wasn't fair to anyone. Cindy was at rest; for that he was thankful.

He didn't know where he would go next or what he planned to do about the pictures that Warren had drawn for him. He didn't know if they mattered anymore. He had found what he was looking for and all he needed at that point was to go home and sleep.

He made his way through the woods and back to his car, putting the cliff behind him. Just as he began to drive away, Mark spotted a light in the woods, on the other side of the road.

As he drove past this light, he caught a glimpse of a small house. It looked an awful lot like the picture that Warren had drawn for him.

52

Tami drove straight home after leaving the cemetery. After everything that happened, she would have been happy to go back to her normal world and pretend that the night had never happened, but it wasn't quite that easy. The world looked different to her. She'd left that house without her parents knowing, because she was headed to a top secret party where she planned to dance, drink and make merry like any normal teenager would. Instead, she found herself alienated from her classmates and in the aftermath of that social downfall, Tami witnessed true darkness.

She sat in her driveway with the engine turned off, staring straight ahead at her mother's car, which was parked directly in front of her. Her father's was off to the side. They were both home. She could go inside and wake them up and she knew that as crazy as she would undoubtedly sound, her family would be there for her. She knew that not everyone was so lucky and she hated the fact that she could do nothing to help the people who had been like family to her for as long as she could remember.

The night was cold. The world was dark. She saw that darkness inside of Mr. McKeller. It was a part of him now; a part of all of them. Until she saw that darkness face to face, she couldn't have possibly identified it inside of people. After it came for her, she saw it everywhere. It was overwhelming and scary, and she had no idea what she was supposed to do with this revelation.

She left him there. As soon as she had pulled away from the cemetery, she regretted it. She wondered if she had done the right thing. She wanted to go back, or to call his family and tell them, but what could they do? What could anyone do? If he was determined to chase the darkness, she would have been a fool to follow him.

At least, that was what she told herself.

Tami was clutching Cindy's cross, which hung around her neck, nervously running her thumb over its edges as she sat there, trying to find the nerve to walk from her car to the house.

In all honesty, she didn't think that it made much of a difference if she was outside or in the car. The shadows—or whatever lived within the shadows—could be anywhere. The car made her *feel* safe and protected. There was no wind blowing her hair, forcing her to relive the touch of the unseen thing in the cemetery; there was only silence and calm. It was entirely misleading, but comforting nonetheless.

She took a deep breath, trying to build up enough nerve to open the door and step out of the car. She closed her eyes and tightened her grip on the cross as she silently counted down from five, planning to open the door and force herself out once she reached zero, but the plan failed. She remained in the car.

While silently cursing her own weakness, she prayed for help. She prayed for the strength to take action. She prayed for someone to find her and somehow put an end to that horrible night once and for all. She prayed for the sake of praying, which was becoming a habit with her. If anyone at school found out, she'd be a laughingstock. She'd be forced to eat lunch with the Bible Club and plan pancake breakfasts for charity.

"C'mon, Tami," she urged herself in a half-whisper. "Stop being such a wuss and get out of the damn car. Just like last time and the time before that. There's nothing out there tonight that hasn't been out there every other night."

Even as she said it she could hear her own voice inside of her head, calling her a liar. She knew that something *was* different. Whatever balance existed out there was thrown off. She saw things that she should never have seen.

As she argued with herself, both out loud and inside of her mind, she found herself suddenly interrupted by a thought that seemed louder and more pressing than all of the others. It was one word: *Go!*

Without hesitation, she opened the door and stepped out of the car. She wasn't quite sure if the thought had come from herself or from some other place, but everything inside of her compelled her to listen to it.

As she closed the door behind her, Tami stood in the driveway and looked across the lawn in front of her house. Each tree cast a shadow; each bush and blade of grass. The shadows were everywhere, but she didn't see any of them moving—Not at first.

She knew that she should have run for the door as soon as her feet touched the ground, but she didn't. She stood there, waiting and watching, knowing that it would be coming.

There was a feeling on the top of her ear, as though someone's finger was lightly touching her. The feeling moved downward, until it reached her jawline and then it stopped.

She could barely breathe. The feel of that touch made her want to shed her skin, but she didn't move.

From the corner of her eye, Tami saw that familiar shadow which seemed to dash across her neighbor's lawn, keeping low but running fast. She turned to see the shadow, but it was gone by the time she could focus her vision.

Tami didn't walk toward her front door. Instead, she walked to the center of the lawn. She knew she was crazy. She knew that any normal person would run for their lives, but she didn't think about her fear. For some odd reason, the only thought that ran through her mind was the memory of Cindy's funeral.

During the day, the cemetery was beautiful and peaceful. Though usually well kept, the grass in the cemetery was longer on the day of the funeral. As Tami listened to the minister, she watched deer grazing not too far away. She watched them until the groundskeeper shooed them off.

There was something slightly whimsical about the cemetery on the day of Tami's funeral. The way the light hit the grass and the deer, and the shadows of the headstones on the ground made the place look like something out of a fantasy.

As Tami made her way into the center of her front lawn, she held onto that memory so tightly that she could almost hear the minister's voice as he spoke over Cindy's coffin. She could almost smell the flowers.

In the car, Tami had been gripping Cindy's cross so tightly that even as she stood in the lawn, she could feel the edges of the cross in her palm. She balled her fist, holding that phantom cross as tightly as she had the real thing.

She could see the shadows beginning to shift in the grass near her feet and her heart began to pound in her chest. There was a very strong urge to run into the house and scream for her parents, but that same voice inside of her, which had urged her to get out of the car, was now telling her to remain calm. The thought of standing there and allowing the shadows to twist and stir all around her sent a chill through the core of her being, but she held her ground. Somehow, she knew that she had to.

She could feel something gently touching her right leg. At first, it flicked the bottom of her pant leg, almost playfully. The flick then became a gentle tug. When she didn't run screaming, the tug became a steady movement up her calf before the touch finally went away.

She wanted to throw up.

Tami closed her eyes tightly, not wanting to see the shadows any longer. She conjured the image of that sunny day at the cemetery and she held that image almost as firmly as she gripped the phantom cross. It was peaceful and calm. The minister's voice was soothing. The shadows were present on that day, but they did not consume her. She did not allow them inside.

She felt her hair moving across her face, as it had in the cemetery. There was a sensation near her ear, which felt almost like someone exhaling with their lips nearly touching her, but there was no breath.

It wanted to scare her. It wanted to defeat her and claim her as its prize. She wanted to run, but that voice inside of her would not allow it. The more this unseen thing pressed her, the stronger that power inside of her became.

She felt something touch the small of her back, and the urge inside of her shifted. She didn't want to run any longer. She was done running. From the shadows. From the kids at school. From herself.

"Enough," she said as her eyes shot open.

She saw the shadows moving all around her, waiting for her to break. She did not give them the pleasure. Instead of collapsing, she stood tall. Instead of retreating, she stepped forward.

The shadows parted before her.

"Leave," she demanded, in a tone less threatening than it was blunt; as though she were talking to a house guest who had overstayed their welcome.

The shadows danced and twisted along the ground for a moment, as though challenging Tami. She, in response, took another step forward and said, "Now."

At her command, the shadows bolted. They seemed to move between the blades of grass as they pulled away from Tami.

She took in the sight of the shadows obeying her and she couldn't help but grin just slightly. She was the boss of them. Those shadow-things were creatures of the dark, usually hiding and creeping in unseen, preying on the weak and vulnerable. Tami was neither of those things. They could taunt her and touch her and try their best to break her down, but for as long as she refused to let them in, they could not harm her.

The memory of Cindy's funeral remained heavy in her mind, and the sound of the minister's reciting of the twenty-third Psalm.

53

"Were you married? Did you find someone who saw you for what you were and who loved you for it?" Marion asked, and Obell couldn't believe the nerve.

She had been going back and forth all night, trying to decide why this woman had come into her home and who had sent her. There were times when the woman's story was almost believable. The way she spoke was not outright threatening, but her comments could often be read in different ways.

The reference to the man who had cast his spell on Obell, causing her to lower her guard and to be taken in by petty, irrational emotion was a dead giveaway. How would this stranger possibly know about him, unless he had been the one to send her in the first place? He had tried poison, and that didn't work. He had tried sending his henchmen after her, with no success. Once she saw through his act, she was no longer a victim of his power.

"People are disposable," Obell replied, with a tone that she hoped would convey both disinterest in her enemy, and a threat toward the woman who had been sent to weaken her once again.

Marion was holding onto a granite ashtray. Though Obell didn't smoke, she kept the ashtray around for the burning of incense, spell scrolls and insects.

"What happened to him?" Marion asked with that sickly sweet tone.

Marion. Marion. Obell repeated the woman's name in her head over and over again. To know someone's name gave a witch power over them.

It was genius; sending a soother, rather than a warrior. In self-defense, a person with Obell's power would lash out and use that power. The only way to weaken them was through manipulation. Marion's form of casting spells was not through chants and theatrics. Her spells were crafted into penetrating dialogue.

Obell's eyes drifted toward the floor as she remembered how she had been attacked before. How her enemy had come into her life, appearing to be a normal man. He claimed to love her, but it was a lie. He preyed on her weakness, giving her the family that she never had growing up, and then that family was taken. First the child—or the projection of a child—was taken from her. Obell had come to the conclusion that it had all been fake. It had to be fake.

Once she was broken by the loss of that child, her enemy tried his best to poison her. He called those capsules *medicine*, but she knew better. And when she refused to buy into his games any longer, he tried to take her down by force.

Her world was full of enemies, living amongst the irrelevant human beings who knew little of the monsters that passed them on the street every day.

Marion spoke again, asking, "Is he alive?"

Obell hated this woman. She wanted her to leave, so that she could try to do the thing that she had set out to do that night. She was so close to controlling Death, and when that happened, there would be no stopping her. She would be more powerful than the most dangerous enemy of all time.

Yet, her spell had gone wrong. It wasn't right. It was something which she never intended to create. She didn't know why. He stood and walked, which is what she was hoping for, yet when she looked into his eyes, she could see that they lacked something vital. The sight of him sent a chill up her spine, and this was not an easy thing to do. She just couldn't explain *why* she felt this way.

Because it's not natural, whispered a voice in her head. *Because you're not meant to control Death. Because at your core, you're just a person. There are no such things as monsters.*

Obell shook off those words. She ignored that voice, which spewed lies to her on a daily basis. It was a mind trick, implanted by her enemy when she was at her weakest.

"You were right about me," Marion admitted at last.

Obell coolly looked up at her and listened to what she had to say.

Marion continued, "I'm not the person that I want people to think I am. I put on this act and pretend that I know how this all turns out. I hide what's inside of me, so nobody else will have to deal with it. So they can't see..."

Obell knew it! She was right. She knew that the creature lurked just beneath the middle-class exterior; behind the soothing voice. Oh, she had had her doubts. For a moment or two, she could have believed that this woman was just a woman. But now, she knew better. She just didn't know *exactly* what this woman was.

Obell cocked her head just slightly and in a soft voice asked, "See what?"

The woman's eyes met Obell's and at first they seemed to be nothing special. They were the eyes of a human woman, filled with pain and anger. But Obell saw something else flash through those eyes. Just as she had seen a shadow from the corner of her eyes earlier in the night, she saw it dart across Marion's pupil now. It was inside of her.

Marion seemed to notice something to her side and glanced to her left, just for a moment before turning back to Obell.

Obell listened as the Marion said, "One year ago, my daughter Cindy was killed. On that day, Death came into my home. He's been there ever since, and none of us had the nerve to kick him out. The truth is, when someone dies like that, there is a hole inside of you and it hurts. And if you try to sew up that hole, it just hurts more, so you let it fester. It grows. It devours you. And Death...After a while, he doesn't just live around you anymore. He lives inside of you; inside of that hole. Everything you are is defined by him—everything you feel. Suddenly, you didn't just lose one person anymore. You've lost everyone. You're alone. You're weak. You're scared. And you're desperate for it all to just be over."

A tear fell down the Marion's cheek. It was as black as oil and dripped down onto her shirt.

Obell was surprised to see this black tear, and caught herself gasping. She blinked, and when she opened her eyes, Marion was wiping this tear away. It was now as clear as any normal tear would be.

She didn't know if what she had seen was an illusion or a trick. She didn't know what it meant.

Marion looked around the room and squinted her eyes as though the lights had suddenly become brighter. Obell's interest was piqued by the woman. She wondered if Marion knew about her black tear. She wondered if Marion had accidentally shown her hand.

Obell walked toward Marion, staring her directly in the eyes. She was waiting for the next sign of that beast within the woman and while she did not see that shadow passing through Marion's eyes, she would not allow herself to be lulled into a false sense of security. This woman was a beast, like Obell herself, but far more foolish. She was an underling; a servant of Obell's enemy.

Or, whispered that voice inside of Obell's head, *she is just a mother who lost a child.*

Obell shook her head in response to that stray thought. She would not allow herself to be fooled.

Marion tried to back away from Obell, but Obell would not allow it. Marion backed herself into a small table and as she tried to correct herself and move around it, Obell rushed toward her.

"I see the thing inside of you!" Obell screamed, happy to tell the woman that she knew exactly what she was. "I see the black tears. I see the lies in your words."

"There is nothing inside of me," Marion replied, weak and pathetic as she was.

"Death is inside of you! You said it yourself."

As Obell got closer, Marion attacked her, swinging the ashtray as hard as she could, hoping to smash Obell's skull. Obell was expecting this attack and managed to grab Marion's arm before it was too late. She twisted it, and the ashtray dropped to the ground, taking a chunk out of the hardwood floor.

"I was using a metaphor," Marion insisted, wincing in pain as Obell twisted her arm harder and pushed her backward.

Obell shook her head, not buying into the woman's story as she said, "I see the Death in your eyes. I know why you're here. You want my power. You know what I've done and you want it back."

"I want what?"

"I've unleashed it. I didn't even mean to do it, but I set it free. That's why it could walk, isn't it?"

"Why *what* could walk?"

"The corpse!"

Marion looked at Obell as though she were crazy, but Obell knew better than to believe that this woman had no idea what she was talking about. There was a reason why she showed up on this night, of all nights.

As Obell pushed Marion and held firmly onto her arm, Marion stumbled and fell to one knee.

"Fight back," Obell insisted. "I know you want to."

"You're hurting me. Please, stop," Marion cried.

"Make me stop. Make me end the pain."

"I can't make you."

Obell twisted Marion's arm so hard that she thought it would break.

Marion screamed.

54

Marion's eyes were closed as Obell twisted her arm and the pain shot through her body.

Obell was crazy. There was no other way of looking at it and no professional way to avoid using the word. She needed help. She needed to be institutionalized. She was a danger, not only to other people, but to herself.

Of course, none of this was Marion's primary concern. In that moment, all she could think about was the pain that she felt in her arm and the fact that she was incapable of fighting back. She hated the helplessness of her situation. She hated her inability to end the pain. She hated the fact that no part of her fate was in her own hands at that moment. She was alone—or so she thought.

"No!" came the voice of a man, so familiar, yet not. It was a panicked, guttural yell.

The twisting ended. The pain began to fade. When Marion opened her eyes, she saw Mark pulling Obell away from her. She was struggling to break free of his grip, screaming as she swatted his arms until she finally pulled herself away. As she broke free, Obell stumbled over the ashtray that had fallen to the ground earlier. She fell, hitting her head on the corner of the kitchen table and didn't get back up. She didn't move at all.

Mark raised a hand to his mouth as he looked down to Obell, wondering what just happened and looking terrified at the thought that he might have killed someone. His eyes then shifted toward Marion and they looked at each other for a moment, as though neither quite believed what was happening.

"She was attacking you," Mark explained, as he bent down to check Obell's pulse. "I didn't have a choice."

Having found Obell's pulse, Mark stood and looked back to Marion. He didn't seem to know that to do or say next.

"I know," Marion replied.

She stood up and found her eyes filling with tears as she wrapped her arms around her husband. She allowed herself to cry as he held her and gently brushed his hand through her hair. They stood silently for a moment, holding onto each other in a way that they hadn't since Cindy died.

Finally, Mark spoke. He asked her, "Did she say that she made a corpse walk?"

Marion couldn't help but laugh. It was not funny, but her night was so absurd that she could think of no other way to react to her situation.

"She needs help," Marion assured him.

"Yeah, but...Do you think she did?"

Marion pulled away from Mark and looked him in the eyes to see whether or not he was joking. She thought that he surely had to be, but his expression was serious.

"You wouldn't believe the night I've had," he told her. "I'm talking about remote viewers and shadows attacking Tami..."

Marion took a step backward and looked at Mark like he might have been dipping into Obell's liquor cabinet. Still, there was something about the night that she'd spent with a witch that made it all seem strangely possible, and thinking back on it, she could have sworn that she had seen a shadow or two herself.

"Is she okay?" Marion asked.

"She's fine. I sent her home," Mark replied and then looked around the room. A troubled expression came over him as he asked her, "Where's Winnie?"

"I can't find her. I was looking for her and I... We have to find her."

In that moment, both Marion and Mark knew that they needed to find their daughter. As bizarre as the night had been for both of them, nothing could overpower the sense of urgency that they felt in regards to Winnie.

They hurried for the door and toward their cars. As they rushed, Mark asked, "You don't think there's really a corpse out there, do you?"

"Now's not a good time to ask me what I believe," Marion replied.

She started to move toward her own car, but Mark stopped her, saying "Wait. I think I have an idea about where to find her."

He ran to his own car and opened the passenger-side door. From it, he pulled a stack of papers and began to fish through them. Marion joined him and looked at the papers. They were rough sketches, each depicting a different location. Their home, Cindy's grave, Obell's house, a cliff...

"That remote viewer I mentioned—Warren Oster—drew these earlier tonight," Mark said.

"How could he have known? I mean, our house, I understand. But Obell's house?"

"Obell?"

"The woman you hit," Marion said, looking back toward the house. "We should call someone. We need to get help."

"We will. After we get out of here," Mark replied.

He pulled one last picture from the stack and showed it to Marion.

"It looks familiar, but I don't know what it is," he said.

When Marion looked at the picture and studied the structure, it did not take long for her to recognize the building. It was the last place on Earth where she wanted to find Winnie, but she knew exactly where they had to go.

55

As they walked down the road together, Winnie could no longer manage to let her mind wander. She found herself constantly scanning the area for any sign of people or the headlights of an approaching car.

The mysterious stranger didn't seem concerned with any of those things. He walked at a steady pace, never hesitating for a moment. His feet made slapping sounds on the pavement with each step that he took. The sound was not very loud, but Winnie was certain that someone would hear them from inside one of the buildings along the way. She was sure that she would have to explain why she was walking down the road with a naked dead guy.

She tried planning her explanation, but there didn't seem to be an angle at which to approach the subject without her sounding insane and stupid. She didn't *feel* stupid, but there was no logic to what she was doing. Every ounce of reason that she possessed was telling her that this was not a good idea, and yet she could not deny the feeling that she was meant to be there. She and the stranger had some unexplainable connection.

He had to feel it too, even though he showed no sign of feeling anything. He waited for her in the woods and pulled her off of that cliff. He saved her from the coyote attack.

As they rounded a curve in the road, Winnie saw lights. Her first instinct was to grab the stranger's arm and prepare to pull him off the side of the road, where they could take cover in a ditch. Before she could do this, she realized that those lights weren't moving. They were the lights of a building in the distance.

She knew this road. She should have been able to identify that building without any problem, but it was the middle of the night and she was on foot; this was not how she normally saw these surroundings. She needed to find a landmark. She needed something which would tell her exactly where she was.

As she stared at that building up ahead, she spotted more lights. These were red, flashing lights. At first, she only saw the light bouncing off the side of a wall, but she soon saw where they were coming from. An ambulance was pulling up to the building.

It was a hospital.

That realization brought her surroundings into focus. She knew this place. She had been to that hospital a few times. Now, it made sense.

The stranger was leading her there. He was a guy who had come back from the dead. His feet were injured. He had fallen into freezing cold waters and didn't have a shred of clothing to protect him from that cold—not that clothing was helping Winnie all that much either.

She stopped walking and asked him, "You do feel it, don't you? You're hurt?"

The stranger didn't stop walking. She couldn't blame him for wanting to get to the hospital as quickly as possible, so she hurried to catch up and keep pace with him.

"I'm sorry. I thought you couldn't feel it. Y'know, cause you're dead," Winnie told him, feeling stupid just hearing those words. "You are dead, right? Maybe I took your pulse wrong."

She put her fingers to the stranger's neck to feel for a pulse, but he did not slow down enough for her to get a proper feel. His walking caused her fingers to bounce up and down on his cold flesh.

Winnie pulled her hand back and walked next to her strange friend, feeling suddenly more awkward than she had at any other point in that night. She stopped walking.

"I can't believe I was so stupid," she told him, pulling out her cell phone, which was unfortunately still not working. "I can't call for help. I should have tried. I should have done something to help you."

The stranger stopped walking and turned around, looking at

Winnie with those metallic eyes of his. He stood in that spot for about five seconds before turning away and resuming his walk.

Winnie took this to mean that he wanted her to walk with him. For some reason, he wanted her to be there when he got to the hospital. She began walking.

After remaining on the road for two or three more minutes, they were getting close to the hospital's main entrance, but the stranger did not walk toward it. Instead, he turned and walked off the side of the road. Winnie followed him, but she was confused. She could see the emergency room from that spot, and he was not walking in that direction.

"Where are you going?" she asked. "The ER's that way."

She tried to grab his arm and pull him toward the emergency room, but he would not allow for his heading to be changed. He knew where he was going, even if she did not.

As they walked through the field which surrounded the hospital, Winnie kept her eyes peeled for some clue as to where he could be going. She didn't know why she trusted in his instinct, but she could feel that he knew what he was doing. Still, she only had to wonder why he wanted her there, if it wasn't to have someone holding his hand in the emergency room.

She could have asked where they were going—again—but she knew that doing so would be useless. He did not speak. She didn't even know if he could.

Winnie followed him through the field, just as she had followed him through the woods and down the road. She stayed by his side, with no idea who he was, where he came from, or where he was going. She was not ordinarily a creature of great faith, but some part of her was just as compelled to walk as he was.

He turned once again. This time, he walked toward a patch of trees which stood between the two of them and the hospital. Winnie kept pace, more curious than ever to see where they were going.

"Are you a patient?" she asked him. "Did you run away? Is that why you don't have clothes? I mean, there are those gowns, but they're kinda pointless and you could have—You know what? I'm just going to shut my mouth now and let you do your thing."

In response, he walked.

Their path led them through that patch of trees, which had thick weeds and grass growing between them. While the mysterious stranger seemed to make his way through that patch with ease and grace, Winnie stumbled more than once and nearly fell on her face.

When she emerged from the patch of trees, she found herself stepping into the hospital parking lot, looking directly ahead at the stranger's destination.

It seemed so obvious to her, once she knew where they were going. It was the only place for a person like him to go, since he didn't seem to have any interest in killing people or eating their brains.

The stranger walked toward the automatic doors which led inside. He was on the last leg of his journey.

Winnie made it as far as one of the stone pillars which held the roof of the covered driveway. Once she reached that pillar, Winnie froze. She could not bring herself to take another step, and she suddenly felt much colder than she had before.

From the corner of her eye, Winnie could have sworn that she saw a shadow move across the driveway. It could have been a person, coming to see what she and the stranger were doing there. It could have been another coyote that wanted to attack her. She didn't turn to see what it was. She could not take her eyes off of the sign above the door, which read: *MORGUE.*

It was such a simple word, but so very loaded. All at once, it piqued a hint of curiosity and scared the living crap out of her.

As the mysterious stranger neared the automatic doors, they slid open for him. He walked closer, nearly walking inside, before he stopped and once again turned to look at Winnie.

He expected her to go with him.

That whole night, he had waited for her to catch up to him for a reason. It was because he felt a connection to her, just as she felt toward him. They had something in common, which compelled them to walk together. She couldn't explain that connection before, but as he stood there looking back at her from the doorway to the morgue, Winnie put it all together.

Something about the way she looked or the way she carried herself—something inside of Winnie gave him the impression that she belonged with him; that she was like him. That she was dead.

That thought sent a chill up her spine. Yet, perhaps even more disturbing was the fact that she had felt drawn to follow him that entire night as well. She was led to that place, not just by curiosity, but by a nagging feeling in her gut which told her that wherever he went, she should go as well.

She stood there, in the driveway of the morgue, looking at the mysterious stranger and the darkness which awaited him beyond those doors. She didn't know exactly what would happen to her if she chose to walk with him for those last few feet, but she knew that if she walked through those doors, she would not be walking out again.

Her heart was pounding in her chest. She was breathing heavily and could feel pressure building in the back of her nose.

Winnie McKeller had spent the better part of a year lingering on the brink. Now, she finally had to choose a side. She had to choose to walk those last few steps toward her sister, once and for all, or else she needed to walk away and never look back.

56

The first thing that Mark and Marion did when they pulled out of Obell's driveway in their separate cars was to find an empty parking lot. Once there, Mark parked his own car and hurried to join Marion. After he was inside, she wasted no time in pulling back onto the road and speeding toward their destination.

"Tell me again," Marion said to him. "What happened? Where did you get the pictures?"

"I went to meet with a psychic—or, a *remote viewer*. He doesn't consider himself psychic. I asked him to help me. I've—uh... I've been investigating..."

"You've been looking for Cindy. I know. Winnie found one of your recorders at the grave."

Mark froze, and in his mind he went back to the house where

he found the recorder and heard Winnie's voice. He had ignored her segments of the recording entirely. In fact, he had been annoyed at her for ruining his investigation.

He couldn't help but feel like the worst father in the world. He was so self-involved; so uncaring. How could he have not seen what was happening sooner?

Marion allowed the silence to linger for longer than Mark would have liked. He wanted her to say something for once. He wanted her to react. He wanted her to scream and curse his name for violating the memory of their daughter. He wanted some sign that she still felt anything at all, because he knew that those feelings had to be in there, somewhere.

"I'm not mad at you," she said.

He looked straight ahead. She was never mad at him. She was never sad about Cindy's death. She was always calm and collected, and that was the worst lie of them all. For as long as she pretended to have herself completely together, he felt completely alone.

"I can't blame you for doing what you did. I can't get upset that you've kept secrets," she said, in a tone that he hadn't heard in a long time. It was weak and pathetic, and exactly what she should be feeling, for once. She continued, "I've been keeping secrets too. I've been trying to keep the family together by pulling away and ignoring everything that's happened. Instead of going through it with you, I've been trying to let you get through it alone, while I watched from a distance."

Mark turned his attention to her, though she kept her eyes on the road. Instead of looking at him, she placed her hand in his and held it tightly. She didn't explain herself any more than that. She didn't burst into tears right then and there and they didn't embrace each other while violin music played in the background. He could have pressed her into a longer conversation about the state of their relationship, but he had neither the desire, nor the time for such a conversation. The moment was what it was: A step.

The sight of the hospital in the distance caused Mark's stomach to turn. He hadn't been there since Cindy died and he had no desire to go back. Everything about that day was a blur to him. He didn't remember the paperwork or what anyone said to him. For some strange reason, the memory which stood out the most for him was holding onto Cindy's purple backpack and looking down at its white straps, which had smudges of ink on them. He remembered thinking about Cindy getting ink on her hands and picking up her bag without noticing, all while her death seemed to be happening around him.

Marion's grip grew tighter around his hand as they neared the hospital. As she turned her car into the parking lot, she took a deep breath.

They had identified the body of one daughter there, and now they were going to find another. They didn't know whether Winnie was dead or alive. They didn't know how she had gotten there. All they knew was that this was the final picture that

Warren had drawn and if Winnie wasn't there, they had no idea where else to look.

Mark only vaguely remembered the morgue, which was why he couldn't easily identify it when he saw Warren's drawing. When Marion drove around to the back of the hospital and approached the covered driveway in front of the morgue, he took in just how accurate that picture had been.

"I don't see her," Marion said, driving up to the front doors. He couldn't tell whether she was scared or relieved by that fact.

As soon as the car stopped, Mark and Marion were unbuckling their seat belts and opening their doors in one fluid motion, and in nearly perfect sync.

"Maybe she's inside," Mark replied.

"That doesn't make me feel better."

Mark was headed for the front doors and watched as they slid open in front of him, but he stopped when he heard a noise from behind him; the sound of a sneaker twisting on the pavement. Both he and Marion turned at the same time, and they found Winnie sitting on the ground, leaning against one of the stone posts which held up the roof of the driveway. She had her knees pulled close to her chest. She was soaking wet and shivering, but what stood out the most for Mark was that his little girl was crying. As horrible as she looked, the only thing that seemed important or urgent to him at that moment was wiping those tears from her cheeks.

Marion reached Winnie before Mark could, but he ran as fast

as he could to get to her. He dropped to his knees hard—quite possibly drawing blood, but he didn't care. All that he cared about was her.

He put a hand on her head and urged her to look at him. She kept her eyes on her own knees, sobbing. She didn't say anything right away and didn't leap into his arms, but she also didn't pull away.

"Are you okay?" Marion asked her, taking off her own jacket and wrapping it around Winnie.

When Winnie didn't answer, Mark pressed her more, asking, "Are you hurt? Did something happen?"

Winnie's eyes finally met his, but she didn't seem to know what to say. Her mouth moved as though to speak, but she couldn't find the words.

Seeing her speechless and crying brought tears to Mark's eyes. It broke his heart to see her like this and to know that he could have prevented it if only he had opened his eyes sooner.

Marion pulled Winnie close to her, and rubbed her shoulders in an effort to warm her daughter up. By the time Winnie closed her eyes and allowed her mother to comfort her, Marion was crying just as hard as Winnie was.

Earlier that night, Warren Oster told Mark that if he followed those pictures, he would be led to the daughter that he had lost. As Mark sat on the ground in front of the morgue, holding his family and mourning with them for the first time, he finally came to understand what Warren really meant.

57

It walked into the morgue without thought or emotion, and headed straight for the room from which it had been taken.

As the corpse moved toward that stainless steel table where his autopsy had been conducted, shadows surrounded it, but it did not see them.

It climbed onto the table and placed its hands across its chest. It put its head down on the table and looked toward the ceiling with empty eyes. The shadows moved through every crack and corner of the room, but it did not notice.

After it was settled, the corpse did not move. Its journey was over. Now, it waited.

Something had been forced from the body after he was stolen

from the morgue. It was the only thing that would ever truly be his again, and while everyone who ever lived had been given one upon the moment of their conception, only his could fill the void left when it was removed. While the corpse was incapable of missing it or longing for its return, the thing that belonged to that body pined for him. Every second that they were apart was a moment stolen from eternity.

To the side of the corpse, it darted across the room, waiting to see how he would respond. He didn't.

It inched closer, waiting for the corpse to recoil with fear, but it remained still.

It hovered just above the corpse, unable to comprehend how their separation had come to be. And finally, it worked its way inside of that body, returning nature to its proper balance.

Death was home at last.

58

Winnie was asleep in the back of Marion's car as she drove. It had taken them two hours to have Winnie's ankle looked at and bandaged—It would have undoubtedly taken longer, if Marion hadn't known several of the doctors who worked the night shift at the hospital—and now her daughter was alive and in one piece, and they were now together as a family, free to go home.

But Marion wasn't on her way home. Instead, she drove the dark and hidden road which led to Obell's house. She wasn't sure that she wanted to go back there, especially with her family, but she had no choice. Obell needed help, and though she and Mark had already called the police, Marion needed to be sure that help had arrived.

Mark was sitting in the passenger seat, staring out the window. The night had suddenly become very calm and quiet. Whatever had caused that feeling in the air—as though something was urgently off balance—was gone. In fact, Marion felt lighter than she had in months. The world seemed clearer and lighter.

Though the car was quiet, her family was speaking volumes. Their silence was not filled with anger or pain. They had each wandered into the darkness alone that night, but their paths brought them together. The ride was peaceful.

Marion listened to the sound of Winnie breathing in the back seat of the car, and she felt at peace—Not entirely whole, but she was finding a new balance to life. She was no longer running, or attempting to observe her pain from the outside. She ran toward it, and by accepting that pain, she could allow Cindy to rest.

Mark looked over to Marion and watched her drive the car. When she looked back to him, he seemed to be experiencing the same revelation. Neither had fully explained how their night had unfolded and how they were led to that point, but there would be time for that. In that moment, on that night, all they needed to know was in the silence. Words couldn't possibly convey what the lack of words was able to.

As she looked toward the road once again, Marion saw a strange glow which had not been there earlier. Mark looked forward as well and when he saw this glow, he straightened in his seat.

The sound of a fire truck rose behind Marion's car, and she pulled to the side to allow it to pass. She came to a stop on the side of the road and looked toward Obell's house, which was now nothing more than a violent display of flames and swirling plumes of smoke.

They watched as the fire department attempted to put the fire out, but there was no hope of anything surviving inside of the home. If Obell was still in there, she would now be dead.

Marion couldn't bring herself to drive away for the longest time. She and Mark simply watched, without comment.

She had been there only a short while earlier. She had occupied the same space as Obell. She breathed the same air. She fought the same demons, only Marion had survived that battle. Obell had been consumed by Death.

Marion found herself saying a silent prayer for Obell. Though Obell was undoubtedly of a different belief system entirely, Marion couldn't help herself. She prayed for what remained of Obell's humanity. She prayed that if Obell was inside of that house and if she was now dead, she would finally find the sort of peace that she could not find in life. She prayed that if Obell survived, those fragments of humanity would fight through the darkness inside of her.

Marion had gone back to that house, hoping to find some way of helping Obell. She was willing to fight for the woman who had tried to do her harm, because when she looked into Obell's eyes, the reflection that she saw was her own.

All she could do now was pray.

59

The sun shone down upon the schoolyard the following Monday afternoon. The air was cool, with just enough of a nip to it to tell Winnie that winter was that much closer. She breathed deeply.

As she carried her lunch through her school's courtyard with a crutch under one arm, Winnie watched all of the other students eating and talking. They laughed with their friends and goofed around like children. She watched them and wondered what it would be like to feel that way again, but she could never go back. Too much had happened and she could not be the girl that she had once been.

She passed a table where Tami was sitting by herself, nibbling at her own lunch with eyes glued to the screen of her cell phone.

She wondered why Tami was alone. It was unusual to see her without a group of friends and a smile on her face.

When Winnie had replaced her cell phone the day before, she checked her voicemail and listened to a message which Tami left for her. In that message, she could hear the terror in Tami's voice. She could hear the hopelessness and the loneliness. She heard Tami say goodbye and she wondered why Tami chose to call her, of all people.

Though Winnie had heard the story of what happened to Tami from her father and she knew that Tami was safe, that call haunted her. It was what kept her from moving away from Tami that afternoon in the courtyard. It was what caused her to turn back and walk to Tami.

As she approached, Winnie caught a glimpse of what Tami was reading on her cell phone. It looked an awful lot like a Bible passage, which Winnie thought was strange, considering the fact that Tami had never been very religious, as far as she could tell.

Winnie placed her tray on Tami's table and waited for Tami to look up and see her. She wanted to be sure that Tami wouldn't tell her to leave before she sat down. She wasn't sure how Tami would react to seeing her after their last encounter.

When Tami saw Winnie standing over her, she smiled and said, "You're late. By about a year now."

Winnie sat and tried to think of something clever to say, but all she could think of was, "You better not let Mrs. Kinsey see you reading that. Katie Bishop had her cross confiscated last week.

Apparently, it's a gang symbol now."

Tami's smile grew and she put the phone down. She didn't say anything at first, which made their conversation seem awkward and uncomfortable to Winnie. She wasn't sure how they would manage to get over that awkwardness and start talking like normal people again. It seemed like such an impossible hump to get over.

Finally, Tami said "I had a really long weekend," as though the two of them had never stopped talking to each other at all.

"I heard," Winnie replied, with a bit of hesitation at first, but eventually just going with it. "So... I'm glad that you didn't get killed by evil shadows."

"You mock all you want, but what I saw out there was real. I can't begin to explain what happened to me, but it was real."

"Dad says that he didn't find anything in the cemetery."

"They followed me home."

Winnie tensed up. She hadn't heard this part of the story, and even with Tami sitting in front of her, she found herself worrying.

"They—It...Whatever those shadows were," Tami explained. "They were everywhere. They were touching me and trying their best to bring me down. I had no idea how to stop them. I had no idea how to fight them."

Tami trailed off. In her eyes, Winnie could see that she was in that memory, reliving that experience. Yet, Tami didn't seem scared.

"What happened?" Winnie asked.

"I was all set to run to Mommy, you know? I was friggin' terrified. And then... I wasn't. It was like this realization came over me. I kept thinking about Cindy's funeral. I kept thinking about you and the things that you said to me; the look in your eyes."

Winnie looked down to her lunch and said, "Yeah. Sorry about that."

"No," Tami told her. "It made me realize that I might not have seen those shadows before exactly, but I've been fighting them for a long time. They had me. There was nowhere for me to run. They should have taken me, but they *couldn't*. Not if I didn't let them. *I* had the power."

Winnie found herself smiling at Tami's realization. It seemed like everyone she knew had some sort of story to tell from that night.

Tami continued, "I kept hearing the minister's voice in my head, from Cindy's funeral. I kept thinking about what he was saying, but I can't remember it exactly. So, I'm looking for the passage."

"Are you, like... a gangsta now?" Winnie asked, feeling awkward and uncomfortable with the topic.

Tami looked at her for a moment, first trying to figure out what she was saying and then considering her response. Once she knew what she wanted to say, she looked down at her cell phone and started to spin it nervously with her fingers. Finally, she said, "I've seen things. And I did things. And I felt... I don't know. I guess I just...I think I might be. I don't know."

Tami's eyes shot back to see how Winnie would react to that declaration. She then looked around the area, checking to see if anyone else had heard her.

Winnie did not think that Tami was crazy. She wasn't entirely comfortable having that conversation with Tami, but she gave Tami a reassuring look, just to let her know that she didn't think she was a freak. Winnie then moved on, saying, "So, I met a guy that night."

Tami perked up and asked, "Cute?"

"Umm...Kinda. In a naked sort of way."

"What?! What happened?"

"Nothing! Well... not nothing. Which one is the base that includes fondling? Because I kinda got to that one. But it turned out that he was a zombie, so I was like...Yeah, that's not my type. Too much drama, you know?"

From that point on, it was like they'd never stopped talking at all. They laughed and talked, and exchanged dating horror stories. Somehow, Winnie always seemed to win the contest of worst date ever, since she always had the *zombie* card to play.

It felt good for Winnie to laugh. As it turned out, she enjoyed spending time with the living. It was a pleasant change of pace.

60

There were no mourners at the funeral which was held for the John Doe who had been killed nearly a month before. Though efforts had been made to track down the young man's identity or any clue that might lead officials to his family, nothing was ever discovered. He was destined to be put to rest in a grave which would not be inscribed with his name or year of birth. His death would not be felt by anyone. At best, he would be an unanswered question to some distant family.

As the grave diggers stood nearby and watched, Reverend Jonas Clark stood over the young man's casket. He volunteered his time to this service, because he believed that no soul should be unmourned or forgotten. Nobody should die alone.

He held a Bible in his hand, though he had no need to read the passage from it. It was the same passage that was used at most funerals: the twenty-third Psalm.

"The Lord is my shepherd; I shall not want. He maketh me to lie down in green pastures: he leadeth me beside still waters. He restoreth my soul: he leadeth me in the paths of righteousness for his name's sake. Yea, though I walk through the valley of the shadow of death, I will fear no evil: for thou art with me; thy rod and thy staff they comfort me. Thou preparest a table before me in the presence of mine enemies: thou anointest my head with oil; my cup runneth over. Surely goodness and mercy shall follow me all the days of my life: and I will dwell in the house of the Lord for ever."

As a cold breeze blew across the cemetery and the reverend walked away, the casket was lowered into the ground. Before the dirt could be placed over the casket, heavy snow began to fall, covering it in a blanket of white.

The gray of winter was looming.

Find Strange Fall Online:

www.AuthorKyleAndrews.com/StrangeFall

facebook.com/AuthorKyleAndrews

@StarletteNovel

Find Kyle Andrews Online:

AuthorKyleAndrews.wordpress.com

kyle@AuthorKyleAndrews.com

If you enjoyed **Strange Fall**,
be sure to check out...

Now available on Amazon.com